Shadows on the Levels

ALSO BY DAVID HODGES

DETECTIVE KATE HAMBLIN MYSTERIES
Book 1: Murder On The Levels
Book 2: Revenge On The Levels
Book 3: Fear On The Levels
Book 4: Killer On The Levels
Book 5: Secrets On The Levels
Book 6: Death On The Levels
Book 7: Poison On The Levels
Book 8: Witch Fire On The Levels
Book 9: Stalker On The Levels
Book 10: Venom On The Levels
Book 11: Watcher On The Levels
Book 12: Storm On The Levels
Book 13: Diamonds On The Levels

STANDALONE NOVEL
Slice

SHADOWS ON THE LEVELS

DAVID HODGES

Detective Kate Hamblin Mysteries Book 14

Joffe Books, London
www.joffebooks.com

First published in Great Britain in 2025

© David Hodges

This book is a work of fiction. Names, characters, businesses, organisations, places and events are either the product of the author's imagination or are used fictitiously. Any resemblance to actual persons, living or dead, events or locales is entirely coincidental. The spelling used is British English except where fidelity to the author's rendering of accent or dialect supersedes this. The right of David Hodges to be identified as author of this work has been asserted in accordance with the Copyright, Designs and Patents Act 1988.

No part of this book may be used or reproduced in any manner for the purpose of training artificial intelligence technologies or systems. In accordance with Article 4(3) of the Digital Single Market Directive 2019/790, Joffe Books expressly reserves this work from the text and data mining exception.

Cover art by Nick Castle

ISBN: 978-1-83526-946-6

This book is dedicated to my wife, Elizabeth, for all her love, patience and support over so many wonderful years and to my late mother and father, whose faith in me to one day achieve my ambition as a writer remained steadfast throughout their lifetimes and whose tragic passing has left a hole in my own life that will never be filled.

AUTHOR'S NOTE

Although the action of this novel takes place in the Avon & Somerset Police area, the story itself and all the characters in it are entirely fictitious. At the time of writing, there is *no* police station in Highbridge. This has been drawn entirely from the author's imagination to ensure no connection is made between any existing police station or personnel in the force. Some poetic licence has been adopted in relation to the local police structure and specific operational police procedures to meet the requirements of the plot. But the novel is primarily a crime thriller and does not profess to be a detailed police procedural, even though the policing background, as depicted, is broadly in accord with the national picture. I trust that these small departures from fact will not spoil the reading enjoyment of serving or retired police officers for whom I have the utmost respect.

David Hodges

BEFORE THE FACT

December 1989. The night was crystal clear, the ground silvered by a heavy frost in the blaze of winter moonlight. The old woman walked slowly and carefully along the slippery lane for fear of losing her balance, tapping the ground in front of her with her walking stick. She was muffled in a tattered, khaki overcoat which still bore the rank insignia of the army officer who had once worn it, and her thick, woollen shawl was drawn closely over her head and shoulders to keep out the biting cold. Every so often she stopped beneath one of the big trees that bordered the lane and bent down to pick up a small piece of fallen branch lying on the verge, which she slipped into the plastic bag she carried over one bony wrist with a smile of satisfaction. The spindly branches would help to fuel the fire she would soon light in her tin shack to warm her old bones, and every piece was a bonus.

Annie Evans had been on the road for round about twelve years now, ever since her husband had died and alcoholism, followed by financial ruin and a mental breakdown, had forced her out of her home and into a life of vagrancy. She was well-known on this part of the Somerset Levels and to most people she was regarded as a bit of a local celebrity, to be pitied and provided with little handouts whenever the mood took them. Others, however, particularly the superstitious members of the isolated communities, saw her in a more sinister light. A witch, to be shunned whenever she put in an appearance, in case she took it into her head to lay a curse on whoever she took exception to. Some even saw her as Somerset's own legendary "Woman of the Mist", the "Night Hag" of ancient folklore, who it was said, sought out wrongdoers and sat on their chests while they slept to suffocate them. Children were told to stay clear of her and were kept in line by their parents with the threat that old Annie would come for them in the middle of the night if they did not behave.

The reality was that the old woman was no threat to anyone. True, she was well into her seventies and wildly eccentric, with a propensity to mutter away to herself and shoot hostile glances at people as she passed by, but Annie Evans was totally harmless and only wanted to be left alone. Sadly, Fate had decreed otherwise.

The five close friends had been on a pub crawl to celebrate their graduation from university, and they were well-oiled when they were virtually thrown out of the last hostelry at around eleven. On the promise of more cider at the home of their "chauffeur" for the night, Danny Aldridge, whose parents were away on holiday, they decided to go back to his place to continue partying, despite the fact that Aldridge was by now in no fit state even to ride a bicycle, let alone get behind the wheel of his father's powerful Volvo 240.

Full of raucous cheer, they bellowed and shrieked their exuberance through clouds of cannabis fumes as they pulled out of the car park, narrowly missing one of the gateposts, then fishtailed along the lane for several yards before straightening up and racing off into the black void beyond the pub's security lights. Aldridge felt good and, with a joint held firmly between his bared teeth, he put his foot down hard on the accelerator, determined to impress his passengers with his flashy borrowed toy. To start with, he just about managed to focus on the moonlit road as the car struck out across the marsh. But in his inebriated state, his brain was a little too sluggish to react to the road's sudden disappearance, as it suddenly plunged into a gloomy tunnel formed by overhead tree branches, which bored through a patch of woodland bordering the narrow, frosted strip on either side.

He glimpsed the bent figure in the headlights a fraction of a second before he mounted the verge. The next instant, he felt the sickening impact as he fought with the wheel to return the car to the road and something dark was thrown up in front of his horrified gaze. Slamming his foot on the brake, he skidded to a halt, staring in shock through the windscreen at the clouds of vapour rising from under the bonnet as the engine continued to turn over as if nothing had happened.

Jennifer Talbot, sitting beside him, groaned and touched her head with one shaky hand, thankful that she had been wearing a seatbelt. 'I–I hit my head on something,' she said. 'I think I'm bleeding.'

'What the hell did you *do*, Danny?' Lizzie Johnson screamed from the back seat. 'You nearly killed us.'

'Did we hit something?' another voice joined in. 'I felt a thump and . . .'

Julian Grey, sitting to one side of Lizzie, threw open the passenger door and scrambled out, nearly losing his balance on the ripped-up verge as he steadied himself with one hand against the side of the car to make his way round to the front.

'Bloody Nora!' he shouted through the windscreen. 'Looks like she's dead.'

Aldridge snapped out of his trance in a moment and, throwing open his own door, clambered unsteadily on to the verge. 'Dead?' he said hoarsely. 'What–what are you talking about? Who's–who's dead?'

He soon found out when he got to his friend's side. Annie Evans had been struck with such force that she had been propelled high into the air and had landed in the middle of the road several yards away. She was clearly visible to him in the blazing headlights of the Volvo, which had come to a stop with the front wheels buried in the verge, partially facing back out across the road. She was lying in a contorted heap, in the middle of the tarmac, her arms trapped beneath her body and her legs thrust out from under a long, badly ripped overcoat like some grotesque parody of a shop mannequin dumped from a passing car. Her head was twisted round at an unnatural angle, the side of her face closest to where he was standing horribly smashed and bloodied and seemingly staring straight at him through the gore. Unable to control himself, he turned away from the horrific sight and, doubling up, vomited on the ground in a series of long retching spasms.

Other car doors then opened, and the remaining passengers joined Aldridge and Grey by the body. Robert Chalmers was even more doped up than the rest and he stood there, swaying unsteadily for a moment, unable to fully comprehend what was going on.

'What–what's happened?' he blurted in a slurred voice. 'Where are we?'

'Pagan's Clump,' Talbot replied, grabbing his arm to steady him as he stared down at Annie Evans's bloody remains. 'You must remember? Where we used to play as kids.'

He peered through the trees to his left. 'Pagan's Clump,' was all he could manage to repeat.

Aldridge stared wide-eyed at the others, in a state of shock. 'I–I didn't see her,' he mumbled, and wiped his mouth with a large handkerchief.

'Didn't see who?' Chalmers queried, still out of it.

'It's the old crone, Annie what's-her-name,' Jennifer Talbot said quietly. Her voice was strained, and blood trickled from a deep cut in her forehead. But otherwise, she was surprisingly calm, despite the circumstances.

Aldridge shook his head repeatedly. 'My dad will crucify me for this,' he choked. 'He forbade me ever to borrow his car after I was disqualified.'

No one seemed to pick up on the fact that his first concern seemed to be for his own welfare rather than the fate of his innocent victim.

'Disqualified?' Grey exclaimed. 'You mean you're banned?'

'That's usually what disqualification means, Jules,' Talbot said sarcastically. 'You're in deep poo this time, Danny, never mind what your dad might do to you.'

'I never knew you were banned,' Chalmers put in, still failing to appreciate the seriousness of the situation, and he glanced round at his other friends, bleary-eyed and obviously still confused. 'Anyone else?'

There was a collective shake of heads.

'It was in Birmingham six months ago,' Aldridge blurted. 'Third speeding offence. I–I was too embarrassed to tell anyone about it—'

'Never mind his bloody ban,' Lizzie Johnson cut in, retching at the gruesome sight in front of her, but somehow managing to keep her natural reflux under control, 'will someone check *her* out? She could still be alive.'

Grey bent over the old woman and carried out a cursory examination. 'She's dead all right,' he said. 'Looks as if she broke her neck in the collision. Her head is also split wide open and one of her legs is so badly twisted, I reckon it must be busted.'

'So, what are we going to do?' Johnson whispered. 'We need to call someone. What about an–an ambulance or–or the police?'

'She's *dead*, Lizzie,' Grey repeated sharply. 'No one can do anything for her now. And if we call the police, not only is Danny toast, but they're bound to spot the fact that we've all been smoking weed.'

'But–but we can't just leave her here.'

'Then what the hell do you suggest?'

'We bury her.' Talbot's voice was very quiet, unemotional, and the others stared at her. Sensing their disbelief at the apparent callousness of her suggestion, she grimaced, then added, 'Well, no one will miss her, will they? She's a vagrant. A loner. And we certainly can't bring her back to life.'

'But–but bury her?' Johnson echoed. 'That would make us accessories. We would be in the same shit as Danny.'

'Would you rather we shopped him, and had him put away then?' Grey said. 'You know, death by dangerous driving, driving while disqualified and obviously no insurance? Maybe you'd like to be a witness for the prosecution?'

'Don't talk wet, Jules. I'm simply stating the bleeding obvious.'

'Yeah, but the bleeding obvious doesn't need to be stated here, does it? All of us have been close friends since we were kids. We were born in the villages round here, went to the same schools, and you and Bob are even engaged now. Hell, we've known each other like forever, and we have always stuck together. That's the way it's got to be now.'

'He's right,' Talbot added. 'And think on this. After all the years of graft at uni, each of us is in the market for a really good job. What do you think would happen if we were to be embroiled in a scandal like this? You know, rowdy, drunken yobs mowing down a homeless old woman after being thrown out of a pub stoned?'

'But it was nothing like that. It was an accident.'

'Think the press will see it that way, Lizzie?' Grey went on. 'We'd be hung out to dry. And what self-respecting firm is going to take us on with that sort of baggage? Even Danny's dad couldn't hang on to him in his real estate business, despite his respected position as a local magistrate. *Persona non grata*, that's what we'd become. Outcasts, not only workwise, but socially too.'

Johnson closed her eyes tightly for a few seconds, as if trying to blot out the whole thing, leaving Grey free to press home his argument.

'Right then,' he said, 'all in agreement? We keep schtum and bury the old girl here, like Jenny suggested?'

Before anyone could respond, Aldridge called out sharply, panic in his tone. 'Headlights!'

The vehicle was approaching from the direction in which they had just come and, although still some way off, it was only seconds away.

'Get her off the road,' Talbot shouted. 'Quickly!'

The dead woman seemed made of little more than skin and bone and the three boys picked her up easily between them and carried her in among the trees. Moments later, a big, black saloon drew up alongside the Volvo. The front passenger window slid down with a faint hum and the outline of a figure in a dark coat and cloth cap stared in their direction from the passenger seat, though the driver remained hidden in shadow.

'You people okay?' a male voice queried above the rhythmic thud of a powerful engine.

Talbot came up with the first thing she could think of. 'A fox,' she lied, walking over to the car, then stopping cautiously a few feet from it. 'Ran right out in front of us.'

Dark eyes studied her from a lean, pale face. 'Anyone hurt?'

Talbot shook her head. 'No, shaken up, that's all. Thanks for asking.'

'Need an ambulance or a breakdown?'

'No, we're fine, thanks.' She glanced over her shoulder, seeing him stare past her at the three boys emerging from among the trees, and forced a laugh. 'Lads needed a leak after a shock like that.'

There was no answering chuckle. 'Did you hit it?'

'Hit what?'

'The fox. You said there was a fox.'

Talbot cursed her stupidity. 'Oh y–yes. There *was* a thump, but it ran off.'

'Could be injured then?'

'I suppose. But nothing we can do now.'

'Have you looked for it?'

'Er, the lads did try, yes, but no joy. It's probably gone to its burrow somewhere.'

'You mean earth, don't you?'

'Earth?'

'They call foxes' burrows earths, I believe.'

Talbot frowned. This guy was getting to be a pain. Why all the questions?

'Oh right. Look, thanks for stopping, but we're okay, honestly.'

'Not a very good way to end the night's partying, though, was it?'

'I beg your pardon?'

'Weren't you the crowd celebrating at the pub down the road?'

'Oh, er, yes.'

'Thought so. My friend and me were in there too. Asked to leave, weren't you? Shouldn't have been driving at all, I would suggest.'

Talbot didn't answer him but saw the man ease back into his seat and heard the car's engine note start to change.

'Well, if you're all okay then, we'll be off,' he called out.

Talbot tried not to let her relief show. 'Fine. Thanks again for stopping.'

But the car was already pulling away at speed and her eyes followed its red tail-lights until they disappeared around a bend in the road.

'Brilliant, Jen,' Aldridge mumbled and, still shaking, he stepped forward to squeeze her arm. 'You couldn't have handled that any better.'

'Pretty cool,' Grey agreed, then added, 'but why all his third-degree crap? What was that about?'

Talbot shrugged. 'No idea. Perhaps he was a curious type.'

'But–but what if he was a cop and he suspected something?' Johnson asked, fear back in her voice.

'Hardly likely, is it?' Grey answered. 'Otherwise, he would have got out the car and had a look around. And how would he have known what happened anyway? No, he was simply a nosey prick doing some fishing.'

'Whatever,' Talbot replied, impatiently. 'Let's get this job done before anyone else happens along. Is there a spade in your boot, Danny?'

Aldridge nodded. 'Father always carries one at this time of year, as a precaution. He's that sort of guy. You know, snow and all that.'

'Then let's find a spot and start digging. Ground should be quite soft under the trees, despite the frost.'

'Should we say a prayer or something?' Johnson suggested.

'Don't be stupid.'

Grey found a spot a couple of yards inside the wood and the three boys took it in turns to dig, using the spade from the car. It turned out to be a lengthy, more difficult task than they had anticipated as the soft, crumbly soil kept folding in on itself. Their backs were breaking by the time they had finished. But fortunately, there were no further unwelcome interruptions and only one car came by while they were doing the digging. By then, though, Aldridge had had the good sense to straighten the Volvo up on the verge and the other vehicle didn't even slow, the driver and whoever might have been with them possibly assuming it had broken down or run out of petrol.

In any event, Annie Evans was finally laid to rest and her unmarked grave backfilled with the earth that had been dug out of the hole, before being carefully tramped down and covered with fallen leaves. It wasn't a very professional job, but it was as good as it could be under the circumstances and, as Grey said, who was likely to be walking through that isolated wood and inspecting their handiwork any time soon anyway?

There was nothing that could be done about the blood at the scene or the gouges in the verge's soft earth made by the Volvo's wheels, however, but cool-headed Talbot dismissed their concerns, pointing out that anyone passing by the spot in the morning would simply assume the mess was due to yet another of the prevalent roadkills and think no more about it.

'What's done is done,' she summarised. 'All we've got to do now is to put the unpleasant business out of our minds for good and get on with our lives.'

'Yeah,' Grey agreed. 'It never happened, okay? It was nothing more than a bad dream.'

'More like a nightmare,' Johnson muttered, still shivering. 'Let's hope it isn't one that comes back to haunt us one day.'

Grey stared at her. 'Haunt us? How do you mean?'

Johnson hesitated, now looking embarrassed. Then she gave a shaky laugh. 'Well, you know what the superstitious folk round here used to say about the old crone who lived in the haunted wood at Pagan's Clump. They called her the "Night Hag" after the legendary figure in folklore who punished wrongdoers by creeping into their homes at night and, er, suffocating them by sitting on their chests so they couldn't breathe.'

'What?' Grey snorted. 'The Night Hag? Oh, come on, Lizzie. I know you've always been into séances and the spiritualism thing, but you don't still believe all that bogey woman crap, do you? As kids, it was only fed to us by our parents to frighten us into toeing the line. You know, "behave yourselves or old Annie will come for you one dark night".'

Johnson shrugged nervously. 'You can laugh,' she replied tersely, 'but as a child, old Annie frightened the hell out of me and I'm still not over it.'

'Well, she can't frighten you anymore, can she? She's a corpse several feet underground with the worms.'

'Let's hope she stays there then,' Johnson muttered.

Behind them, the trees rustled sibilantly in the still air . . .

CHAPTER 1

Christmas 2023 was a distant memory, and Detective Sergeant Kate Lewis had butterflies in her stomach as she followed her detective constable husband and partner, Hayden, up the steps of Highbridge police station on a cold, blustery day in late January 2024. She knew deep down that it was stupid to feel the way she did. After all, with so many years of police service already under her belt, a large proportion of which had been spent as a DS at Highbridge, she should have had no qualms at all about rejoining the department. Yet in a peculiar way, she felt like some spotty-faced newbie on their very first day at work in the big city.

Not that you could describe Highbridge as anything like a city. In fact, it was an unremarkable, rather drab, former market town and one-time centre for the old Somerset and Dorset Railway engineering works. Next door to the seaside town of Burnham and in the shadow of sprawling Bridgwater, it stood on the edge of the flat, marshy plain that was the Somerset Levels with its criss-cross pattern of drainage ditches, or "rhynes" as they were called in this part of the world. But as Kate knew only too well, her old patch had plenty to offer the keen detective in the investigation of serious crime. Too much, in fact, which was why she and

Hayden had chucked in the towel in the spring of the previous year to take a much-needed sabbatical in their newly acquired cottage in rural Pembrokeshire to unwind and recharge their batteries.

Sadly, things hadn't worked out as they had planned. Persuaded by her former DI into assisting with a major police inquiry, set up by the National Crime Agency, Kate had taken on an undercover role involving close surveillance of a dangerous target criminal living in the village. Overall, the police operation had been a success, but once again it had put her in grave jeopardy and had almost finished her marriage. Now back home in Somerset, after putting their Welsh cottage in mothballs, she and Hayden had been given the opportunity by the force hierarchy of picking up where they had left off.

In Hayden's case, that opportunity had not been greeted with too much enthusiasm. Highly intelligent, but lacking in any real drive or ambition, he had never professed to be the most committed detective, and he had initially shown little desire to return to his former role. But in the end, he'd had to acknowledge that it paid good money and he wasn't blessed with any other professional skills that would have allowed him to do something else.

For Kate, the issues were different. She had always wanted to be a police officer and she had proved herself a courageous and dynamic go-getting detective in her time on Highbridge CID. But although she was tingling with excitement at the prospect of starting over again, she was also conscious of the fact that she was carrying a lot of personal baggage. Almost losing her life in another investigation some years before, she had suffered serious mental trauma, and had ended up in a psychiatric hospital with a near nervous breakdown. That, coupled with her tendency to be impulsive and to rub senior officers up the wrong way by disobeying orders — earning herself the nickname "Maverick" or "Go It Alone Kate" — had had an adverse effect on her career. In particular, it had resulted in any prospect of actual promotion to inspector rank being held in abeyance for the time being, despite having previously passed the sergeant to inspector promotion selection board. To be honest, she was surprised she had been allowed back in "the firm" at all, but she knew she owed this to her DI and some powerful influencers in the NCA, following her recent undercover role in Pembroke. It was up to her now to demonstrate she still had what it took to be a supervisory detective. It was her last chance. But she couldn't help wondering what sort of reception she was likely to get from her old colleagues when she walked through the double doors of that general office on the first floor.

There were several people standing around in the front foyer when Kate followed Hayden into the building; most of them from the usual flotsam and jetsam of street life that turned up in many a police station around the country during the average day. One was standing to the side of the front counter, writing inside a black A4-size book. She recognised it as the station's signing-in register for those reporting on police bail. An emaciated looking man, who had to be well into his sixties, with dirty, shoulder-length blond hair and a face pock-marked from senior acne, she knew him immediately. He was one of her former snouts. Billy James, a sly, treacherous article who had spent much of his life in prison for drugs and petty crime. The last time she'd had dealings with him, maybe eighteen months before, had been when he was on his way to court-imposed rehab for heroin abuse.

She gave a cynical smile. So, Billy was back to signing in on police bail, it seemed, which meant he was still committing crime even while acting as a police informant. Why didn't that surprise her? At the same moment he pushed the register back to the civilian station duty officer (or SDO) and turned for the door to the street, almost colliding with Hayden in the process. His gappy teeth formed a crooked grin through his stubble and he threw Kate a wink as he walked past her. Things never changed, did they? she thought as Hayden pressed the security button beside the counter. Same old, same old.

The SDO glanced up and nodded in recognition as he hit the button on his side of the front counter and a bleep sounded from the box attached to the door, allowing them to walk through.

'Welcome back, both,' Tom Grain said with a broad grin. 'Couldn't stay away, could you?'

'We should have our warrant cards re-registered for the card reader after today,' Kate told him. 'Then you won't have to open up for us again.'

'You're staying for good this time then?' Grain said.

'Wished we'd never left,' Hayden lied with a scowl.

They met no one on their way up the stone staircase to the first floor and they got a surprise when they pushed through the double doors into the CID general office. The place was in total darkness, the heavy blinds pulled down across the windows against the grey day and only the outlines of the double row of computer workstations visible in the gloom, but even in the poor light they could see that the office appeared to be completely deserted.

'Where the hell is everyone?' Hayden exclaimed. 'Why are the lights switched off and all the blinds closed?'

Kate reached for the bank of light switches. 'Well, someone should have been here,' she replied. 'It's only after nine . . .'

But her words were drowned by a chorus of cheers and as the lights flickered on, several familiar figures emerged from their crouched positions behind the workstations, grinning and clapping their hands. A banner suspended from a strip light on each side of the room bore the words, *Welcome Back*, and beneath it a small table bearing the weight of a large, iced cake and stubby bottles of what looked like lager, had been set up between the two rows of workstations.

As they stood there gaping at it all, a slight, dapper man with jet-black hair and a lean, pale face stepped forward and treated them to a broad grin. 'So, late as usual then?' he said, 'We thought you two had chickened out.'

Kate shook her head slowly and stared at her old friend and boss, thinking that the last time she had seen Detective Inspector Charlie Woo, it had been at the debrief following the largely successful conclusion of the surveillance operation in Pembrokeshire.

'We did consider doing that,' she said wryly, glancing past him at her other old colleagues. 'But then we thought you wouldn't be able to manage without our expertise.'

There was a roar of laughter, and everyone then homed in on the table with much back-slapping and mickey-taking, as they concentrated on the cake and bottles of drink that had been provided.

After a decent interval, Charlie Woo drew away from the rest and signalled Kate to join him in his glass-panelled inner sanctum at the end of the room, leaving Hayden on his third slice of cake, complaining over the fact that the beer in the stubby bottles had turned out to be alcohol-free.

Closing the door of his office behind them, Woo waved Kate to a chair in front of his desk and dropped into the swivel behind it. The former Hong Kong police inspector, who had got out of the territory hours before China took it back, looked tired and strained. Kate recognised the signs only too well. Her face had looked very much the same before she and Hayden had taken the plunge and put in for their sabbatical in Pembrokeshire. Not that the relaxing break they had been desperately looking for had turned out to be what they had envisaged in the end.

'Good to have you with us again,' Woo said, leaning back in his chair. 'I expect you know that I was promoted from acting DI to the substantive rank while you were away?'

She flicked her eyebrows in acknowledgement. 'Congratulations,' she said, unable to completely conceal the deep-seated envy and resentment she felt, knowing that she had come so close to that temporary promotion herself all those months ago, only to foul everything up at the final hurdle by disobeying orders and living up to her nickname of "Go It Alone Kate".

'The successful result in that last Pembrokeshire operation have something to do with it?' she said brutally before she could stop herself.

He winced. 'I'd like to think it had a lot more to do with it than that one job, Kate,' he replied quietly, making her feel small. He hesitated a fraction. 'Look, I know how much you wanted DI, even before I was appointed to the acting rank and I'm really sorry it didn't work out for you . . .'

She shrugged. 'I think we had a similar conversation before, Charlie, but it's no big deal and it's all water under the bridge now anyway.'

He nodded. 'Well, I'm glad to hear it, but as we've been friends for such a long time now, I wanted to get that out of the way to start with.'

He pursed his lips for a moment, then leaned forward and studied her intently. 'You should know that things haven't changed in the department since you were last here,' he warned. 'We're still light of another DS and a couple of DCs. For the past twelve months during your absence we had a skipper seconded here from Bridgwater to replace you on a temporary basis, but he was pulled off last week when it was known you were returning. So, we're back to square one on staffing, though Hayden being here now as well will be of some help. There's an additional complication too . . .'

His voice trailed off and he stared down at his desk for a second, as if trying to decide how to phrase what he needed to say.

'The thing is, Kate, the old hostilities that existed in certain quarters before you cleared off to Pembrokeshire a year ago haven't gone away and the prospect of your return hasn't exactly been welcomed by everyone.'

'You mean the DCI?' she interjected with a bitter smile, thinking of the man who had caused her so much grief in the past.

Another nod greeted the comment. 'Between you and me, when Mr Ricketts heard about your application, he did his level best to prevent you being accepted back into the fold by slipping some poison into the ear of the Assistant Chief Constable, Personnel . . .'

'What a surprise.'

'Absolutely! But after the brilliant close surveillance work you carried out on that National Crime Agency operation in Pembrokeshire last year, he got a flea in his ear from ACC (P) instead.'

'I bet that wound him up even more?'

'So much so that he brought up the subject again at "morning prayers" last week,' he said, referring to the briefings that took place with the station's superintendent on local crime and other issues every morning, 'but the boss also slapped him down. Now, I don't want to appear disloyal by telling you all this, but as a friend, I felt bound to warn you in the strictest confidence that you have made a powerful enemy there, Kate, and you should watch your back from now on.'

She smiled again. 'I'll be the soul of restraint and discretion, Charlie. Honestly. Poor old Toby Ricketts will think I've had a charm injection.'

Woo sat back with a snort. 'Yeah, which is about as likely as Hayden winning the British Fashion Awards for Best Dressed Man.'

Then abruptly he saw something over her shoulder and broke off, flashing a warning sign with his eyes. A second later, the door was thrown open and Kate turned to see the very man they had been talking about standing there, staring at her.

In his thirties, tall and slim, with blond hair and a luxuriant blond moustache Kate remembered he'd always had a habit of stroking with his index finger when perplexed, Detective Chief Inspector Toby Ricketts was the epitome of elegance and good taste. He was dressed in an expensive-looking Italian-style blue suit, matching university tie and black patent leather shoes and, as he paused in the doorway with his hand raised against the edge of the door, Kate glimpsed the flashy gold Rolex watch he always wore on his wrist. Like her, he had joined the force straight from university as a graduate-entry candidate, but there the similarity between the two of them ended. Fast-tracked to his present rank, he had once been seen as one of the chief constable's high-fliers, or "blue-eyed boys" as they were called by the lesser mortals in the job. But somewhere along the line the whizz-kid had lost much of his whizz. No one seemed to know what had happened, but it was generally believed he had blotted his copybook in some way, and he had been DCI now for far longer than he or anyone else had ever anticipated.

Filled with bitterness and totally ruthless about regaining his former foothold on the ladder to chief officer status, his mission in life now seemed to be to make everyone else's life as unpleasant as possible. He had taken an especially strong dislike to Kate because of her rebellious, single-minded approach to the job and her barely concealed contempt for him and what he represented. As a result, he had used every opportunity available in the past to try and humiliate her and bring her down.

Kate rose to her feet at the same time as Charlie Woo and turned to face her arch enemy with a stare as cold as his.

'What's going on out there?' Ricketts snapped before Woo could say anything. 'I didn't realise we went in for parties in this department.'

'It's a welcome back for Kate, guv,' Woo replied. 'It was only for ten to fifteen minutes.'

Ricketts glared at him. 'Drinking alcohol on police premises is a disciplinary offence,' he went on. 'Aren't you aware of that, Inspector?'

The DI shook his head, the suggestion of a triumphant gleam in his eyes. 'I'm well aware of it, guv,' he replied. 'Which is why I ensured it was all alcohol-free.'

Ricketts passed over his explanation without offering any apology and fixed his gaze back on Kate. 'Well, you're back with us, it seems, Sergeant,' he commented. 'I thought you and your husband had decided to embark on careers more suited to your, er, alleged talents? Nothing out there for you then?'

Woo tensed and glanced quickly at Kate, as if fearful that she might rise to the bait. But instead, she treated the DCI to a wry smile. 'Not at all, sir,' she replied. 'We missed all the camaraderie here. You know, the feeling that we were part of one big, happy family.'

Ricketts's eyes narrowed as the shot went home and there was a noticeable tic in his cheek as his mouth tightened. Before he could think of something else to say, Woo's phone rang and there was silence for a moment while the DI engaged in a short "Yes, No. Right" conversation with someone at the other end before finishing the call.

'Control room, guv,' he said to Ricketts, moving out from behind his desk. 'Some skeletal remains have been found buried in a wood called Pagan's Clump out on the Levels. I'd better get over there to take a look.'

Ricketts smirked. 'Oh, I don't think it will be necessary for you yourself to go at this stage, Detective Inspector, not until we know exactly what we've got there. It could be nothing more than a dead cow or sheep and I am quite sure our *ace* detective is experienced enough to be able to tell the difference. Really sorry to break up the welcome party, Sergeant Lewis, but you must be bursting to get back into the swing of things . . .'

* * *

The scene of the incident was not difficult to find. A marked police patrol car was parked on one side of a narrow lane which cut through a wooded tunnel behind a couple of open-backed lorries. One had its tailboard down and was laden with a large tree trunk and a tangle of lopped branches. Several hard hats were leaning against the lorries smoking, as if awaiting instructions. The traffic lights at each end of what was obviously a tree-felling operation were still there, changing regularly through the phases, but for the moment there were no other vehicles passing or waiting for a green light to proceed.

As Kate arrived with Hayden in the CID car, a middle-aged policeman wearing a yellow flak jacket over his uniform tunic emerged from a gash which had been torn in the line of trees on the blocked side of the lane. A heavily built workman with a red hard hat followed close behind him.

Kate flashed her warrant card at the policeman, and he glanced at it suspiciously for a moment, maybe thinking she was press.

'Detective Sergeant Kate Lewis,' she said, and waved a hand towards Hayden. 'My partner, DC Hayden Lewis.'

The policeman raised his eyebrows, then grinned, but said nothing. Kate knew what he was thinking. Those who hadn't met them before were always taken aback by the fact that they were a husband-and-wife team, as it was normally taboo in the force for couples to work in the same station, let alone on the same department.

'You've got some bones,' she said, more as a statement of fact than a question.

He nodded. 'Been buried near one of the trees they were taking out.'

'Digger had to go down deep, under the roots,' the man in the red hat said at Kate's elbow, 'and there it was. Bloody horrible too.'

'And you are?'

'Lazenby. Derek Lazenby. I'm the gang foreman.'

'You'd better show us then.'

There was a big yellow excavator, with the shovel raised, parked among the trees, the driver still sitting in his cab, also smoking and looking bored. A couple of powerful-looking chainsaws were lying on the ground nearby.

'There,' Lazenby said, pausing on the edge of a large hole that had been dug out of the ground, close to the stump of what had once obviously been quite a big tree.

Kate bent down to peer into the hole. The skeletal remains were still half-buried, but her eyes picked out what looked like part of a human skull and some ribcage bones, the latter still with bits of cloth attached. The rest of the body was mostly covered in soil, and it was impossible to tell whether the remains were those of a man or a woman.

'How long before we can resume our work, do you think?' Lazenby asked, rubbing the stubble on his chin.

Kate straightened up. 'We'll have to get the pathologist and a forensics team down here first,' she said, 'but I reckon you'll all be off the site for at least a few days now.'

'Days? But–but this is all part of a new road-widening scheme. We can't down tools and sit on our arses while someone ponces about in the hole. Delays cost money. I could easily get the digger to lift out the bones for you.'

Kate stared at him incredulously. 'You'll do no such thing. I'm having the whole area cordoned off now and all work here will have to cease until further notice.'

'Bloody hell, boss will do his crust. Wish I hadn't reported it now.'

'If you hadn't, you could have found yourself on a criminal charge,' she snapped back. 'Think on that, Mr Lazenby.'

'You reckon it was a murder then?'

'I have no idea, but corpses don't usually bury themselves, do they?'

CHAPTER 2

Charlie Woo finally arrived on the scene about the same time as a leather-clad figure riding a Triumph Bonneville motorcycle, who pulled up behind Kate's car, removed their full-face crash helmet and placed it carefully on the seat. The rider was a young woman in her thirties, with spiky green hair and an assortment of silver-coloured facial piercings. Kate recognised her immediately. Once seen, not easily forgotten, she mused. Debbie Moreton, the crime reporter for the very anti-establishment *Bridgwater Clarion* newspaper, had been a thorn in Kate's side for a long time and the personal animosity between the two of them had run deep after Moreton's attempts on a number of previous cases to trash Kate's reputation in her news coverage of local crime.

'How did *she* get to know about this business?' Kate breathed as the reporter walked quickly towards them. 'She's pure poison.'

Also recognising her, the DI glanced across at one of the workmen leaning against the side of the lorry laden with tree branches. The man met his gaze briefly, then looked away and concentrated on studying the screen of his mobile instead.

'I wouldn't be surprised if one of the tree-fellers hasn't slipped her the wink,' he replied drily. 'It would be a nice little earner for him.'

Kate faced Moreton squarely on her approach, blocking her way into the trees, her smile as cold as that of the reporter's. 'Out for a joyride then, Debbie?' she asked. 'I didn't realise you had a motorcycle.'

Moreton craned her neck to see past the two detectives to where Hayden and the uniformed police officer, who had been first on the scene, were standing talking in front of the police crime scene tape that had been strung across the gap between two trees to prevent unauthorised access to the prospective crime scene.

Moreton ignored the remark. 'A little bird told me you'd found some bones buried here, Sergeant. Man or woman?'

'No idea yet,' Kate said. 'Too early to say.'

'Murder, is it?'

'Don't know about that yet either.'

'Can I take a look? I won't touch anything.'

'No,' Woo put in emphatically.

'The public have a right to know.'

'No, they don't,' Kate countered, 'and neither do you — or the *Bridgwater Clarion*.'

'I'm not with the *Clarion* anymore. I've got my own news agency now.' She produced a business card and waved it under Kate's nose.

'Very smart,' Kate replied, reluctantly taking the card and slipping it into her pocket, thinking that the press office at headquarters would have to be advised of the new player in the game anyway.

Moreton held up her camera. 'So how about I take a quick snap of the scene? Then I'll leave you in peace.'

'The answer is still no,' Woo repeated.

'But there *are* human remains in there, I assume?'

Woo hesitated. 'What we believe to be human bones have been found buried in the wood, yes, but that's the only comment we are prepared to make at this stage.'

'What condition are these bones in?'

'We're not qualified to say.'

'But very old, or relatively recent, do you think.'

'No comment.'

'But you do believe it could be murder?'

Woo sighed. 'We're not saying anything of the sort, so don't try and put words in my mouth. Now, if you don't mind, we have work to do.'

He turned his back on her and began to pick his way carefully across the verge towards the taped-off area, only to swing round again to stare quizzically at Moreton as she made to follow him.

'That's as far as you go,' he said.

'It's a free country.'

'Not here, it isn't,' Kate said blocking her attempt.

She smirked but made no attempt to go round her. 'I heard you'd left the force, Kate,' she said. 'Gone to "Welsh" Wales or somewhere.'

'Did you? Well, I'm here now, aren't I? So, why don't you climb back on that flashy motorbike of yours and head off to investigate a few potholes?'

For a moment, it was touch and go, as the two old enemies faced each other. But then Moreton capitulated and, with a sneer, turned round and flounced back to the Bonneville.

'That one's going to be trouble,' Kate said, joining Woo in the wood.

He made a face. 'Maybe, but there'll be a whole pack of hyenas like her descending on us when the rest of the media gets wind of this job,' he replied. 'We'd better have SOCO out here with their tent PDQ. Then at least the scene will have some protection against the weather and the pathologist and forensic team will be given some privacy in which to work.'

Kate pulled out her mobile and set things in motion immediately with the control room, then joined him by the macabre excavation.

'So, what are your first impressions?' Woo asked her.

She crouched down at the edge of the hole and studied the exposed bones for several minutes. 'Difficult to draw any positive conclusions from the remains as they are, but it's obvious that they have been here for a very long time — years, I would say. The bones themselves are yellowed and they have certainly been picked clean.' She held on to the edge of the hole and peered closer. 'But there is something else down there among what appears to be part of a ribcage that looks suspiciously like a part-corroded brass button . . .'

'Brass?'

'Yeah.' She straightened up. 'That's what it looked like. Embellished with something too. Couldn't quite make it out.'

'Military, do you reckon?'

She shrugged. 'Long shot, but could be, I suppose. Someone who deserted or went AWOL. That might mean dog tags are also buried down there under the rest of the earth, which could save us a lot of trouble re identification.'

'I never get that kind of luck, Kate, and don't forget, a lot of youngsters now wear ex-army gear as a sort of fashion statement. Makes 'em look tough, I suppose. They can buy it in any army surplus store too.'

'Well, whoever they were, they obviously didn't expect to end up being dumped in a wood, miles from anywhere and it certainly doesn't look like they died solely from shortage of breath. Even at this distance, you can see that the top part of the skull appears to have been badly fractured and there are also breaks in the one visible leg bone . . . Tibia, isn't it?'

'Can't remember which is which . . . But equally on that point, the bones could have been crushed by the actions of the digger?'

'True, but with a bit of luck the forensic pathologist will have some early thoughts on things when they arrive.'

'Might be a tad difficult with most of the bits still largely buried.' He gave a short laugh. 'Pray we're not the ones that are expected to dig them out.'

She shook head soberly. 'Well, you know what they always say in the job: if you can't stand a joke, you shouldn't have joined.'

* * *

The arrival of the tent and the crime scene investigation team, together with a few more uniforms made Kate feel a lot more confident about the security of the site and she left Hayden to supervise the setting up of a tighter, more well-defined cordon around it, using the yellow crime scene tapes, prohibiting access, and an outer ring of blue and white police perimeter tapes, keeping the press and other unauthorised visitors even further back.

Debbie Moreton tried a number of times to slip through the outer cordon but gave up after her third attempt and the threat of arrest from one of the uniformed officers. By then, as Woo had anticipated, there were a lot more reporters on the scene, plus a few cameras and a small local television unit, but for the most part they behaved themselves, only trying it on a couple of times, then uncharacteristically giving up.

A short statement by the DI, giving more slightly guarded information on the situation helped to satisfy most of the media that were there and, learning that it was only a collection of bones that had been found and not a nice, fresh, juicy corpse, most of them then drifted away, though Moreton was one of those that remained.

The forensic pathologist created a little bit more interest when she arrived about two hours after the discovery of the body, but apart from a few shouted questions as she disappeared into the tent, everything quietened right down then and even Moreton chose to leave with an aggressive roar of her Bonneville.

The pathologist was a tall, slender blonde well into her forties who looked more like a thirty-five-year-old beautician than someone who spent much of her working life sorting through human body parts. Lydia Summers was an old friend of Kate's and she had worked with her on many different cases in the past. Not that these particular remains looked like being able to tell her too much on this occasion.

'Afternoon, people,' Summers said cheerfully, staring down into the hole that was now flash-lit by SOCO's powerful equipment. 'Thought you'd thrown in the towel and escaped to Pembrokeshire, Kate?'

'She couldn't live without us, doc,' Woo cut in with a grin. 'Had to slink back to the fold.'

Summers raised both eyebrows. 'That true, Kate?' she retorted, her gaze staying fixed on the grisly remains in the hole. 'Then more fool you,' she said. 'You should have kept on running.'

Kate shrugged, giving a faint smile. 'I might have done if I had known this was waiting for me,' she replied.

Summers pursed her lips and bent down on the edge of the hole for closer scrutiny of the bones. 'Not much for me here, though, is there?' she said. 'I prefer nice juicy cadavers. Bones don't do a lot for me. In this instance, most of it is still buried too. You'll need a forensic anthropologist if you want the remains securely recovered without loss of possible evidence in the process. I can certainly conduct a PM of sorts, but if you need to analyse the skeletal remains in more detail and have a biological profile put together for assistance with age and identification, you'll need the bone man.'

Woo frowned. 'I was afraid of that,' he replied. 'So, we're talking about a protracted site investigation before we can do anything?'

Summers gave a waspish smile. ''Fraid so, Inspector. Unavoidable if you really want answers.'

'Guv'nor won't like it,' the DI commented to Kate gloomily. 'It'll take a big lump out of his budget.'

'It's his call,' Summers added.

Woo sighed. 'Can you give us anything unofficially as a possible starter for ten? I mean, from what we can see, it seems very likely that the deceased suffered some sort of severe fracture to the skull and one of the leg bones appears to have been shattered. Can you at least tell us whether you think those injuries might have been inflicted deliberately by someone or may have been caused by the work being carried out by the digger driver who found the remains?'

There was a spark of anger in Summers' grey eyes. 'I don't gamble or give off-the-cuff opinions that are not backed up by scientific evidence, or at the very least, by qualified expert opinion, Inspector,' she said. 'This is not a game show and, as I haven't yet had the opportunity of carrying out any kind of proper examination of the remains, I am unable to tell you anything — officially or unofficially. You will have to curb your impatience in the meantime.'

Kate inwardly winced and couldn't help feeling sorry for Charlie Woo. Lydia Summers could be quite caustic if she felt she was being leaned on, and Kate guessed that for all his usual professionalism, as a new DI in post, Woo was anticipating the rough ride he was going to get from Ricketts over the hit to the DCI's budget. This was what happened, she thought, when a DCI with no previous CID experience was put in post for his own career development rather than to fill the position with the most suitably qualified candidate. The trouble was, the department was now stuck with him, as the powers-that-be had doubtless discovered he was a wally no one else wanted, and as a knock-on effect, his inadequacies rubbed off on everyone else.

'Well, that was telling me, wasn't it?' Woo said ruefully to Kate, as they watched the tail-lights of Summers's car disappear into the gathering dusk.

Kate laughed. 'Don't worry about it, Charlie,' she said. 'The doc can be a bit testy at times. She'll be as right as rain tomorrow when we resume, and at least she'll have everything set up for us. We've got the scene secured with a couple of woodentops for tonight and there's nothing more we can do now until tomorrow.'

'Try telling that to Ricketts,' he said sourly. Then throwing open his car door, he accelerated away at speed without another word.

'Problems?' Hayden asked Kate when he climbed into the CID car beside her.

'Charlie had a bit of a run-in with Doc Summers,' she replied. 'I think Ricketts has been giving him a hard time since he made DI, so he tried to push things along a bit with her and got bitten.'

Hayden grunted. 'Ouch! From what I've seen of the doc in the past, that wouldn't have been a good move.'

'No, it wasn't. But when you've got an arsehole like Ricketts constantly on your back, you *are* likely to make unwise moves from time to time.'

He grinned in the semi-darkness. 'You should know, old girl. You're a past master at it.'

She started the engine. 'Flattery will get you nowhere, fat man,' she retorted as she pulled away.

CHAPTER 3

Charlie Woo was already in his glass-panelled inner sanctum when Kate and Hayden arrived at Highbridge police station the following morning. Leaving Hayden to head for the canteen — old habits died hard, especially where Hayden and food were concerned — she hung up her coat and grabbed two black coffees from the machine in the corner before sauntering across to Woo's office.

Tapping once on the door with her knee, she stepped inside and plonked one of the mugs on the desk in front of him. She got the impression he wouldn't have noticed she was there at all if he hadn't smelled the coffee.

'Ah, er, Kate,' he acknowledged and looked up from the newspaper he appeared to have been reading with a worried frown. Then he slid the newspaper towards her. 'We appear to have made the news.'

'That was bloody quick,' she replied, setting her mug down on the corner of the desk. Grabbing a plastic chair, she sat down in front of his desk and reached forward to pick up the morning's copy of one of the local rags. The photograph hit her first. It occupied nearly a third of the front page of the tabloid under the eye-catching headline: *BURIED IN*

THE WOODS. It was a slightly hazy photograph of what was obviously the collection of bones she and Woo had been studying the day before. Underneath the main picture were several smaller photographs of a parked patrol car, plus one of the CID cars and the digger itself, as well as several recognisable figures.

'How the hell did they get hold of all this?' she exclaimed. 'The scene was cordoned off and we had a plod, plus Hayden there to prevent unauthorised access.'

He sighed. 'If you check the pics again, you'll see that they were taken from the other direction,' he said, 'and *before* the tent was erected. The close-up of the bones in the hole appears in the foreground of that main pic with the partially unearthed tree stump to the left of it, which means it was captured from inside the woods on the other side of the hole.'

'Debbie Moreton,' Kate breathed.

He nodded in resignation. 'My thoughts entirely. She must have got a photographer to sneak in earlier through the woods at the back of the site while you and me were actually by the road. If you look at one of the lower pics, you can see us there talking to her on the verge. This would have been even before we went to take a look at the scene. She was keeping us occupied while her colleague did the business.'

'But Hayden and the plod were standing by the police tape. They would have seen anyone creeping out of cover with a camera.'

'Not if the photographer came in from behind, through the trees. You can see our plod's shoulder and epaulette in the left-hand corner of one pic and it's obviously a rear view. Both he and Hayden would have been facing towards the road with their backs to the hole.'

Kate released her breath in a sharp, explosive hiss. 'Well, Moreton certainly stitched us up this time, didn't she?'

'Not only with the pic of the bones either,' he said, nodding towards the newspaper that was still across Kate's lap. 'You might want to read on.'

Her eyes narrowed as she caught his drift, and she turned her attention to the news report underneath the photographs.

> *Highbridge Police are investigating the discovery of human remains on the Somerset Levels near Wedmore. A collection of bones was unearthed yesterday afternoon in an isolated wooded area known as Pagan's Clump. Council worker, Ron Finch, was digging out a tree stump as part of a new road-widening scheme when he discovered them. Mr Finch said he thought the remains, which consisted of a badly damaged skull and at least one broken leg bone, had been there a long time. Police refused to comment on the macabre discovery, other than to state that inquiries were ongoing. They were unable to confirm whether the skeleton was male or female, and refused to say whether they believed this was a case of murder. Nevertheless, one of the lead investigators, our very own Detective Sergeant Kate Lewis, apparently told Mr Finch that "bodies don't bury themselves". A rather flippant remark for a senior police officer to make in the circumstances, we thought, but the sort of comment we've come to expect from Kate Lewis, who has only recently returned to duty from a year's sabbatical in deepest Pembrokeshire after taking time off for stress. We trust the good sergeant has fully recovered from her illness now and will not find this investigation too much for her to handle.*

Kate's face was ashen. 'That snidey little cow,' she snarled. 'I could wring her scrawny neck.'

'Don't let her get to you,' Woo said sharply. 'That's what she wants, you know that. She's done the same sort of thing to you in the past. So, be patient. She will get her comeuppance sooner or later.'

Kate dumped the newspaper back on his desk and snatched up her mug, her hand trembling with suppressed fury as she gulped down some more coffee.

'At least the *Clarion* didn't get the story first anyway,' she said, finally resigning herself to the situation after a long, thoughtful pause. 'But that's about the only plus here. I bet Moreton deliberately offered the story to the *Clarion*'s rival to get back at her old editor, Theodore Rainer. Rainer will be really pissed over the fact that the other paper got in first.'

Woo made a grimace. 'He won't be the only one who's pissed,' he said. 'The DCI will be next in line when he sees the story this morning, especially after the row we had yesterday evening over bringing in a forensic anthropologist to recover the remains.'

Kate looked astonished. 'Don't tell me he's opposing it? As DCI, he must be aware that in cases like this we have no choice if we are to preserve what is likely to be a crime scene and recover any evidence that might be there?'

'It's all about money, Kate, money and time — *and*, of course, ensuring he doesn't face criticism from the hierarchy for overspending his budget. He feels that any skeleton must have been there for yonks and therefore any evidential traces will have been obliterated long ago.'

'But it isn't simply the evidential aspect. We haven't the faintest bloody idea who the stiff is, their probable age, whether they are even male or female and how long they're likely to have been buried there. These issues are fundamental to the investigation and the anthropologist is our best bet for coming up with some answers.'

'Don't you think I know that?' He shrugged his shoulders in obvious frustration. 'But Mr Ricketts is a university import who was shoe-horned into the job under the graduate entry scheme . . .'

'Careful. So was I.'

He treated her to a brief smile. 'Yeah, but there's a difference. You are an experienced detective with a lot of time at the coal face behind you, but he hasn't been on CID five minutes. He's been hopping from department to department for most of his service, and he doesn't see things the same way as a dyed-in-the-wool CID man. In short, he thinks bringing in what he regards as yet another kind of expert would be a waste of time and money.'

'Are you saying he's knocked it on the head? I think Lydia Summers is likely to have something to say about that when she hears.'

'No, he agreed to it in the end, but he's been on to HQ and a Major Investigation Team is being sent down to take over the inquiry under a DCI Maurice Skindle. They'll have one of the force's major incident wagons on site and they'll handle things from there initially. That gets him off the hook and Skindle will carry the investigative responsibility.'

'Typical. So, we're out of it anyway?'

'Initially, yes. But depending on what they turn up, we are likely to be providing support later in the form of local inquiries. The DCI and myself are liaising with the new team down at the scene later this afternoon.'

'I must admit I'm more than a bit pissed off. This looked like being an intriguing case. We should have stuck with it.'

'Maybe we should, but with the department so short-handed, we have enough on our plate to deal with at present without this as well, and a protracted inquiry like this is ideal for one of the major investigation teams to take on.'

She missed the sudden wicked gleam in his eyes.

'I saw our office manager, Ajeet Singh, fill your in-tray near to breaking point before he went off yesterday evening,' he said mildly. 'Furthermore, as a newbie, you'll probably find the department's caseload daunting enough as it is . . .'

Her response was like a whiplash. 'I *have* done this before, Charlie,' she reminded him tartly, failing to pick up on the underlying mickey-take in time. 'Grandmother really doesn't need to be taught how to suck eggs, you know . . .'

Her voice trailed off as it abruptly dawned on her that she was being had.

'Then Granny better get her skinny, wrinkled arse in gear and get on with the job, hadn't she?' he said, dissolving into an unexpected fit of laughter — only to knock over his coffee as a result.

* * *

The mountain of paperwork was a real sight for sore eyes, and Kate needed another cup of coffee before she could even begin to tackle it. The general office had filled up substantially by the time Charlie Woo was collected by the DCI for the liaison meeting down at the crime scene and those of Kate's colleagues who were not actually out investigating the multitude of crimes, big and small, that had been reported right across the Highbridge police area in the last twenty-four hours, were at their laptops in the large general office, completing crime reports, internet searches and background inquiries into other reported cases that had been allocated to them. Even Hayden found himself tied to his desk for a while, though, predictably, that didn't last long and after about an hour and a half he managed to slink away down to the canteen, banking on the fact that amid the constant noisy banter which was such a regular part of CID life, his departure would go unnoticed.

He was wrong. Kate knew him too well and spotted him slink away. But then she was distracted by a phone call.

'A Rev. Arthur Taylor is on the line for you, skipper,' the switchboard said.

Relieved at being given an excuse to push her paperwork to one side, albeit for what was likely to be a few minutes' conversation, Kate told the operator to put him through. She was right about the shortness of the call, but to her relief it provided her with the opportunity to abandon the mountain of crime reports and case files for a lot longer than a few minutes and to head out into the fresh air.

She found Hayden in the canteen, straddling a small plastic chair like some kind of Buddha look-alike, with a coffee and the remains of a currant bun on the table in front of him.

He started when he saw her, one podgy hand poised over the last morsel of bun, a sickly smile on his face. 'Ah, Kate, old girl,' he said. 'I, ah, needed a quick bite. Low blood sugar and all that, you know. Feeling quite faint.'

'Don't give me that old chestnut, Hayd,' she snapped back. 'You know you shouldn't be down here again. You've already had one break this morning and it looks bad to the rest of the team. And for the umpteenth time, do *not* call me "old girl" at work. It's embarrassing. I've told you about that before.'

He flushed. 'Er, like a coffee?' he asked. 'Lot better here than that stuff upstairs.'

'No, I don't want any coffee,' she replied, 'and you can forget it too. We've got a job on.'

He stuffed the last bit of bun in his already half-full mouth and tipped some of his coffee in after it.

'A job?' he prevaricated, wiping his lips on the back of his hand. 'Why us?'

'Because everyone else is tucked up at the moment and, as this is only our second day back and we are now free of the inquiry we were dealing with, we are available.'

'Rushing like this could give me bad indigestion.'

'Oh, do me a favour, Hayd,' she retorted. 'Your stomach is tougher than a cast-iron boiler. So, come on. Out to the car, like now!'

Several faces turned towards her with sympathetic grins from nearby tables at her raised voice — everyone knew Hayden — and he stumbled to his feet like an obedient Labrador, gulping down the remains of his coffee on the way.

'So, what's this all about?' he queried grumpily as they drove out of the police station yard.

'Call from a local clergyman, the Rev. Arthur Taylor,' she said. 'Seems he disturbed someone breaking into a shed on his property, but the man ran off.'

Hayden frowned. 'No plod patrols to cover it then?' he asked sourly. 'CID don't usually respond to shouts like this until Uniform have attended.'

'No Uniform mobiles available,' she said. 'Besides which, for some inexplicable reason he asked for me personally.'

She threw him a wicked sideways glance. 'As for your beef that CID don't usually attend these incidents first, CID don't usually sit around stuffing their bellies in the canteen when there's work to be done either.'

There was immediate silence in the passenger seat beside her. Hayden was strangely tongue-tied.

CHAPTER 4

The Reverend Taylor lived in a cottage with a red brick and grey flint facade and pitched tiled roof that was reminiscent of the architecture Kate had once seen on a holiday in the Chilterns. It occupied a sizeable, well-manicured plot on the outskirts of a small hamlet not far from the village of Wedmore and the driveway was occupied by an early reg black Volvo XC90, which, from the noticeable scratches evident on the bodywork, suggested it had seen a lot better days. The churchman was in his garden, on the front lawn, pruning part of the roadside hedge when they pulled up outside and he spotted them immediately.

'Ah, Sergeant Lewis,' he said, limping towards them to open the wicket gate. 'Thank you for coming.'

Kate studied him curiously. A tall, thin man in what she judged to be his late seventies, he had long, spindly-looking legs and a slightly stooped back. A thatch of snow-white hair and gold-coloured half-moon spectacles gave him a slightly eccentric air, but the blue eyes that studied her from under bushy, white brows were sharp and focused. He was not wearing the customary dog collar, although there was an ornate silver-coloured crucifix hanging on a chain around his thin neck, and he was dressed in faded tweeds and brown brogues that were plastered in dirt and hedge cuttings, which dropped off as he led the way along the garden path to the open front door, with what seemed like a permanent limp.

'You said an intruder?' Kate said, as she and Hayden walked through the door after him. 'Yes, yes, yes,' he said over his shoulder, seemingly unaware of the trail he was leaving behind him on the hall carpet. 'Long gone now, I'm afraid.'

'It's quite a warm day,' he said, showing them into a small square library and indicating two floral-patterned armchairs with a wave of one hand. 'Can I offer you some tea, or a cordial perhaps?'

After plonking himself in the nearest chair with an expectant look on his face, Hayden then hurriedly climbed to his feet again, looking disappointed to see that Kate had remained standing. 'No, thank you, Reverend,' she said. 'Can we have a look at this shed of yours and you can tell us what happened?'

'Of course, of course, come through.'

Preceding them along a hallway, through a large farmhouse-style kitchen, he led the way along another path at the back of the cottage, which wound its way among mature shrubs, to a second lawn with a wooden shed in a corner at the far end.

Even as they approached, Kate could see the jagged hole in the half-open side window and the glass shards glittering on the lawn beneath.

'Only gardening stuff in there,' Taylor said. 'It's where I keep my mower too.'

Kate and Hayden jointly examined the window, then followed the old man inside the shed. They were met by the musty smell of old wood and stale oil. There was a workbench to one side, opposite the window, and hessian sacks were piled up in a corner. The usual tools hung from a number of hooks on the far wall and low shelving under the window held an assortment of bottles, pots and spray cans.

'Anything missing, Reverend?' Kate asked.

He sighed and shook his head. 'Not as far as I know and there wasn't really much in here *to* steal. But it was rather unnerving to walk down my path and see someone sprinting away towards my back gate.'

'When did this happen?' Hayden put in.

'Oh, about ten minutes before I rang your station.'

Kate glanced at her watch. 'So around twelve?'

'Must have been, yes. I was on my way to get some tools out when I heard the sound of breaking glass and saw the man running away.'

'Was he coming out of the shed?'

'No, the door was still locked. The impression I got was that I had disturbed him after he had smashed the window.'

'Can you describe him?' Kate said.

'Not really. Average height and build, that's about all. I only saw the back of him, and he was wearing one of those hooded coats. Black, I think.'

'Well, there's not a lot we can do on the information you have to hand, and this isn't something we would normally send our scenes-of-crime team out to examine.' Kate shrugged. 'Broken window, no entry gained. No apparent sign of injury to the assailant from the glass. It isn't the sort of break-in where fingerprints, fibres or DNA might have been left behind. I assume the stone lying there was from your own garden?'

He nodded and pointed to a gap in the line of similar stones lining a rectangular border opposite.

'From there, it would seem.' He shrugged. 'I thought I would report it, to be on the safe side.'

'Of course.' Kate frowned. 'But tell me, what made you ask for me when you rang us?'

He led the way back towards the house. 'Well, I saw your details in the newspaper about those human remains being found out at Pagan's Clump and, having got hold of a name, felt it sensible to ask for you personally. How's that investigation going incidentally? Do you know who the unfortunate soul was?'

'No, not so far. It is likely to take some considerable time, as we have no means of identification yet.'

'But do you even know whether the person was male or female?'

'We have no idea. At the moment, we simply have a collection of bones. Not much to go on really.'

'How old do you think the remains are? I mean, could they be from a previous century perhaps? You know, medieval even?'

'Maybe they could, but that doesn't seem likely.'

'Oh, so you have reason to believe they are from this era?'

'At this stage no one can say. But what makes you think the bones might be medieval specifically?'

He shrugged. 'I'm not suggesting they are. I'm merely offering that up as a possibility. Pagan's Clump has an unenviable reputation. It has long been reputed to have been used by Satanists over the centuries for black magic purposes, and it is possible sacrifices of some sort were once carried out there.'

'How do you know all this?'

'Well, I have always been a bit of a historian and in my spare time I have made a point of researching local legends and folklore. The Clump is one of many places on the Levels linked to devil worship. You will find that a lot of superstitious local people here still believe the wood is cursed and that, for masters of the black arts, it acts as a gateway from our world to the lower echelons of Hell or–or for the, er, Devil.'

Kate raised her eyebrows and treated him to a faintly crooked smile. 'I trust that in your position you do not share that belief.'

He laughed now. 'Hardly, Sergeant. I am merely passing on what I have heard.'

'Very good of you to let me know too, Reverend. I'll bear it in mind.'

He opened the back door and ushered them through ahead of him. 'And the discovery of these bones, do you suspect foul play then, er, as the newspapers are now saying?'

Kate stopped by the front door and turned to face him, becoming a little irritated by his constant questions. 'Look, we have no idea yet who the person was or how they died, but the fact that they ended up being buried in the manner that they were obviously requires investigation.'

He nodded. 'I see your point. But is it true what they are saying in the local newspaper, that the deceased had head injuries and a broken leg?'

Kate controlled herself with an effort. 'I cannot go into details, Reverend. What you have read amounts to nothing more than press speculation . . . Why are you so interested in this particular matter anyway?'

He made a face. 'I hate to admit the fact, but I suppose it's partly due to morbid curiosity. Ministers of religion are no different from anyone else with regard to basic human frailties, I'm afraid. Also, as the former minister for the diocese in question, I cannot help wondering whether this deceased soul was once a member of my own flock during my term as parish priest.'

'So, you are no longer the local minister?'

He shook his head with a soft laugh. 'Good gracious me, no. I am now seventy-seven and I retired with ill health some years ago.'

'And when you *were* the priest, can you remember any member of your parish going missing?'

He thought for a second. 'Not on a permanent basis, no. As with communities right across the country, people were and still are, I am sure, reported missing from home from time to time, but I am not aware of any of my former parishioners remaining unaccounted for during my ministry here. Do you believe the remains you have found are those of some unfortunate missing person then?'

'The jury is still out on that, Reverend,' Kate replied. 'But if anything should subsequently occur to you that you feel may be of interest to us, it would be most helpful if you could contact Highbridge police station.'

'But of course. Thank you for responding to my little crime complaint so promptly.'

'All part of the job, sir . . .'

'Well, that was a total waste of time,' Hayden growled as they drove away. 'Things have certainly gone downhill since we were last here if CID are having to respond to garden shed break-ins like this.'

'If it *was* a break-in,' Kate replied with a grim smile.

'Ah, so you noticed too?'

'Couldn't really miss it, could I? The glass from the broken window and frame was lying on the lawn instead of inside the shed where it would have landed if the window had been smashed from the outside.'

He nodded. 'The naughty old reverend was fibbing and did the job himself?'

'Precisely, like another case we dealt with a few years ago, remember?'

'Then why not tackle him about it there and then? I was surprised you didn't. Wasting police time is a criminal offence.'

'I couldn't see the point. It was much too trivial an issue to pursue. It would also have been almost impossible to prove anyway without forensic examination, which I certainly wasn't about to call for. He was an old man and was probably lonely and seeking a bit of attention.'

'Do you really believe that?'

She made a grimace. 'No, I don't. He obviously did it to get me out here so he could quiz me on the remains that have turned up.'

'Do you think he might have had something to do with the stiff's death then?'

'No idea, but I think we should keep the Rev. Taylor in mind as a possible person of interest, if the business is ultimately determined to be a homicide.'

'So, are you going to pass the info about him to the major inquiry team then?'

'No, not yet.'

'Why not?'

'Well, what have we got to tell them? That there's a retired local priest we suspect of breaking his own shed window to get us out to his home so he could quiz us about the discovery of our pile of bones. I'm sure that little snippet of crap would go down a treat with the SIO in the circumstances!'

'At least it would forestall any allegation that you are doing your usual "Go It Alone Kate" thing, for which you've been criticised in the past.'

She snorted her contempt. 'Do me a favour, Hayd. Nothing at all is known about those remains yet or how they came to be where they are. We'd look pretty damned stupid fingering the Rev Taylor as a potential suspect for some heinous crime, only for it later to turn out that there is no crime at all and the bones are, in fact, those of a twelfth-century monk, or a Cavalier from the English Civil War! Archaeologists are forever finding ancient remains like that across the whole country and there are a few that have been uncovered in Somerset.'

'That's not the point. It could merit looking into.'

'I think it's every bit the point, and I'm surprised you care one way or the other, as it could involve that dreaded thing called work if the SIO were to ask us to do the looking into.'

He shrugged. 'Insults will get you nowhere. Do what you want. It's your funeral.'

'No, it isn't, Hayd,' she retorted. 'That position has already been taken by someone else and, since the DCI feels we should no longer be part of the investigation into their ID and how and why they died, I intend leaving it there. I will be getting on with the shitload of paperwork in my in-tray instead. Any other bright suggestions?'

He scowled, 'Do you have to use abusive language all the time to describe things? Rather than the way you said what you said, why couldn't you simply say "a lot of paperwork"?'

She grinned. 'Because it isn't simply a lot of paperwork, Hayd. It's a bloody shitload!'

* * *

DCI Ricketts was waiting for Kate when she and Hayden got back to the police station. He was standing in the DI's office to one side of her boss's desk, staring out of the window. Of Charlie Woo there was no sign and Kate guessed Ricketts had left him down at Pagan's Clump. The DCI had his back to Kate, but he seemed to sense her presence and he swung round to beckon her in to see him. Hayden gulped and promptly disappeared behind the computer on his desk and the civilian officer manager, Ajeet Singh, who was sitting at another desk a short distance from Kate's, winced at her and appeared to try to burrow further into his chair. Ricketts had a newspaper in one hand and as she warily approached the door, he thrust it belligerently at her.

'Seen this, Sergeant,' he snapped, and his eyes glittered like polished glass.

She nodded, without looking at it. 'The DI brought it to my attention before I went out on a job, sir,' she replied.

'Well? What have you got to say for yourself?'

She shrugged. 'Nothing much I can say, is there, sir? The press were bound to find out about the discovery of the bones sooner or later.'

'I'm not talking about that. I'm talking about the facetious comment you made to that site foreman about the dead not burying themselves. You can't help yourself, can you? Your tongue will be your downfall.'

Kate stared at him, incredulous that he could be making such a song and dance about such a minor issue in the face of a potential murder investigation.

'It was an observation, that's all, sir,' she said, 'and Debbie Moreton was bound to make something of it when he mentioned it to her. She has always been anti-police and especially anti-me—'

'I'm not surprised,' he cut in. 'It was a stupid, unprofessional remark to make.'

'Point taken, sir,' she said, without meaning it. 'Is there anything else you wish to see me about?'

His mouth formed a hard line. 'You insubordinate little—' he began but didn't finish the sentence. Then he said, 'But yes, there is. From now on, you will not talk to the press at all. No official comments, or off-the-cuff remarks. You will pass any inquiries that are made to a senior officer or headquarters press office. Is that clear?'

'Very clear, sir. But does that include radio and television?'

'What did you hear me say?'

'Yes, sir, but reference to "the press" specifically, is usually taken to mean newspapers and magazines. I assume you mean the media generally then?'

She thought he was about to explode. 'Get out of my way!' he shouted and almost knocked her over as he barged past her and marched across the general office at speed, disappearing through the double doors at the end and practically colliding with DCs Jamie Foster and Indrani Purewal in the process.

'Bloody hell, skipper,' Foster exclaimed, staring after him. 'What have you done to upset the guv'nor?'

She smiled almost with glee. 'Oh, I think he must have had a bad day,' she said. 'He'll get over it . . .'

* * *

Robert Stephen Chalmers was every bit the company man and he certainly tried to look the part in his neat blue suit and shiny black Italian shoes. He had "crawled" hard to get to where he was on the board of the IT management firm, G & S Solutions, and he had his eye on the deputy chairman's position when the present incumbent retired. But at fifty-three, with double chins and a noticeable paunch already developing, and the bald patch in his thinning brown hair expanding faster than his expensive hairdresser could cope with it, he knew he was running out of time. He was in an industry that revered young, dynamic executives, who could walk the walk, talk the talk, and use all the right buzzwords, even if they hadn't a clue what these meant any more than anyone else. The IT industry had always been a bit like the fairytale of *The Emperor's New Clothes*, adhering to the principle of bullshit baffles brains, and Chalmers knew he was fast losing his grip on the edge of the career precipice he had been dangling over since his fifty-first birthday. He couldn't afford any major faux pas now.

Small wonder then that he was not best pleased when the call came through on his mobile in the middle of an important board meeting. Colouring up under the smouldering gaze of the company chairman, which focused on him from the head of the long table, reducing him to a mumbled 'Sorry', he shut off the strident notes of "When the Saints Go Marching In", cursing his own stupidity for failing to switch the phone to "silent" before the meeting.

An hour and a half later he checked on the "miscreant" who had unwittingly embarrassed him so badly in front of all his smirking colleagues, determined to give them a hard time — only to find it was his former wife whom he'd not long divorced.

Lizzie Johnson sounded breathless when she answered his call.

'Robert, thank goodness . . .'

'Lizzie,' he snapped, angrily cutting her off, 'do you realise what you've done? You rang me right in the middle of a vitally important board meeting.'

'Bugger the meeting,' she said, unrepentant, 'I needed to get hold of you urgently.'

'Oh yeah?' he sneered. 'Don't tell me you broke a fingernail?'

She ignored the sarcasm. 'Robert, this is bloody serious. Haven't you heard the news?'

'News? What news? How the hell could I have heard any news if I was at a board meeting?'

She swore. 'Listen to me, Robert, will you! It's about Pagan's Clump. They've found human remains there.'

'Pagan's Clump? What are you talking about?'

'Surely you haven't forgotten the old dosser Danny totalled all those years ago? Annie Evans — remember? We stuck her in the ground at Pagan's Clump.'

An icy claw snatched at his vitals as everything suddenly came back to him in an ugly flashback. 'Shit! How do you know?'

'How?' He picked up on the tremble in her voice and heard her catch her breath. 'Local radio, that's how, Robert, local bloody radio! Now half the county knows about it. It's in all the newspapers too.' Her voice rose to a higher pitch. 'I said that would come back to haunt us. Police have sealed off the whole site. Hells bells, they're digging her up even as we speak! What if they find something there that links us to her death? What if–if we left something behind all that time ago? What if—'

'Shut it, Lizzie!' he snapped, conscious of the fact that he was now sweating. 'Calm yourself down. You're jumping to stupid conclusions. That business must have been over thirty years ago. Anything that was there then will be long gone now. Use your head.'

'Her bones aren't long gone, though, are they? The police have got them—'

He gripped the phone so tightly that it gave off a loud crack. 'You don't know what they've got,' he retorted in the most authoritative tone he could manage, acutely aware of how emotionally fragile his former wife could be in a crisis and how easy it was for her to become hysterical, which was the last thing they needed. 'Get a grip, will you? Now, are the others aware of this?'

'I've no–no idea,' she wailed. 'Maybe . . . But how would I know? I haven't heard from any of them for ages.'

'Right, so we need to get everyone together again for a meeting asap. Do you still have their mobile numbers?'

'I'm–I'm not sure. I think so . . . I'd have to have a look.'

He grimaced and shook his head irritably. 'Okay, okay, forget that. I think *I* have, so I'll bell them all about the meeting myself. I should be able to make it tomorrow night, if that suits. Can we use your place? My flat in Bristol is hardly big enough.'

'Yeah, cool but–but Robert, what if—?'

'Eight o'clock tomorrow then,' he said, cutting her off, 'and don't talk to anyone in the meantime. Do you understand? *No one at all.*'

CHAPTER 5

Lizzie Johnson lived in a converted barn outside the village of Blackford. Life had been good to her over the years. Embarking on a career in teaching at a prestigious private school after leaving university, she had retired on an ill-health pension at the grand old age of fifty-two, following a dubious but successful tribunal claim of work-related mental stress. This had provided her with a nice lump sum — which, coupled with her subsequent lucrative divorce from childhood sweetheart, Robert Chalmers, three years ago on the grounds of infidelity — had enabled her to buy her current dream home.

Good luck had stayed with her too. Plunging headfirst into the world of literary fiction, aspiring to be a romantic novelist, she had made the bestseller list with her debut novel and had secured an ongoing contract for at least two more novels with a major London publisher.

Her future had seemed assured — but that was until she had turned on her radio that morning and learned about the macabre discovery at Pagan's Clump. Suddenly a blot had been put on everything and, in her guilt-laden panic, she had involuntarily conjured up a mental picture of her whole world collapsing around her. Bob Chalmers saw the dramatic change in her the moment she answered the door to him on his arrival for the meeting the following evening. Although they were divorced, they had always kept in touch, and he had seen her only two days before when they had bumped into each other in Bristol during his lunch break. He was astonished at the change that had been wrought in her since.

A once attractive strawberry blonde, with a trim figure, flawless ivory skin and clear blue eyes that, even in her fifties, had seemed to retain an enticing, flirty invitation, she now looked shrunken and haggard, with dark patches under her over-bright, staring eyes and a noticeable tic in her left cheek, suggesting she was close to a breakdown.

Not that he was in much better shape himself. He had slept hardly at all the previous night after going through the local newspapers and catching up on the discovery at Pagan's Clump. His brown eyes seemed sunken, and the chubby face had developed a tight, haunted look. Although he had been at pains to reassure Lizzie, he was in a pretty bad place himself and his reliance on strong spirits to keep him going in times of stress hadn't been much help.

The others were already in the house, lounging on chairs and sofas with drinks already in their hands, and he took stock as they raised their wine and whisky glasses in perfunctory welcome as he walked into the room.

The original author of all their woes, Danny Aldridge, was spread out nonchalantly across a two-seater settee as if he hadn't a care in the world, a glass of red wine in one hand. Dressed in a blue jumper and faded blue jeans, he seemed to have hardly changed since the old days. True, his shoulder-length black hair was streaked with grey, and he sported a full beard, but he didn't look the fifty-odd years Chalmers knew he had to be by now.

Jennifer Talbot did look her age, though. Sitting bolt upright in an armchair in the corner of the room, resting a glass of white wine on the chair arm beside her, she was wafer thin, with short, grey hair and tinted blue glasses. In her sensible grey suit and lace-up shoes, she seemed every bit the hard-bitten, fifty-three-year-old spinster he had always thought she would one day become. He noticed that she wasn't wearing a wedding ring.

Julian Grey was perched on a windowsill, clutching a large glass of whisky. Dressed all in black — an open-necked silk shirt and corduroy trousers under an unbuttoned shortie car coat — he also appeared a lot thinner than Chalmers remembered all those years ago. He had no doubt recently been somewhere in the sun too. His clean-shaven, aquiline features were nicely tanned, and he was wearing a gold stud in the lobe of his left ear, as if trying to make a statement about something. Though all of fifty-two by Chalmer's reckoning, he appeared to be much younger than his years, and his head of coiffed jet-black hair would have been the envy of a thirty-year-old.

'Bobby, my man,' Grey said as, at Johnson's invitation, Chalmers poured himself a brandy from a cut-glass decanter standing on an attractive fawn-coloured cocktail cabinet by the door. 'Good to see you after so long.'

'Yeah,' Aldridge agreed, unwinding his legs and dragging himself up into a sitting position on the settee. 'Though, according to Lizzie, it seems we have a problem?'

Chalmers took a gulp from his glass and nodded. 'Filled you all in then, has she?' he asked.

They all nodded as one. 'Not that she needed to,' Talbot said sharply, 'as by lunchtime yesterday we had all seen the news reports ourselves.'

'Bit of bad luck the road being dug up there now after all these years,' Aldridge said almost too casually.

'Bit of bad luck, Danny?' Johnson echoed, the tremble back in her voice. 'Is that what you would call it? Bad luck? It's a b–bloody disaster!'

'Steady, Lizzie,' Grey soothed from his windowsill. 'Don't get yourself all worked up. That won't get us anywhere.'

'Oh, won't it?' she retorted derisively, and she was shaking now. 'Well, if that stupid bastard over there hadn't mowed the woman down in the first place because he was too pissed to drive, we wouldn't be in this position at all.'

'Oh, come on, it was an accident,' Aldridge shouted. 'That daft old bitch shouldn't have been hobbling along that lane in the dark.'

Chalmers winced and, fearing a slanging match between the two of them, he took Johnson firmly by the hand, and led her with her glass of scotch across the room to a vacant armchair, pressing her down on to it. 'Jules is right, Lizzie,' he said, ignoring Aldridge's outburst, 'we need to stay calm and work out what we are going to do.'

Talbot's cold, hard voice cut in straight away. 'As far as I can see, there is nothing we *can* do,' she said, 'except keep our heads down and get on with things as usual.' She could see that she had the floor, so carried on speaking. 'The newspapers say that all the police have is a collection of bones. They have no idea who they belonged to — they don't even know whether they were male or female. We left absolutely nothing at the scene. I think Danny said afterwards that his Volvo was undamaged . . .'

'Not a scratch,' Aldridge confirmed. 'The old girl must have bounced off the big bumper bar. And I hosed the car down when I got home too. Not even my father noticed anything when he got back from his hols.'

'There you are then. There's nothing for the police *to* find, and think about it, the accident happened some thirty-five years ago. If we had left any forensic traces behind, the elements would have destroyed them by now. We're completely in the clear.'

Chalmers sighed heavily. 'I've already told her precisely that, Jen,' he said, though inside himself he was less confident than he tried to sound.

'So, what about the guys in the car who stopped to ask us what had happened?' Johnson persisted. 'What if one of them made a note of the car number or something?'

Grey shook his head. 'Hardly likely, is it? If he had, they would already have done something afterwards, and we'd have heard about it long before now.'

'All we've got to do is hold our nerve,' Talbot went on. She looked straight at Johnson. 'Not do anything stupid, like talk to someone outside this room, for instance.'

Johnson picked up on the dig and glared at her. 'Me, you mean? Why would I do that anymore than anyone else here?'

'I'm not saying you would, but the wrong word in the wrong ear could put us all at risk.'

'Yeah, right, but there's maybe something much more important that we should be worried about than a visit from the police.'

'Such as?'

Johnson squirmed a little but seemed reluctant to qualify what she was getting at.

'Well, go on?' Talbot persisted, looking as puzzled as the rest. 'What else should we be worried about?'

Johnson looked down at her feet, colouring up and twisting the neck ties of the blouse she was wearing round and round in her fingers like a little girl. Then abruptly Talbot somehow sussed what was on her mind and released a derogatory snort.

'Surely we're not back to all that nonsense about Annie Evans being the so-called Night Hag, are we, Lizzie?' she exclaimed.

Johnson looked up, her face wearing a defiant scowl. 'You can scoff,' she retorted angrily, 'but it's not nonsense. I warned you all against what you were proposing to do when you decided to bury that evil old woman at Pagan's Clump. Now the police have opened up her grave and she'll be out looking to punish us for what we did.'

Grey swore and, downing the rest of his drink, pushed off his windowsill and crossed to the cocktail cabinet to pour himself another whisky.

'You keep talking like that, Lizzie,' he said over his shoulder, 'and you won't have to worry about the police finding something; the men in their white coats will be turning up at the door to take you away!'

Johnson didn't reply but returned to morosely studying the carpet. There was an awkward silence. Grey strolled back to his windowsill, shaking his head in resignation and Talbot fixed Chalmers with an intense, meaningful stare. As for Aldridge, after his own run-in with Johnson, he seemed to have opted out of any further involvement in the issues that were being discussed and had sunk deeper into his settee, sulking and interrogating his mobile.

'So, what is everyone doing now?' Chalmers said suddenly, in an effort to break the silence and get everyone talking about something else. 'Funny when you think about it that, out of the whole country, we all eventually chose to come back to live and work in this same area after uni—'

'Except you then buggered off to Bristol,' Aldridge pointed out.

'Only because me and Lizzie split up,' Chalmers qualified defensively, shooting a quick embarrassed glance at Johnson, though she still stared down at her feet as if in a trance, without commenting.

'You mean when she threw you out?' Grey pointed out good-naturedly.

Chalmers ignored the remark. 'Thing is, with my parents gone and their house sold, I couldn't find a decent place to buy in my old village, so I had to go elsewhere, and I know none of you fared any better either. Even you had a problem, didn't you, Danny? Despite the fact that you inherited your late father's real estate business and should have been in the best possible position.'

Aldridge stirred and nodded. 'Yeah,' he agreed. 'But the business is all I got. As you know, I had to sell the parental mansion to pay for the old man's care when the old woman died, and he ended his days with Alzheimer's in that rip-off home. Had to settle for another place I bought at a knockdown price, which I'm still in. But it's so old, it's falling down and has had to be partially propped up with scaffolding at one end while repairs are carried out. The stink I'm getting from all the turps, paints and other noxious inflammables the workmen leave behind when they're not actually working on the place is driving me nuts. So, I haven't gained much of an inheritance when you think about it. Also, the house is way out in the sticks near Glastonbury and half an hour's drive from the "shop" in Wedmore, which is far from convenient. The housing market I rely on is in an even worse state now too. Once upon a time, everyone wanted the perfect rural pad. You know, blue skies, loads of fields and cows around them everywhere, and fresh country air. But the cost-of-living crisis and then the high interest rates have virtually killed everything off. There's hardly any money to be made in domestic real estate anymore and the daily grind isn't worth what there is. So, I reckon I'll be selling the business in the next few months, if I can, and taking early retirement.'

'Lizzie has already done that,' Chalmers said, encouraging Johnson to join in the conversation, but she continued to sit there, staring into the glass of whisky she was holding, as if it were a crystal ball.

'What about IT, Bob?' Talbot called across the room. 'That still a booming business, is it? Looking forward to taking on AI when it comes in?'

Chalmers snorted. 'I hope I'm well clear of all of it by the time that it becomes a global reality,' he replied. 'I can see a big shitstorm heading our way . . . What about you? Still in teaching?'

Talbot gave a grim smile. 'For another couple of years, probably,' she said. 'As you already know, I'm head of our old primary school and I was fortunate in being able to find my little cottage a short distance down the road from the school. But the job is not what it was. Too many silly, woke ideas crushing education and indoctrinating the kids. I aim to do a Lizzie soon and also retire early.'

'All this talk of retirement,' Grey put in sharply, switching off his mobile. 'It depresses me. Like Jen, I was lucky to find my nice Georgian place in Mark and I plan on staying there and continuing to run my business from the Bridgwater office until there are no investment opportunities left.'

'Glad about that!' Chalmers responded. 'That group investment you set up for us has proved to be a nice little earner. Long may it continue.'

Grey laughed. 'Don't you worry, old boy. The returns are getting bigger by the month, as you will have seen from the statements everyone's been receiving. We certainly invested at the right time, I can tell you.'

'That's if we're not all behind bars — or worse — before the year's out,' Johnson chimed in.

But no one answered her, for they were all thinking the same thing . . .

CHAPTER 6

More strange noises in the stillness of the night. Lizzie Johnson awoke suddenly and stared up at the shadows thrown across the ceiling of her bedroom by the moon blazing through the glass-panelled balcony doors. Her bedside clock registered the time as eleven thirty. Her heart was thumping and her throat felt dry and sore, as she listened intently for a repeat of the sounds that must have awakened her.

Several weeks had elapsed since the old gang had met up downstairs in her living room and, though the others had confidently dismissed any possibility that they could be connected to the bones discovered at Pagan's Clump after so many years, Johnson had not been convinced. Ever the pessimist, she had seen nothing but disaster ahead of them after what they had done, and she had not slept properly since their tense, unproductive get-together. Her worries had continued to linger, not so much on what the police investigation might reveal, but with her long-held belief in the supernatural, what the paranormal entities of that terrifying other world had in store for them now that old Annie had been released from her earthly bondage.

Okay, so there had been no ghostly manifestations or scary incidents to suggest anything was brewing, but she had certainly heard a lot of unusual noises at night, which she could not explain — like now — and no matter how hard she tried to rationalise her fears, nothing could allay them. When Bob Chalmers, her former husband, had slammed the phone down on her after her fourth call in the last particularly stressful week of seeking some sort of reassurance, she had defied the rest of the group by taking her fears to a local priest she felt she could trust. After all, priests had to keep confidences, didn't they? He had done his best for her, but no amount of prayer had helped, and she found little faith in the protection allegedly afforded by the wooden Christian cross he had given her, which now stood on the dressing table. Annie would come, she was sure of that, if not tonight, the next night or the night after that, and there was nothing anyone could do to stop her.

Swallowing hard, she retreated further under the bedclothes, peering through the glass panels of the balcony doors with her hands clenched tightly together, her nerves on a knife's edge.

Silence. Nothing stirred inside or outside the house. She eased up a little higher in the bed, her eyes probing the shadows of the room where the moonlight failed to reach. Again, nothing. The room was quite large, but there was nowhere for anyone to hide — except . . . She glanced quickly at the door of the ensuite, which was slightly ajar. Had she imagined it, or had she seen it move a fraction?

She was shaking now, cold perspiration breaking out on her forehead. Driven by a kind of perverse compulsion to check things out, despite her fears, she pulled back the duvet and tentatively swung her legs halfway out over the edge of the bed, without taking her eyes off the door. It remained in the same position, unmoving. Maybe her imagination was getting the better of her. She gritted her teeth and wriggled until her bare feet touched the cold floor, stopping there for a second to pluck up a little more courage.

Then, trembling nervously, she crept slowly towards the ensuite — just as the door suddenly flew open from the inside and a nightmare apparition lunged at her through the gap.

She caught a momentary glimpse of blazing yellow eyes and vicious snarling teeth as she crashed back on to the bed with a terrified, high-pitched scream — only to stare in disbelief at the large blue Persian cat now streaking away across the duvet on which it had landed, fleeing through the half-open bedroom door into the galleried hallway beyond . . .

Then she simply couldn't help herself, but creased up with hysterical laughter. The noises. The intruder. It had all been down to Rufus. She had been frightened out of her wits by nothing more sinister than her pet cat. What a turn-up. She couldn't help feeling a sense of relief that none of the others had been there to see what a fool she had made of herself.

But her relief didn't last long. The next instant she jerked up on her elbows, once more staring wide-eyed around the room, her body shaking inside the thin nightdress. The noises she had heard this time had certainly not been made by a cat, but by someone or something infinitely bigger, and they were coming from directly beneath her in the living room. The sounds consisted of a series of heavy footfalls, each followed by a long scraping sound, as if someone were dragging their other foot behind them, and they seemed to be moving incredibly slowly across the room in the direction of the stairs — the stairs that led up to her bedroom! Immediately she thought of Annie Evans, the road accident and the old woman's broken leg. She was gripped by a nameless dread. Scrambling off the bed, she raced to the door to peer along the moon-splashed gallery beyond.

Nothing at first. Only the gleaming brass handles of other bedroom doors and small items of furniture. But then she stiffened. Something had moved at the bottom of the stairs but she couldn't quite make out what it was. A dark mass, like a misshapen figure, which rose up out of the gloom, as if it were in the process of climbing the stairs. At the same moment she heard the hollow clump of a footfall on bare wood, followed by a familiar, if more clumsy scraping sound as another foot was pulled up after it.

In a panic, she ducked back into her room and slammed the door shut behind her, leaning back against it with her eyes tightly closed. God help her. There was no key. She couldn't lock the door even if she wanted to. Moaning softly, she listened to the "thump, scrape" of the intruder advancing slowly along the gallery towards the room. *Barricade the door*, a voice shouted at her from inside her head. *Don't let it in*.

Darting forward, she grabbed a chair from the corner of the room and wedged the back under the handle. Then she took hold of the dressing table in the alcove beside the door and used all her strength to haul it out and drag it up behind the chair for extra strength.

Leaning against the dressing table moments later, she felt the door shake behind her and heard the handle rattle several times. But it remained steadfast and after several attempts, the intruder appeared to give up. Shortly afterwards Johnson heard the laboured "thump, scrape, thump" of them retreating back along the gallery, until the sounds faded into nothing, and the night was still once more.

Feeling her legs start to give way with the shock of it all, she sank down on to the floor with her back resting against the dressing table, sobbing and whimpering like a small child. It was over. Annie's vengeful spirit, or whatever else it was, seemed to have gone — at least for the time being. But she was taking no chances and she stayed there for a good half hour before she felt confident enough to climb back up. Even then, she made no attempt to remove her improvised barricade from the bedroom door to check the gallery outside. No way. That could wait until daylight.

Still shivering, she crossed the room to close the ensuite door, then made her way back to the other side of her bed, helping herself to a large glass of scotch from the bottle she always kept on her bedside cabinet. She had just raised the tumbler to her lips when she happened to look out through the glass doors accessing the balcony. Uttering another shrill scream, she staggered to her feet, the whisky glass flying from her hand and rolling across the floor, spilling its contents across the carpet.

An old woman in a long, dark coat and shawl, leaning on a stick, was standing on the balcony paving with her face pressed up against one of the doors, her hideous ravaged face leering at her through the glass as she scraped the long nails of one hand along the pane. At which point Lizzie Johnson collapsed in a dead faint.

* * *

'Oh, come on, Lizzie, you had a bad dream, that's all?'

Robert Chalmers didn't even try to conceal his scepticism as he followed Johnson into her living room around ten the following morning, having taken the day off work. He was followed by Julian Grey, whom he had rung after Johnson's panicky phone call two hours before.

'It wasn't a bloody dream,' Johnson shouted, turning to face him. 'She was here, I'm telling you! She was as clear to me last night as you are now, you *have* to believe me.'

Chalmers shook his head. 'How can I? A ghost? Do me a favour. Lizzie, you've got to accept, it's all part of your ongoing neurosis, nothing more.'

Her eyes blazed. 'Neurosis?' she shouted. 'I'll show you sodding neurosis!'

Storming across the room, she led the way upstairs and along the gallery to her bedroom.

It was a bright winter's day, and the room was bathed in fragile sunlight.

'Is that neurosis then?' she said, pointing at the glass balcony doors.

Both men gaped. The word had been scrawled across one of the glass panels in red letters at least eight to ten inches high:

MURDERER!

'What the hell!' Grey exclaimed. 'Is that someone's idea of a joke?'

'If it is, it's in pretty poor taste,' Chalmers breathed.

'It isn't a someone,' Johnson quavered, her aggression melting into panic once more. 'It's a *thing*, and the message is not meant to be funny. It's a warning.'

Grey snorted disparagingly. 'Oh, grow up, Lizzie! A warning about what?'

'You know very well what. We're all to be punished. I've told you that so many times and here's the evidence.'

Chalmers grunted and, turning the key in the lock, opened the door and stepped out on to the balcony. Then he bent down to study the writing before scraping one of the letters off with his fingernail.

'As I thought,' he said, straightening up. 'Lipstick. This is not the work of some enterprising ghost who happened to have a tube of lipstick tucked under a wing, but a sicko prankster.'

He checked the paving stones in front of the door. A second later he released a sharp exclamation and bent down to pick something up.

'There you are,' he said triumphantly, holding up what he had found. The sunlight glinted on the little gold-coloured tube. 'The top of a lipstick holder. Whoever did this obviously didn't realise they'd dropped it afterwards.'

He and Grey exchanged meaningful glances as he stepped back into the room again.

'Why don't you take Jules back downstairs, Lizzie, and pour a couple of drinks, eh?' he suggested quietly. 'Have you a cloth or flannel of some sort? I can soon remove that lipstick with a bit of soap and water while you're doing that.'

'No!' she exclaimed, alarm in her expression now. 'You have to leave it there . . . for–for the police to see.'

'Police?' Grey visibly started. 'You haven't contacted the police, about it, have you?'

'Well . . . yes . . . They're sending someone over in a couple of hours.'

'Lizzie, you can't have the police here? Use your head. If you tell them about all this, they'll suspect there's some sort of nutter on the loose round here and launch an investigation.'

'Dead right,' Chalmers agreed, an edge to his voice now. 'They'll be asking questions as to why someone would take the trouble to write something like that on the door. Bloody hell, it could drop us all right in it if they were eventually to somehow link this to the Pagan's Clump business.'

Johnson bit her lip. 'I–I'm so sorry, I didn't think.'

Chalmers took a deep breath. 'No worries, love, but what did you tell them?'

'That I'd had a break-in.'

'Did you tell them about the message?'

'No, only that I'd had a break-in and someone was in the house.'

'Right. Well, what's done is done. You and I will see them together when they arrive.'

Johnson nodded uncertainly. 'Okay, but–but what about me?'

'I don't follow you.'

'I need protection if that thing decides to come back. That's why I rang the police.'

Grey mentally counted to five and gently took hold of Johnson's hands. 'Lizzie, there is *no such thing*. It's some idiot trying to wind you up.'

'But I saw the old hag, right there on the balcony.'

'You thought you saw her, Lizzie. It was obviously someone dressed up.'

'But why? And–and how did they know to do that? Unless . . .' Her eyes widened 'Unless this was one of those two guys who stopped on the night it all happened, and–and he recognised me at the time . . . Maybe he's after all of us?'

Grey shook his head. 'If it is one of those guys, which I sincerely doubt after all this time, he will want money to keep quiet about it. What we need to do is to sit tight and do nothing — certainly not tell Old Bill — and wait to see if he makes some kind of demand.'

She nodded again. 'If you're sure.'

'I'm certain.'

'Would you like me to stay here with you for a couple of nights as it's coming up to the weekend and I won't be at work?' Chalmers went on.

Johnson breathed a sigh of relief. 'That would be good.'

'Then it's settled. *I* will now remove the lipstick message and then we'll wait for the arrival of Mr Plod.'

Grey glanced at his watch. 'If you're going to do that job I might as well be off. I've skived off work to come over here and, though it's my own business, I've still got one or two jobs I really must finish before the weekend.'

Chalmers nodded. 'Fine. Lizzie, why don't you pour those two drinks for us, and I'll see Jules off.'

'What do you think?' Grey asked as he climbed into his Porsche parked at the front of the house.

Chalmers shrugged. 'Lizzie obviously dreamed the whole thing. The story is too wacky to be true. Best to simply humour her.'

'And the writing on the balcony door?'

'Did it herself while she was under the influence after a few too many. You must have seen the number of empty whisky bottles in the kitchen. I thought she'd stopped all that nonsense, but she's obviously back to heavy drinking again. On top of that, she's always been flaky and neurotic, you know that from the old days. Always into the paranormal and things that go bump in the night. The news about Pagan's Clump must have sent her over the edge.'

'She could be dangerous if she blabs to the wrong people in another panic attack.'

'You leave that with me. I'll make sure she doesn't do anything stupid from now on.'

Grey smiled and clapped him on the shoulder. 'Excellent. If you need me, you know where I am.'

'What about the others? We should tell them.'

'*I'll* do that, in case she contacts any of them. We all have to be singing from the same hymn sheet.'

'Amen to that.'

Chalmers watched Grey drive away with a worried look in his eyes.

* * *

Kate and Hayden had no idea what they were about to be drawn into when they arrived at work on the same morning that Grey and Chalmers had dropped in on Johnson after her scare the night before. Even as Chalmers turned back into the house and Grey left, Charlie Woo was on his way over to Kate Lewis's desk.

'Nice easy one for you today,' he said, handing Kate the single A5-size note that she knew from past experience of single A5 notes usually meant the allocation of the sort of "just job" that promised to be pure aggravation. 'Report of another sus break-in.'

Kate frowned as she studied the address. After weeks dealing with mundane run-of-the-mill commitments, including bicycle thefts, indecent exposures, domestic assaults and criminal damage, as well as wading through a never-ending stream of boring crime reports and files submitted by her colleagues for supervisory approval, she wasn't complaining. At least this could be something that was a bit more interesting.

'Uniform attended?' she asked automatically, as she had in respect of the dubious break-in at the home of the Rev. Taylor.

He shook his head. 'All available units assisting the Glastonbury neighbourhood policing team in a search for some old boy who's gone walk-about from an old folks' home in his pyjamas. I said we'd follow up on this one.'

'So, history is repeating itself then?'

He grimaced, sensing what he thought was resentment. 'I'm not *asking* you to do it Kate. I'm telling you, okay?'

She chortled. 'Oh, I do like it when you're forceful like this, boss. It's so manly.'

Realising he had been had, he scowled. 'Get out there, will you?' he said. 'And take Indrani Purewal with you. It's about time that lazy sod, Hayden, got some of his paperwork done.'

She glanced across at her other half, who was hiding behind his computer, munching on a chocolate bar, and smiled affectionately. 'Then you'd better nail his hands to the desk before he smells breakfast in the canteen,' she said. 'I hear they're doing a special on bacon butties today.'

CHAPTER 7

'Nice place,' DC Indrani Purewal commented as Kate drove on to the gold-coloured gravel hardstanding at the front of Lizzie Johnson's house, noting admiringly the sleek, black Mercedes saloon, boasting the latest registration, parked next to a new, dark-blue Jaguar and an expensive-looking red Porsche with personal number plates. 'Looks like a converted barn.'

'Yeah,' Kate agreed, switching off the engine and climbing out of the CID car. 'A bit of money here, I should think. That Porsche must be worth a fortune, never mind the Jag and the Merc.'

'Maybe the reason for the break-in,' Purewal finished.

But she was proven wrong about that from the outset. A plump, balding man, dressed in smart, casual clothes put her right the moment he opened the front door to them.

'Sorry,' he said after Kate had introduced them, 'but I fear you've had a wasted journey. There's been no burglary, as such.'

He seemed reluctant for them to go any further, and stood in the hallway, blocking the way, looking suitably embarrassed.

'There's been what you might call a misunderstanding, you see. The lady who rang you rather jumped the gun, and

I only learned you had been called a few minutes after I had arrived here following her call to me.'

Kate frowned. 'And you are who, sir?' she asked politely.

'Oh, yes, Bob Chalmers. I'm, er, a friend.'

'Of the complainant?' Kate consulted her piece of paper. 'A Ms Lizzie Johnson?'

He nodded. 'She telephoned me after she had made her call to your control room. I live in Bristol and came straight down here.'

'So, can we speak to Ms Johnson?'

'But of course.' He glanced quickly over his shoulder. 'Though I think I should warn you, she is not very well.'

'I beg your pardon?'

'She is rather neurotic. Has, er, hallucinations and sometimes sleepwalks, imagining things that aren't there.'

'Like what, sir?' Purewal butted in.

'Well, er, ghosts and that.'

'Ghosts?'

'Er, yes. She's into the supernatural and all that rot, you see. Drinks a bit too much too.'

Kate shook her head irritably. 'Look, can we see her, please? She rang us, so we need to speak to her.'

He stepped to one side. 'But of course. She's down here, in the living room. But I would ask you to take anything she says with a pinch of salt, if you know what I mean.'

A fifty-something, blonde woman, dressed in a smart, green trouser suit, was sitting on a two-seater settee in a large, vaulted living room with a beautiful woodblock floor scattered with poster-colour rugs and furnished with expensive-looking, dark wood furniture. Behind her a wooden staircase ascended to a long gallery with other doors visible on the far side of it through mauve-tinted glass panels. The room's effect on the senses was quite striking and both detectives took it all in with undisguised awe.

The woman rose from her settee with what seemed like a nervous smile and Kate studied her curiously. It was apparent to her that Lizzie Johnson had once been a very beautiful woman and even now she was blessed with the well-moulded features and near-perfect ivory skin that any woman half her age would have envied. But it seemed something had happened to her, perhaps fairly recently, and her face looked strained and drawn, with dark patches under her eyes and a dullness in her expression, which suggested a recent trauma of some kind. Even her smile lacked warmth and there was a tic in her left cheek that was quite noticeable.

'I–I'm so sorry to have called you out under what now seems like false pretences,' she said, waving them both to a pair of armchairs, a slight tremble in her voice. 'I have been rather under the weather lately and sometimes I tend to overreact to things.'

Kate nodded slowly, propping herself on the edge of the chair. 'Are you saying you haven't been burgled then?' she asked.

Before she could answer, Chalmers said quickly, 'It's as I said to you, Sergeant, Lizzie has been under a lot of strain lately and—'

'I would be grateful if you could let Ms Johnson answer for herself, Mr Chalmers,' Kate cut in firmly. 'She is, after all, the complainant.'

'Yes, yes, of course,' Chalmers replied, sitting down on the edge of another chair.

Turning her head slightly, Kate was curious to see him staring past her at Johnson with a keen intensity, almost as if he were trying telepathically to will her into what to say.

'I–I thought I had when I rang,' Johnson replied, returning to her settee. 'But since then, I've come to the conclusion that I must have imagined the whole thing.'

'But what put the idea into your head in the first place?' Purewal asked. 'You must have seen or heard something that alarmed you.'

'I really don't know. I remember waking up in a panic for some reason, but it must have been a bad dream. I get them a lot.'

'Did you catch sight of anyone prowling about?'

Johnson glanced quickly in Chalmers's direction. 'Er, not exactly.'

'What do you mean by "not exactly"?'

'Well, I felt sure I'd heard noises, like dragging footsteps, inside the house. Then I thought I saw a shadow . . . on the stairs to the gallery, but the next moment it, er, disappeared.'

Out of the corner of her eye Kate saw Chalmers tense, as if that answer was not in line with what he'd got her to agree to.

'Disappeared where?'

'I don't know. It–it, well, vanished.'

'Like a ghost?'

'I know it sounds stupid, but yes, like a ghost.'

'Were all the doors and windows locked when you went to bed?'

'Always, yes.'

'Have you checked to see if any have been forced or tampered with?'

Before Johnson could answer, Chalmers chimed in again. 'We've both been round the whole house since I arrived and everything's secure. No sign of any forced entry.'

Kate nodded and turned back to Johnson. 'Does anyone else have access to the house?'

'Only my cleaner, Mrs Rowlands. She comes in three days a week, every Monday, Wednesday and Friday.'

'So presumably she has a key?'

Johnson shook her head. 'No, I don't hand out spare keys to anyone.'

'So how does she get in if you aren't here?'

Johnson looked a little shamefaced. 'I, er, always leave her key under the loose paving stone at the back door.' Then, sensing what Kate was about to say in response, she added in a rush, 'But no one else knows it's there.'

Mentally, Kate closed her eyes in resignation. 'You do realise that that is the worst thing you can do, don't you?' she admonished gently. 'Professional burglars are fully aware that people leave keys in such places; under paving stones, flowerpots, loose bricks, they know all the regular spots and will always check them out first.'

'I–I s'pose . . .' Johnson agreed, looking down at her feet.

'Is the key still there?'

'Affirmative,' Chalmers said. 'We checked.'

'Then I suggest you remove it and find another way of providing the cleaner with access.'

'Point taken,' Chalmers answered again and cleared his throat in a business-like way. 'Now, Sergeant, I feel Lizzie and I have taken up enough of your time. Plainly there was no intruder here and I think Lizzie herself would agree, on reflection, that she probably dreamed the whole thing. So, perhaps we could treat this as nothing but a well-intentioned false alarm.'

Kate ignored him. 'The thing is, Ms Johnson,' she said firmly to make it apparent that she was talking to her and not Chalmers, 'we have no way of knowing whether someone was in here or not last night. Hypothetically, they could have found the key, used it, and left afterwards with no one being the wiser—'

'Ghost don't need keys anyway,' Chalmers cut in sharply again, obviously tiring of the whole thing.

Kate smiled thinly but didn't dignify his comment with a response. 'But in the absence of any physical evidence of a break-in or of any property being stolen, we can only assume, as you have acknowledged yourself, that you might have imagined your prowler. So, I'm afraid, we can only advise that you ring us again if you have any further problems. In the meantime, I would recommend that you make sure you lock up securely at night and contact our crime prevention department if you would like some professional guidance on how to make your property more secure.' Kate leaned forward in her chair and placed a business card on the coffee table, then stood up. 'Their number is on the card.'

Chalmers seemed to breathe a sigh of relief and it did not go unnoticed by either of the two detectives. 'Thanks for your help.' He beamed as he stood up. 'Before I show you out, maybe I could put something in the police welfare fund, or whatever it's called, in recompense for your wasted time.'

'That won't be necessary,' Kate replied. 'No harm's been done, and we are glad to have been of service.'

'Liar,' muttered Purewal in Kate's ear, as they walked out to the car. 'There's something going on here, and you know it.'

Kate slid behind the wheel and gave Chalmers standing at the front door a quick smile and a wave as they drove away.

'So, what do you reckon to it all, then?' Purewal asked.

'Not sure,' Kate replied. 'It's certainly a funny business. A bit like an alleged shed break-in Hayden and I dealt with not long ago, only then it was pretty obvious the householder had done it himself on an attention-seeking trip.'

'Could this be the same sort of thing?'

Kate shook her head. 'No. It's more likely Johnson has suddenly had a touch of the seconds after calling us out, maybe because she's embarrassed by the fact that there's no real substance to her complaint, and she now wants to drop the whole thing.'

'Then why go into such detail? You know, hearing noises and seeing shadows on the stairs? She could simply have dismissed it all as a dream, without any further embellishment and left it at that.'

'Well, she had to say something, didn't she? Something to justify why she called us out in the first place. I actually think she may have unwittingly said too much, and Chalmers isn't happy about her straying from what could be the hastily prepared script he came up with when he arrived. Don't forget, he got here *after* we had been called, so we were already on our way and bound to turn up anyway.'

'But why would he want to scotch her complaint if he's only a visiting friend? It's got nothing to do with him, has it?'

Kate shook her head. 'No idea. Maybe because he knew her complaint was rubbish and didn't want her to look stupid. It's possible he was genuine when he buttonholed us at the front door and warned us not to take anything she said too seriously, because she was prone to imagining things.

One thing I think was pretty obvious is that Johnson was obviously being played by Chalmers. But whether he did that to help her save face, or for some other reason, we have no way of knowing, and I can't think of any other ulterior motive he could have had.'

'So, we've wasted half the morning for nothing?'

Kate shrugged. 'Not really. I have this nagging feeling that this isn't the last time Ms Lizzie Johnson will come to notice one way or the other. I can feel it in my water.'

* * *

'Well, that was a dumb thing to say,' Chalmers snapped at Johnson after the detectives had gone.

'What was?' she replied, pouring herself a glass of whisky.

'About seeing a shadow.'

'Well, I *did* see a shadow . . . on the stairs, and I *did* hear those bloody creepy footsteps too.'

'So you say. But you didn't have to tell them that, did you?'

'I'm sorry, it came out before I could stop myself when they asked me if I had seen any prowlers. I didn't know what else to say . . . I had to give a reason as to why I had called them in the first place.'

'No, you didn't. You could have stayed with the theme of a bad dream, as we agreed beforehand. Now, you've drawn their attention to us and got their noses twitching, and coppers with twitchy noses are the last thing we need with that bloody dig underway at Pagan's Clump.'

She shook her head irritably. 'You're making too much out of this, Robert. I'm sure lots of women living alone make complaints to the police about suspected prowlers. How would my complaint about hearing noises and seeing a shadow on the stairs possibly risk tying me into what's going on at Pagan's Clump? At least I didn't tell them the rest of it.'

His eyes narrowed. 'Rest of it? What are you on about?'

'The old woman on the balcony, peering in at me.'

He looked as if he was about to explode. 'Don't start that crap again. You're giving into your bloody paranoia about that old cow, Annie Evans. She's dead, Lizzie, and she can't become undead, except in a horror film. Okay? So, wise up and join the world of grown-ups.'

She downed her drink and hauled herself unsteadily to her feet. 'I don't need this,' she snapped back. 'I'm going for a shower.'

He ignored her and continued his verbal attack. 'And you might cut down on your drinking too. You're getting too fond of it.'

She turned on him, her eyes blazing. 'What's it got to do with you? In case you've forgotten, we're no longer man and wife. You shot your last bolt when you shacked up with your "Miss Bend Over Backwards"—'

'Yeah,' he cut in, 'and can you see why I did that and walked out on you? You were going downhill even then. Looking at you now, I reckon I got out in the nick of time.'

'You bastard!' she almost screamed. 'Get out of my house!'

He sneered at her. 'You don't want me to stay the night then — in case the wicked old Night Hag comes back?'

'I said, *GET OUT!*'

He grabbed his coat from the back of his chair and turned for the door. 'With pleasure. I wouldn't stay here now if you got down on your knees and pleaded with me to.'

The glass tumbler missed his head by no more than an inch and the whisky bottle shattered against the door as he slammed it shut behind him.

For several minutes after the sound of his car driving away had faded into nothing she stood there, sobbing uncontrollably, and staring at the dark stain spreading down the wooden panelling. She had overreacted, she realised that almost immediately, but in her fragile emotional state, his cruel barbs had really got to her, as they always had done during their turbulent years of marriage. But the end result was that she now faced more nights alone in her isolated home and already her furious outburst was starting to dissolve into a cold, skin-crawling sense of dread.

* * *

The Black Cock public house stood in a small village between Highbridge and Wedmore and it was where Highbridge CID traditionally met up to get together socially and unwind at the end of the week. It had been their local for as long as Kate could remember and the licensee, Mick Braithwaite, was almost one of the CID family, and probably knew as much about what was going on in the area as anyone.

The pub was not that busy when Kate and Hayden arrived in the evening straight from work, but most of the team were already there, the bear-like figure of DC Danny Ferris crouched over a pint at the bar, engaged in a heated discussion with his slim, athletic colleague, Ben Holloway, about football, and DCs Indrani Purewal, Jamie Foster and Fred Alloway sitting quietly over drinks at a corner table.

Kate and Hayden were about to join the threesome when Charlie Woo materialised in the doorway behind her and squeezed her arm. 'A word in your shell-like, Kate?' he said. 'I'll get us a couple of drinks. Red wine, eh?'

She nodded and, somewhat mystified, walked to a seat at an empty table, leaving an affronted Hayden with no option but to join the threesome without her — and to find he had drawn the short straw by being lumbered with the next round.

'How did the attempted burglary job go?' Woo asked when he finally returned from the bar with the drinks and placed a glass of red wine in front of her. 'I missed you before you went off. Meetings and all that.'

'Bit of a funny one,' she replied. 'A neurotic woman and a crappy set of circumstances. She withdrew the thing in the end, so that's it . . . But what have you got to tell me? You said you wanted a word.'

He drank some of his beer and wiped his mouth on the back of his hand. 'Thought I'd pass on the fact that, according to a little bird I've been speaking to, we've got a result,' he said.

'A result?' Kate asked with a puzzled look. 'A result on what?'

'What do you think? The bones at Pagan's Clump, of course,' he said.

'Oh,' she replied with a wry smile. 'I'd forgotten all about that business since it was taken out of our hands by the MIT. It must be around a month since those remains were dug up.'

'Easily, but as you know, forensic work like this takes a fair bit of time, and I reckon they've done well to get a result at all.'

'Okay, so what *have* they got then and who was your "little bird"?'

He shook his head with a fake frown and tapped the side of his nose theatrically with a forefinger. 'I promised SOCO's Roddy Prescott that I wouldn't tell anyone where I got the info from, as he said it was imparted in strict confidence and was for my ears only.'

She released a dry chuckle. 'What, *the* Roddy Prescott — the burned-out ex-DC they used to call the *News of the World*? I might have known. If you want anything broadcast far and wide, give the details to Roddy in confidence. He'll have told half the force by now — only in strict confidence, of course.'

Charlie grinned, fully aware of the fact that Prescott's loose mouth was legendary, despite the fact that he had long retired as a police officer and continued his policing career as a civilian SOCO instead.

'Yeah,' he agreed, 'but to be fair, his info is usually spot on. From what he told me, it seems that with the expert help of a Dr Lawrence Kegman, who is a forensic anthropologist brought in on the job, the remains in question have been found to be female. Don't ask me how they can tell that. Something to do with the shape of the skull and the size of the pelvic bone, etcetera, etcetera, I gather. Roddy was at great pains to explain, but I sort of switched off halfway through—'

'He always did like to try and impress people with his inside knowledge.'

'Well, you know what they say, bullshit baffles brains and all the detail he came up with certainly baffled mine. He also revealed that from a forensic examination of the skeleton's teeth by Dr Kegman and his team and the evidence provided by what Roddy called the ossification process — or the progressive hardening of the different bones in the body over time — it was possible to determine that the woman was probably buried there about twenty-five to thirty-five years ago, and that she was in her late sixties to early seventies when she died.'

'All very clever stuff, I'm sure, but were Kegman and his team able to say how this Jane Doe died?'

He frowned. 'That really is an interesting one,' he replied. 'A trauma analysis of the remains has apparently been carried out jointly by Dr Kegman and Dr Summers, and the visible skeletal damage indicated that the victim's body had suffered from a severe impact with something . . . as in an accident.'

'What, an RTA — a road traffic accident?'

'So it is believed. The view is that she may have been a pedestrian who was struck by a vehicle while out walking, fatally injured and dumped in a hole in the ground by the perp to conceal the crime.'

Kate whistled. 'So, rather than a murder, we could be talking about a hit and run traffic accident that occurred all of thirty years ago?'

'Sounds like it.'

'That will take some investigating.'

'Well, apparently a press release, seeking information from the public, is being prepared as we speak. Should be out first thing on Monday to catch the early editions.'

'A fat lot of good that will do if the thing happened three decades ago. Most potential witnesses will probably be dead by now.'

He nodded. 'True, and if the old girl died that long ago, trying to ID her through DNA profiling is out too.

The national DNA database wasn't even set up until the mid-nineties — 1995, I believe. And even if they're mistaken about the time lapse and she croaked ten years later than they thought, there would be no certainty she would be on the system anyway.'

'Dental records might turn up something?'

'That's another avenue the team are evidently going down, but unless this woman kept her pearly whites up to scratch with a local dentist, that's not likely to lead anywhere either, as any info previously held will almost certainly have long since been destroyed. Dentists are only required to retain records for about ten years minimum, so I doubt there would be anything to see after such a long period of time. Furthermore, where would you carry out your checks? Any dental work she had done could have been performed at a practice anywhere in the UK or abroad. She may not have been local and could have been visiting this area or staying here on holiday. The possibilities are almost endless.'

Kate screwed up her face in thought for a moment. 'So, what about the brass buttons we noticed among the bones? Are the team any the wiser as to the chance of a military connection?'

He shook his head. 'Not exactly. They have been able to establish from minute fibres, plus a belt buckle and so forth, which miraculously survived the years, that she may have been wearing what was once called a "British Warm", an overcoat originally worn by British Army officers in the First World War, a modified version of which is still favoured by some army officers today. They also found a badly tarnished badge bearing the insignia of an army major amongst the bits. But no dog tags or anything to personally identify who she was. Without anything else to go on, the bits they've got are of little use.'

'But those buttons carried some sort of regimental insignia, I'm sure of it.'

'Yeah, so they did. The Royal Artillery, I gather. But as the MOD pointed out, a button is a button and, as I said when you first spotted them, you can buy ex-army uniforms and equipment from a load of army surplus stores. Tracing any such sale would be next to impossible without more information.'

'Which means that, apart from a more or less pointless public appeal, the team are left with nothing more than a troll through misper records.'

''Fraid so. Even that is likely to be a long shot. There are around five thousand plus long-term missing persons recorded on the NCA's misper database at any one time, so it's going to be a difficult, time-consuming process using the sketchy info they have so far. There are likely to be a load of mispers none of the authorities know about too, like foreign nationals who have bypassed immigration and people who have dropped out of the system because of lifestyle choices or simply as a result of bad luck. Vagrants and rough sleepers, for example.'

It was Kate's turn to smile. 'Good job we're off the investigation then, isn't it?'

Charlie Woo grinned. 'If I didn't know you better, I'd say you were gloating.'

'Who, *moi*? Perish the thought . . . Fancy another beer?'

CHAPTER 8

As a child, Kate had always hated weekends. Saturdays had been homework and obligatory "helping Mum out" day, usually with the vacuuming and ironing. Sundays were dead days — church days — when most of the shops were closed and little of interest was going on anywhere. Both were also the days when she'd had to spend a lot more time at home with her drunken stepfather, giving him the excuse to pick on her at every opportunity after rolling home from the pub. His favourite amusement had been to lock her in the garden shed with all the spiders, and listen to her screams, knowing full well that she had a phobia about the hairy, eight-legged horrors. Burning down that shed in her early teens was probably one of the most satisfying moments of her young life, though looking back on that criminal act as a mature adult, she couldn't help feeling a little guilty about it in her present role as a police detective!

Nowadays, due to shift work, weekends were no different to any other days of the week. They were nothing to hate or even to like. They were simply the days that brought the week to a close. To be fair, the weekend following Charlie Woo's revelations in the Black Cock about the Pagan's Clump investigation did seem to have plenty of potential to begin with. Kate and Hayden were both rostered Saturday and Sunday off for a change, instead of on different days of the week, which was more often the case. At the same time, as luck would have it, Hayden's classic car club had arranged their annual treasure hunt for that very Saturday, which offered the two of them the opportunity of enjoying some much-needed quality time together. Kate had been really looking forward to the drive around the Quantocks and a picnic of smoked salmon and a nice glass of white wine afterwards. The day had started off well too, with brilliant winter sunshine greeting them when they got up, but it had ended in disaster and a monumental row between them after a navigational faux pas on Kate's part had resulted in Hayden's prize Mk II Jaguar being bogged down in a muddy field up to its axles and having to be towed out.

Forgiveness for her "crime" was not forthcoming in the short term either. Despite apology after apology, Kate was given the sullen, silent treatment when they got home. The following morning, even after stripping off her nightdress and snuggling up to her other half provocatively in bed, her ardent, sexual advances were rejected with a growl and an irritable shake of his shoulders, leaving her with no option but to give up and flounce naked and humiliated to the bathroom to cool off in the shower. A reprieve from a further day of silence and tension was not far away, however.

The call came through as she was drying her hair. It was her colleague, DC Purewal.

'Sorry to ring you at home when you're off, skipper,' she said, 'but I thought you needed to be told about a job I've been sent to.'

Kate was all ears. 'Go on, Indi.'

'The woman we went to see on Friday? The one living in that beautiful, converted barn who fancied she'd seen a ghost?'

Kate grimaced. 'How could I forget?'

'Remember you said you thought she would come to our notice again before long?'

'I do?'

'Well, she has. She's been found dead in bed. I'm at the house now.'

Conscious of the fact that she had been about to face another day of Hayden in one of his foul, unreasonable moods, Kate's answer carried a touch of relief, which was rather unseemly, given the circumstances. 'I'll be right over,' she replied.

* * *

A marked police patrol car was parked to one side of the house, next to a couple of plain cars when Kate arrived. One of these Kate immediately recognised as a Highbridge CID car. The other vehicle was an ancient VW Beetle she had seen many times before at death scenes and she knew it belonged to the police surgeon. As for the black Mercedes she had noticed parked out front when she and Indrani Purewal had last visited the premises, unsurprisingly under the circumstances, that was still there.

She found a uniformed constable standing in the open front doorway, looking bored. Recognising her, he immediately straightened and nodded to Kate as she walked past him into the hallway, where Indrani Purewal met her at the bottom of the staircase to the ornate gallery.

'Doctor already here and giving the dead woman the once-over,' she said. 'But there don't look to be any suspicious circumstances.'

'Coroner's officer?'

'Already informed, but up to his neck in stiffs this afternoon apparently, so I'll have to act for him from hereon. I gave him the basic details for the coroner, but I'll keep him in the loop and he'll touch base with me later.'

'Who found the body?'

'Cleaner, a Mrs Millie Rowlands. I've let her go home now. We have her written statement and if we need to speak to her again, we know where we can find her.'

'How come she was here this morning? Not cleaning on a Sunday, was she?'

'No. Apparently, she came to give in her notice and to collect her week's money.'

'Why was she giving in her notice?'

'Family tragedy. Elderly father died suddenly on Saturday, and she's off to Essex to stay with her mother tomorrow until a vacancy can be found in a local old folk's home. Anyway, she rang the front doorbell, knocked, but got no response. Seeing Johnson's car still parked there and realising she had to be at home, she went round the back and used the key hidden under the slab to get in.'

'Didn't take our previous advice about the key then?'

'Doesn't seem like it . . . Anyway, once in the house, she got no answer when she called out to Johnson, so went upstairs and found her lying in bed as dead as a dodo.'

'What's this Mrs Rowlands like?'

Purewal shrugged. 'Ordinary. Bit shocked, of course. But she seems quite a steady, capable sort. No reason to doubt her story.'

'We'll need a statement off her.'

'All done, Kate. I only called you instead of the DS on weekend cover at Bridgwater because I thought you would be interested in what has happened so soon after we last visited this place.'

'Quite right too. So, let's see what's what, eh?'

Purewal led the way up the stairs and along the gallery to what turned out to be a large bedroom at the end.

Lizzie Johnson was lying on her back on the big double bed, wearing a thin floral nightdress, which had been pulled right up over her stomach.

Dr Raymond Makepiece, a thin, sallow man, dressed in a shabby sweater and jeans, straightened up from the bed as they arrived, pulling her nightdress discreetly back down over her thighs. He turned quickly at the sound of their approach, closing his medical bag and nodding. It was evident that he had already completed his examination.

Kate moved closer to the bed and studied the dead woman. Her face looked swollen and had taken on a bluish tinge. Her clouded eyes were wide open in a horrified stare that seemed to be directed at the ceiling, and her mouth was also gaping open, the bluish lips stretched back over teeth partially obscured by what looked like congealed vomit, as if in a silent scream.

'Not a good death by the look of it,' Kate commented grimly after introducing herself to Makepiece. 'It's as if she died of fright.'

The doctor glanced back at the corpse and grunted, giving the two detectives a sepulchral smile. 'Depends on what you consider good,' he agreed. 'A rather unpleasant and unnecessary waste of a life. But there again, washing down diazepam tablets with what I would suggest were several glasses of malt whisky, is quite an effective way of ending it all.'

He waved an arm towards one of the two bedside cabinets in a gesture of resignation. Kate saw that it was occupied by a table lamp, and a half-empty bottle of Laphroaig, missing its cap. A small cardboard box carrying an official looking label was lying on the bed in front of the corpse and this had been torn open at one end, disgorging a number of now empty blister packs on to the coverlet, and a cut-glass tumbler lay on the floor close to the police surgeon's foot, where it had no doubt landed after rolling off the bed.

'I found her very much in the position in which she is now lying,' Makepiece said. 'I have taken care not to disturb the scene more than was necessary for my examination.'

'So, barbiturate overdose, you reckon, doc?' she said.

'Not barbiturates, Sergeant,' the medical man corrected. 'We are talking benzodiazepines here, what were once referred to as Valium, although that particular brand is no longer available in this country. The tablets are often prescribed for anxiety and insomnia amongst other things, and they can be addictive if taken for too long. The printed information on the box you see on the bed indicates that it originally contained twenty-one diazepam tablets, of five-milligram strength, which were prescribed locally a few days ago. You will find that the box is now empty, but I have no means of knowing how many were swallowed prior to last night. In any event, multiple tablets taken with alcohol can be fatal, as this case demonstrates. All the telltale signs of a fatal overdose are present. Cyanosis — the bluish tinge to the skin — facial swelling, dilated pupils and a yellowing of the eyes, and a now congealed discharge from the mouth, suggesting a pulmonary oedema. However, the post-mortem will, of course, be the final arbiter as to the official cause of death and I await that result with interest.'

'Nothing suspicious then?'

'Well, nothing that I can find. No defensive marks. No unusual bruising . . . It has all the hallmarks of a tragic overdose, but whether accidental or the result of suicide, I am not really in a position to say, without further information.'

'Time of death?'

Another glance back at the corpse, and Makepiece pursed his lips. 'I noted some stiffness in the limbs, suggesting the onset of rigor mortis. Taking this into account, together with the usual indicators, including the signs of lividity or liver mortis, the core temperature of the body itself, which would have lost its heat more slowly due to the warming effect of the mattress and bed clothes, plus the ambient air temperature of this room, I would estimate approximately six to seven hours ago, but I would emphasise that this is only an estimate.'

Kate glanced at her watch, then pursed her lips reflectively for a moment. 'Which would mean she decided to do the deed well into the early hours. Seems a bit strange for someone to suddenly wake up at, say, two or three in the morning, and decide to kill themselves?'

'Not if they have been lying awake most of the night, brooding over something and drinking heavily, which is very possible.' Makepiece shrugged. 'But that is not for me to determine. I can only give you my professional opinion as to what *looks* like being the cause of death — not why that decision was made in the first place.'

He headed for the door. 'Anyway, you will appreciate, that, apart from certifying the lady as definitely deceased, I am unable under the circumstances to issue an official death certificate. It is likely, however, that there will be an inquest some time after the PM, and I think the official verdict on things can be safely left in the hands of the coroner. Have fun in the meantime, Sergeant. As for me, I am going home for a late Sunday lunch and a glass of fine wine. *Au revoir.*'

Then he was gone and shortly afterwards there was the unmistakable sound of the VW starting up and rattling away.

'So, accident or suicide?' Purewal murmured, staring at the body more closely.

Kate frowned. 'Hard to see this as an accident. For all we know, she could have downed the whole box of diazepam in one hit, going by the number of empty blister packs lying on the bed, and, as the doc pointed out, a large single dose washed down with whisky would have been quite enough to do the business.'

'Suicide then?'

'More than likely, I would think, but it's not for to us to say, is it? That's for the coroner to decide when he has the post-mortem report plus what evidence we can supply. But last time we saw her, she seemed pretty flaky, so it's possible she flipped and decided to end it all. Chalmers did say that she was neurotic, had hallucinations and tended to imagine things, and she herself admitted that she may have been suffering from a bad dream when she thought she had been burgled. It's easy to see what that could have led to once she found herself left in this place on her own. Obviously, the pharmacy who supplied the tablets and the doctor who prescribed them will need to be contacted, to see if anything can be learned about Johnson's mental condition — *if* they can or will tell us anything — but that's a job for later.'

She inspected the corpse as closely as she could without touching it, then turned back to Purewal.

'Nothing obviously suspicious here as far as I can tell,' she said, straightening up.

'Maybe we'll never know exactly why this tragedy happened or what led up to it, but plainly, this poor woman was a mixed-up soul who needed help but doesn't seem to have got any.'

Purewal pointed to the dressing table and a wooden cross that had been placed there against a vanity set of two lidded cut-glass bowls standing on a matching tray. 'Looks like she may have tried to get that help from a higher level, though,' she said.

Kate crossed the room and picked up the cross to examine it. It was about six inches high and carried a handwritten message along the transverse bar attached to the post, *Trust in God for salvation.*

'I wonder who gave her this?' she commented. Then added cynically, 'Sadly, it didn't do much for her in the end, did it? Salvation seems to have been in short supply.'

Carefully replacing it on the dressing table, she continued in a much brisker tone, 'Anyway, there doesn't seem to be anything sinister here to set alarm bells ringing, so there can be no justification for calling out a full SOCO team or the forensic pathologist. Nevertheless, I think it would be sensible to at least get the SOCO photographer to take some pics of the scene for the information of the coroner. Then, while we wait, I think we should have a look around the place, to be on the safe side.'

'What do you mean by, "to be on the safe side"? That suggests you're not happy about this one.'

Kate shook her head. 'Not at all. As I've said, there's nothing here to indicate foul play, and the police surgeon indicated that he was quite satisfied that we're dealing with a straightforward OD. I must admit though that I'm surprised that Johnson ended up like this, so I do have a few niggling concerns. But nothing to justify sending the balloon up. I'm probably being oversensitive in my "old age".' She grinned. 'Could be *I'm* becoming neurotic too.'

Police Control gave Kate an ETA for the SOCO photographer of at least an hour and a half when Kate contacted them. That didn't go down too well with her, especially as she was supposed to be off duty anyway. But it was a Sunday. That meant she had to accept the situation as it was. Biting back the caustic comment which rose to her lips, she shrugged off her annoyance and led the way downstairs.

The back door of the house leading off the kitchen was locked on the inside, with the key still in the lock.

'The key in the door is apparently the spare key the cleaner used to get in, which was left outside under the paving stone as usual,' Purewal said when she saw Kate peering at it. 'The back door was evidently securely locked on the inside when she arrived, with the main house key left hanging up on the nail over there by the cooker, presumably by Johnson before she went to bed.'

Kate glanced across the room, noting the second key, and nodded. 'So, anyone in the know could have used the key Mrs Rowlands used to get into the house.'

Purewal shrugged. 'Well, seeing as we think it's a suicide, that's hardly relevant, is it?'

After a brisk check of the kitchen the detectives carried out a quick circuit of the house, but found there were no other doors, apart from the main front door, and all windows were tightly closed, with nothing to suggest that any had been tampered with. They then turned their attention to the garden, more out of curiosity than anything else.

The house itself stood in around an acre of well-kept grounds, with a sizeable, wooded area at the bottom, which was bordered by a bridleway accessed via a wooden gate. Purewal spotted the deep tyre tracks in the muddy ground on the other side of the gate immediately and they both bent down to examine them.

'Some sort of heavy vehicle,' the DC said. 'Probably a Dagenham Dustbin or something similar. See the depth of the tread?'

Kate shrugged. 'Not a lot of relevance to this job, though, is it?' she said. 'We're not looking at a serious crime, like some sort of burglary with intent, are we? Plus the fact that loads of people probably park their motors on this track regularly while walking their dogs.'

Purewal nodded, but suddenly bent down again, and stuck a pen in the soft ground to dig out something partially buried in the mud, which her eagle eyes had spotted. When she straightened up, and rubbed it clean, Kate saw that it was a cufflink. 'Someone will probably be looking for this,' she said. 'Looks quite an unusual shape.'

Kate took the cufflink from her and studied it curiously. It was of an oval design with two intersecting arcs at one end, like curved tails. 'Unusual,' she said. 'Looks like it's made of silver, and it seems to have been designed to represent a fish.' She held it up in the light. 'It's personalised too with a monogram in a fancy script of what looks like the letters . . .' She read them out slowly '$A — G — J$. Hm, well "Mr AGJ" must be wondering where he lost it.'

'It's badly damaged, though,' Purewal added. 'Looks like someone stood on it or a car ran over it. The toggle on the end of the swivel-bar post is buckled. So, it wouldn't even be worth repairing.'

'Get you!' Kate exclaimed. 'Toggle and swivel-bar post? You should be a jeweller.'

Purewal laughed. 'Used to work in a jewellers' before I came to this country and joined the force,' she said. 'My dad had a shop in Amritsar.'

Kate raised her eyebrows. 'Then I'll know where to come for expert advice on future purchases,' she said, and slipped the cufflink into her pocket.

Her colleague frowned. 'You want to keep it? Whatever for? It's damaged and I would think it's only made of sterling silver. Hardly worth anything really, as there's not even a pair.'

'I'm not thinking of its financial value. But it might be worth hanging on to for the time being. I'll have it put in the nick's miscellaneous property store in the meantime.'

'Why bother?'

'Why not? It might even prove to be relevant in the future, you never know.'

Purewal shook her head in obvious puzzlement. 'I thought you were satisfied at the start that this job was a simple suicide.'

Kate nodded. 'Well, so far, we haven't uncovered any real evidence to the contrary, have we? So, for the present we have to go along with things as they appear. But that doesn't mean we should ignore anything unusual we might come across in the process, does it?'

'Your call,' Purewal replied with a shrug.

Kate smiled. 'Of course it is.'

The SOCO photographer still hadn't arrived by the time Kate and her colleague got back to the house and, since no trace of a suicide note had been found by Purewal earlier, Kate instituted a further search of the bedroom to ensure one hadn't been missed.

It was as she was going through a drawer in the bedside cabinet on which the bottle of whisky stood that she came across the small diary and cursorily flipped through the pages. Most of the content was about mundane things like hair or beauty salon appointments, DIY on the house and bills to be paid. But then an entry made several weeks ago in a neat, though noticeably shaky hand, immediately jumped out at her.

The bitch is free. God help us!

Then, after a gap, another entry read:

Meeting of everyone my place to discuss shock news 8.00 p.m.

Underneath that after another gap, was a third entry, which had obviously been added after the meeting:

Unanimous decision to keep schtum about it. Robert, Jules and Jenny all agreed. Danny not interested one way or the other. Incredible, when all this was his fault in the first place!!! Bastard!

Pressing on through the diary, Kate found another curious entry for the very day she and Indrani Purewal had responded to Lizzie Johnson's complaint about a prowler. But from what was written, it obviously referred to the night before:

Night Hag came as I knew she would. Saw her at top of stairs. Barricaded room. But then she appeared on balcony, staring in at me through door and grinning. Horrible. Rang police, but Robert and Jules say it was a bad dream and to drop complaint when they came. I think I must be losing my mind. So mixed up, I can't think now whether I saw her or not. But terrified she'll come back!

There were no further entries after that, and Kate jumped as Purewal spoke almost at her elbow.

'What have you found, skip?'

She handed her the diary, open at the last entry. Purewal scanned it briefly and gave a sharp intake of breath. 'Night Hag? Who the hell's that? Sounds like some character out of one of the old *Grimm's Fairy Tales*. She must have been more seriously puggled than we thought.'

Kate nodded. 'Sounds like it, certainly. Yet, according to this diary, Johnson *did* see someone on the stairs, as she first claimed when we interviewed her — it wasn't just a dream, as she told us afterwards — and she was supposedly frightened enough to barricade herself in her room. Not only that, but did you not see the rest of the entry about seeing the intruder on her balcony?'

Purewal grunted, handing back the diary. 'Yeah, I saw it, but you don't really believe all that, do you? She was obviously off her trolley. Next, *you'll* be seeing ghosties and ghoulies in your own dreams.'

Kate shivered. 'I hope not. Her Night Hag doesn't sound like a very nice person—'

She broke off as, for the second time that day, Purewal quickly bent down and picked something up from the floor.

'Must have fallen out of the diary,' she said, passing it to Kate.

It was a grubby scrap of paper that looked as though it had been torn from a notebook, and it carried a name and what appeared to be a mobile telephone number. But its effect on Kate was electric.

'Bloody hell!' she breathed. 'Billy James.'

'Who?'

'You must know Billy James?'

Purewal shook her head. 'New to me.'

Kate smiled grimly. 'Well, he's far from new to me. We go back a long way, do our Billy and me. He's a small-time crook and drug pusher and was one of my first arrests way back when I joined the department as a DC. A thoroughly nasty little man, who's as treacherous as they come. And what *I* would like to know is what on earth his name is doing in the back of Lizzie Johnson's diary?'

Purewal raised an eyebrow. 'How do you intend finding out?'

'I'm going to pay snidey little Billy a visit and ask him.'

'What, now? But it's technically your day off. You only turned out because I rang you about this job.'

'Well, I've booked myself back on, haven't I?'

CHAPTER 9

William Arthur Wentworth James, to give him his full name, lived in a semi-derelict cottage left by his late father on the outskirts of the village of Bason Bridge. Much of the roof on one side had been stripped of its tiles many years ago by the ferocious winds that sometimes blasted the Levels in the winter months and a couple of the front windows had long since lost their glass and had been boarded up with cardboard. The approach to the cottage was across a muddy field scattered with the rubbish of the smallholding that had once occupied the site, plus a few chickens and a mangey looking cat, which watched Kate's arrival from an open-fronted shed.

The place looked dead, but Kate was not convinced and, after knocking loudly on the rickety front door, she immediately went round the back — in time to meet Billy exiting at speed through the back door into a low-walled yard, as she'd anticipated.

'Well, hi there, Billy,' she said, blocking his path. 'Going somewhere?'

The little man was dressed as she had last seen him at Highbridge police station. How long he wore the same clothes before changing them was a matter for conjecture, and Kate didn't like to think about the state of his underwear.

'Ah, sarge,' he replied with a lop-sided grin. 'I were just, er—'

'Scarpering, Billy?'

'No, no, noffink like that, honest. I were off to the boozer.'

Kate slowly shook her head. 'That right? And there was I thinking you didn't want to talk to me.'

The grin broadened. ''Course not. Nice to see yer back.'

'You may not think that soon. Let's go inside for a little chat, eh?'

'Sorry, but it ain't convenient right now.'

'Tough. I'll follow you in.'

He stood his ground. 'Sorry, not wivout a warrant.'

'Okay, then how's about I feel your collar as a start, then I might have grounds for a search of your place anyway.'

He gaped. 'Yer freatening to nick me? What fer?'

'Let's say on suspicion of manslaughter.'

'Manslaughter? What yer talkin' abaht, man? I ain't killed no one.'

Kate shrugged. 'Your choice, Billy. Talk to me in there—' she pointed at his house —'or down the nick.'

She waited to see if her bluff paid off, knowing full well that she had no grounds whatsoever for pulling him in, and she was relieved to see his Adam's apple jerk up and down like a lift.

'Okay, okay,' he replied and turned back to the house. 'But this is well out of order.'

He led the way through a kitchen stacked with unwashed utensils, some of which still held remnants of food, and into what served as a lounge, furnished with two threadbare armchairs and a wooden coffee table that was straight out of the 1970s.

James sank into the sagging cushions of one of the chairs, looking pale and apprehensive, but Kate remained standing and walked past him through an archway and into an adjoining dining room, furnished with a plastic garden table and chairs and a battered-looking wooden sideboard.

'Oi!' she heard him shout, and the next instant he was behind her, almost breathing down her neck. 'What's yer game? Yer got no right . . .'

Kate ignored him and, stopping by the sideboard, pulled out one of the drawers to peer inside. Her smile was back as she pulled out a bundle of plastic packets containing what looked like some sort of dark vegetable matter.

'What's this, Billy?' she asked, turning to face him. 'It wouldn't be weed, would it?'

He scowled. 'Yer knows bloody well it is.'

She tutted. 'So, you're still being a naughty boy?'

'It's for me own use? I got arfritis, see, and it 'elps to dull the pain.'

'Bollocks! Where have you got the main product stashed — in that shed outside perhaps, or under the floorboards?'

'Ain't got no more, honest.'

She returned the packets to the drawer and closed it up. It was obvious he was dealing, but she wasn't interested in such a low-level crime, and it would have been difficult for her to prove anything in the present situation anyway, especially as she had no legal right to seize the stuff from his home after what would be seen as an illegal search without a warrant.

'So, tell me, Billy,' she went on, 'what else are you into apart from cannabis? Coke or H? Perhaps some prize skunk or a little acid? Maybe even a few benzos?'

'Ain't into anyfink, I swear. Given up on all that.'

'Yeah, right. So, if I got the team out here to tear the place apart, they wouldn't find a single illegal substance, apart from your hash?'

He wiped his mouth on the back of one nicotine-stained hand, his gaze evasive. 'It's the truf . . . On me muvver's life.'

'I happen to know your mother died yonks ago.'

He grimaced. 'Look, what you at? An' what's all this abaht manslaughter?'

She studied him fixedly. 'Do you know a woman called Lizzie Johnson? Lives in a converted barn out near Blackford.'

She saw the spark of recognition in his eyes. It was as good as a confirmation.

'Never 'eard of her.'

'No? Well, that's strange, because she knows you. Even has your name and mobile number written down.'

'Balls! Yer tryin' to fit me up for somefink?'

'Now, why would I do that to one of my most loyal snouts?'

He licked his lips, then made a sudden decision. 'Okay, okay, maybe I do know 'er. So, what?'

'She OD'd last night.'

'Shit! What on?'

'Never mind that. What I want to know is why she had your name and mobile number. Doing a bit of business with you, was she?'

His Adam's apple was on the move again in a series of spasmodic jerks and he stared at her like a hare transfixed by a pair of headlights.

'You don't fink I 'ad anyfink to do wiv 'er croakin', do yer?'

'You tell me.'

He shook his head several times, panic in his eyes. 'Nah, this ain't on. I ain't done noffink.'

'So, stop pissing me about and tell me what I want to know.'

'Okay, okay, but I need a fag.'

Kate followed him back through the archway into the other room, where he dumped himself unceremoniously into the armchair he had previously occupied. Perched on the edge of the chair opposite, she watched him pull a tobacco tin out of his pocket and start to roll himself a cigarette on his knee. She noticed that his hands were trembling when he finally lit up, coughing and wheezing through the smoke.

'Fing is, I've known Lizzie most of me life,' he said suddenly. 'Ever since I moved down 'ere wiv me ol' man from the Smoke after me ma died. Must've been abaht seven then.

Went to the same primary school as Lizzie an' all 'er stuck-up mates, though we never really got round to mixing much.'

'Well, that *is* a surprise,' Kate said sarcastically, looking at the state of him in the other armchair, slouched, unshaven, unwashed and probably wearing the same clothes he'd worn all the previous week.

He gave her a sour look at the remark. 'Yeah, well, we was on different pavs, weren't we? An' when we was older, 'er an' all them overs went to some fancy private school Bristol way, which 'as gone now, an' after that to university somewhere—'

'You didn't go with them then?' Kate mocked again, and he caught on and emitted a hollow laugh.

'What do you fink? Nah, I ended up bein' sent to a bleedin' secure unit instead, then later, to a stretch in stir for what the beak called persistent fievin' an' drug dealin'. By the time I got out, me ol' man 'ad popped 'is clogs, leavin' me this dump, an' Lizzie an' 'er mates was back from uni an' raisin' the roof round 'ere wiv partyin' an' getting' stoned on booze an' weed an' stuff—'

'Which I suppose you supplied?' Kate finished for him.

He hesitated, then nodded. 'A bit later, when I got into fings proper, yeah, but it were only weed, a little speed and some acid, noffink more. If I 'adn't done it, someone else would've. An' there ain't noffink yer can do abaht it now 'cause it's too long ago an' yer can't prove it anyways.'

Kate acknowledged the truth of that with a slight inclination of her head. 'And I suppose you're still supplying the same crowd now?'

He shook his head. 'Ain't 'ad noffink to do wiv any of 'em for years.'

'So why would Lizzie Johnson still have your name and mobile number?'

The tongue was out again, moistening dry lips. 'This is 'tween us two — right?'

Kate took a deep breath. She could be getting into deep water with this interrogation. If James coughed to something nasty, it could put her in an impossible position, despite any promises she had made. She would have to take the appropriate action, whether she wanted to or not. Otherwise, she could end up being complicit in the suppression of a serious crime. But she had started the ball rolling, and she had no choice but to stay the course and chance wherever this led. So, nodding in agreement, she waited for James to continue.

'A few monfs ago Lizzie bumped into me in the street in 'ighbridge and asked me if I remembered 'er from before. When I said I did, she asked me if I could still get 'old of stuff, like in the old days. I said I could an' she said she needed some molly an' a bit of blow for a party. I give 'er me mobile number, 'cause it looked like bein' a good earner, an' said I would call 'er when I'd got what she wanted.'

'And did you?'

'Yeah, couple days later. But some guy grabbed the phone off 'er an' said if I ever phoned 'er again, 'e'd cut me froat. Frit me to deaf, so I 'ad noffink to do wiv 'er after that.'

'You sure?'

'Gospel, sarge.'

'Any idea who the guy was who threatened you?'

'Yeah, I reckon it were eiver 'er ol' man, Bobby Chalmers, or one of the same crowd she used to 'ang around wiv in the ol' days—'

'You said her old man? You're saying she was married?'

'Used to be once. 'Eard she got divorced recent like, but I seen 'im once wiv 'er in town, so she must still be seein' 'im.'

'And this old crowd you talk about, who are they?'

'Why'd yer wanna know that?'

'Just curious, and it's my business anyway.'

'What's it worf?'

Kate's expression hardened. 'You've got a bloody cheek. I'll pretend I didn't hear that.'

He smirked. 'Okay, okay, only askin'.'

'Well, don't . . . So, answer my question.'

He stubbed out his cigarette on the wooden chair arm.

'Well, there was only ever five of 'em. Lizzie and Bobby, plus free ovvers — one of 'em bein' a bird called Jenny

Talbot, 'oose now the bleedin' 'ead of the ol' primary school we all used to go to. Funny that, ain't it? Then there's Danny Aldridge, who took over 'is ol' man's 'ouse-sellin' firm in Wedmore after 'e croaked, an' a real smoov arse called Julian Grey, 'oose into somefink to do wiv investments. 'E still lives in Mark but 'as an office in Bridgwater. All of 'em still pretty local, see. Must like livin' round 'ere for some reason.'

'How come you know so much about your old school chums all these years later?'

'There ain't much I don't know abaht folk what lives round 'ere. Word gets abaht, see. Like, if someone farts in 'ighbridge, they 'ears it in Wedmore ten minutes later.'

Kate permitted herself a thin smile. She knew only too well how gossip, particularly the poisonous or scandalous kind, could circulate in rural communities, distorting facts and ruining reputations. To snouts like Billy James, whose ear was always close to the ground, it was like manna from heaven, because it enabled him to exploit someone else's weakness or misbehaviour for his own benefit, with a whisper to people like her afterwards.

'What was Johnson herself like then?'

He pursed his lips. 'Bit of a nutter, I always fought.'

'Why? Because she was a user?'

'Nah, not that. But she were always talkin' daft, like — abaht ghosts and spirits an' that. Fought she were bein' follered by somefink from the ovver side,' he laughed. 'A demon or somefink'. Few weeks ago I 'ear she 'ad 'er place done to get rid of it. What do yer call that? Ex . . . sommat—'

'An exorcism?'

'Yeah, that's it. Excism or whatever.'

'Who did she get to do it?'

'Ain't got the faintest. Must 'ave been a right laugh.'

'I bet. So, what grubby little trail are you currently following where Johnson and her friends are concerned?' she queried drily.

He feigned shock. 'I dunno what yer on abaht, Sergeant,' he retorted, shaking his head. 'Far as I knows, they's all nice, 'spectable people . . .' And he grinned. 'But if I was to 'ear anyfink dodgy, yer knows I'd give you a bell.'

'Of course you would — for a price.'

'Market forces, Sergeant, an' I 'ave to earn a crust, don't I?'

She stared at him for a moment. He was up to something. She was pretty sure of that. But without anything to go on, it wasn't worth pursuing her suspicions, and without a lever of some sort, he wasn't about to come clean on anything.

She stood up. 'Okay, Billy, I'll leave you to it — for now. But remember, I'll be watching you.'

Another grin. 'Then it'll be like ol' times, won't it? he replied. 'The sarge watchin' me an' me watchin' everyone else.'

CHAPTER 10

Kate returned to Johnson's house immediately after parting company with Billy James, taking the precaution of radioing ahead to ensure Indrani Purewal was still there. The SOCO photographer had been and gone and the undertaker's van was parked outside the house, with two dark-suited men already loading Johnson's corpse in the back. She found Purewal upstairs in the bedroom, having bagged up the empty box of tablets and blister packs, as well as the bottle of whisky and the diary.

'Thought you'd gone home by now,' her colleague said. 'After all, it *is* Sunday.'

'That didn't bother you when you got me out of bed.'

Purewal chuckled. 'Ouch! So, what did your Billy James have to say?'

Kate shook her head. 'Not a lot. Usual crap.' She recounted what James had told her about the nature of his involvement with Lizzie Johnson.

'Do you believe him?'

Kate snorted. 'You can never believe a scumbag like that. But at present there's no evidence to suggest Johnson died of anything other than a benzo overdose. Unless the PM says anything different, or we can tie James into supplying what Johnson took, he's nothing more than a side issue.'

'And you came all the way back to hold my hand? That is really sweet, Sarge.'

Kate smiled at the good-natured sarcasm and pulled open the drawer of the bedside cabinet in which she had found the diary. She rummaged around for a few moments before extracting what turned out to be a small black book with the word *Addresses* in gold lettering on the front. 'Ah!' she said. 'I thought she might have had one of these.'

Purewal frowned. 'Why do you want that?'

Kate dug her notebook out of her pocket and began carefully checking the four names Billy James had given her against the alphabetically listed entries inside the black book. 'We'll need to let Johnson's next of kin know what's happened to her,' she replied, 'and there will have to be a formal ID. Billy James mentioned the names of four friends Johnson associated with and I wondered if they were listed here . . . Ah, here's one: Danny Aldridge, complete with address and telephone number.' She quickly scribbled down the details. 'Local too. Brilliant! At least that's a start . . . And here's our friend, Robert Chalmers, with a Bristol address. Now for the other two, if they're in here . . .'

They were. She found Julian Grey and Jennifer Talbot moments later, all with local addresses, as in the case of Aldridge. Watched curiously by her colleague, she copied the information down, as before.

'Why did you need all four names?' Purewal exclaimed. 'Surely Chalmers would have been enough? We can get one of the Bristol plods to go round and break the news to him in the absence of any other known relative, and the coroner's officer will then be able to take things from there when he later assumes responsibility for the job.'

Kate shook her head, closing the address book and returning it to the drawer. 'According to Billy James, these were all close, long-term friends of Johnson who had known each other since childhood. So, as well as Chalmers, they are all potential sources of information about her and what sort of mindset may have driven her to take her own life. As it is, I can find no one by the name of "Johnson" in the address book, which could mean she has no other surviving blood relatives we can contact—'

'*If* Johnson was her maiden name.'

'Oh, I think it must have been. Billy James told me she was married to Robert Chalmers at one time, but they got divorced. Looks like she reverted to Johnson again afterwards.'

'Well, there you are then. What could be better than an ex-husband to give us all the info we need?'

Kate raised an eyebrow. 'You think? Don't forget, we have no suicide note or any real evidence that confirms her death *was* definitely down to suicide.'

Purewal groaned. 'Oh, come on, Kate, you're not saying someone could have offed her?'

'I'm not saying anything of the sort. I am making the point that we need to secure all the information we can get on her, and from whatever source is available, to hand over to the coroner's officer. I think he will agree that the coroner would expect nothing less from us in any sudden death inquiry — especially one that is more than likely to be suicide. It would be totally out of order to rely solely on the words of an ex-husband, who — in the worst kind of scenario — could tell us whatever suited him.'

'But that still suggests you're not convinced Johnson died from a self-administered overdose? Is it because of that broken cufflink? You think someone else might have been in the house when Johnson OD'd? That they were somehow involved in Johnson's death, then scarpered, dropping their cufflink on the track as they quit the scene? That's all a bit Agatha Christie, isn't it?'

'Don't put words into my mouth, Indi,' Kate said sharply. 'Her death probably *was* a straightforward suicide, and the PM will no doubt bear this out, but we should never simply accept something like this at face value, however obvious the explanation might seem to be.'

And even as she made those comments, she was conscious of a little worm stirring uneasily deep inside her . . .

* * *

The cottage in Burtle was streaming with light when Kate finally got home as dusk was settling in, and she caught the distinct smell of something cooking. It wafted out of one of the open front windows, although she couldn't see into the cottage, as all the curtains had been drawn. Mystified, she stuck her key in the front door and stepped into the living room. The fire had been lit and logs were blazing merrily in the open fireplace, but there was no sign of Hayden.

Yawning, she shut the front door and tossed her keys on to the half-moon telephone table by the staircase. It was then that she saw that the small dining room table which was usually folded up in the corner, had been erected near the patio doors and was set for dinner, with a bottle of red wine and two glasses positioned in the centre.

Crossing to the stairs, she shouted, 'Hayd, where are you?'

The footfall was light, but she spun round as he emerged from the kitchen, looking sheepish.

'Hi, Kate,' he mumbled, glancing down at his feet. 'Glad you're home.'

She gaped at him and waved an arm towards the dining table. 'Hayd, what *is* all this? Are we expecting visitors?'

He fidgeted from one foot to the other. 'Only us,' he said and suddenly taking the plunge, he stepped forward, grabbed her in a bear hug, kissing her on the lips so fiercely that she felt she couldn't breathe.

'I'm so sorry, Kate,' he said, finally letting her go and stepping back again. 'I've been an absolute pig and — and I wanted to make amends.'

For the first time in her life, Kate was speechless. If he had suddenly admitted to being gay, she couldn't have been more shocked. This wasn't the Hayden she had known all the years they had been married. Hayden rarely, if ever, apologised and after the way he had behaved following her navigational faux pas at the treasure hunt the previous day, his dramatic change in manner came as a total shock to her, and she didn't know what to say.

'Take your coat off and go sit down at the table,' he went on, as she was still struggling to get herself together. 'I hope you like what I've prepared.'

Like someone in a dream, she slipped out of her anorak and, dumping it on the settee in passing, she went to the table and stared at the plate of pâté in the two place settings. He poured her some wine as she pulled out the chair and sat down. Then crossing to the chair opposite, he also sat down and treated her to a nervous smile. 'You do know what today is, don't you, old girl?' he said.

She shook her head.

'It's when I proposed to you all those years ago, and I've been an ass ever since.'

She gulped some wine and said, 'And that's what this is all about?'

He hesitated, then said, 'After you'd gone off today, Ted Parry rang me from the classic car club and gave me some pretty awful news. You remember Jilly, Bill Brace's lovely little wife?'

'I've met her once or twice, yes.'

'Well, she died of an unexpected brain haemorrhage this morning and she was only thirty-six. He–he's devastated.'

'Heavens, that's awful.'

'Yes, isn't it? It worried me all day and I got to thinking, what if–if, you know, something like that happened to you. I–I couldn't bear it.'

'And that's why you set all this up?'

'I wanted to–to let you know how much I care for you, even though I don't show it a lot. I know I'm possessive, grumpy and pretty boorish sometimes, and that we're always rowing over something or other, but–but that doesn't change the way I feel about you . . .'

His voice trailed off and she could feel the tears trickling down her face. On impulse, she reached across with both hands and gripped his wrists tightly. 'You don't need to say anything else, Hayd,' she said, her voice husky and emotional. 'This was a lovely thought. Let's just eat, shall we?'

* * *

The steak dinner was perfect — she hadn't even known he could cook — and, after coffee, they curled up on the settee together, watching castles and bridges building and collapsing among the burning logs in the fireplace, each busy with their thoughts and saying nothing.

Finally, Hayden broke the silence and said, 'I thought you'd walked out on me when you left this morning. I was worried sick.'

'That wouldn't have been the first time, would it?' she said wryly, thinking of the near break-up in their tempestuous relationship that they had faced a few months before while on their short sabbatical in Pembrokeshire.

'Where did you go?' he asked.

'Didn't you hear the phone?'

'Yes, but I was half-asleep and didn't take much notice of it.'

She told him all that happened and waited a few minutes while, true to form, he digested and analysed the information.

'Do you think the death was suspicious then?'

She made a face. 'Not sure. Nothing really significant to suggest that, although I did feel the scene was a bit too "arranged". Too pat and a little overdone — you know, as if it had been laid out like that for the benefit of our visit, presenting us with all the necessary pointers to indicate a suicide, including all those blister packs left on the bed.'

He frowned. 'I must admit, it does all sound a bit fishy, and it would be a subtle way of quietly disposing of someone by making their death look like suicide, but it would not be that easy to pull off. You'd have to be absolutely certain that the overdose would do the trick and that can never be guaranteed, as everyone's metabolism is different.'

She nodded. 'And forcing a load of tablets down someone's throat against their will without causing an injury of some sort would certainly not be an easy thing to do. Even if done surreptitiously, like lacing a bottle of whisky with diazepam, would present quite a challenge.'

He gave a quick smile. 'Then maybe it *was* suicide and you've no need to worry. The woman was plainly flaky, as you say, and her diary entry about the Night Hag seems to suggest she was suffering from some kind of deep-seated guilt complex.'

Kate stiffened. 'Guilt complex? Why do you say that?'

'The Night Hag, or the *Nocnitsa*, as she is known in Polish mythology, is a nightmare spirit, personified by a malicious old crone, who punishes wrongdoers by creeping into their homes at night while they are asleep and sitting on their chests to stop them breathing. Interestingly, a belief by some ancient communities in the existence of the Night Hag and her suffocating technique actually gave rise to the term "hag-ridden", which we use today, and in some communities the spectre of the nasty old woman is also still used as a means of frightening young children into behaving themselves.'

Kate rubbed her hands up and down both arms and shivered. 'Sounds a sweet old thing, doesn't she? And how do you know all this about her?'

He shrugged. 'As you're aware, I majored in history and philosophy at uni all those years ago and part of that involved looking at folklore. The "Nocnitsa" or Night Hag, was one of the superstitions I researched as part of my thesis on seventeenth-century witchcraft.'

She reacted with a characteristic surprised flick of her eyebrows. 'I learn something about you every day, Hayd. So, you're saying Johnson's fear of this legendary old crone was because of something dodgy she had done in the past?'

'Sounds very much like it. Most experts in this particular field point out that rather than being hag-ridden, those allegedly visited by the old crone who survived to tell the tale had probably suffered from the modern medical condition of sleep paralysis or sleep apnoea. But for someone like Johnson, who you told me was deep into the supernatural and was a bag of nerves who saw shadows on the stairs, the so-called Night Hag would probably have posed a very real threat in her mind — especially if Johnson had a murky past.'

Kate sipped some more wine and pondered the issue for a few moments, giving him time to go through to the kitchen for another bottle. When he returned, he found her studying something in the palm of her hand.

'What have you got there then?' he asked, placing the newly opened bottle on the coffee table in front of them and dropping back onto the settee beside her. 'Looks like a cufflink of some sort?'

She nodded. 'Indi found it on a track behind Johnson's house,' she said. 'Nothing significant in it really, just an old cufflink, but it seemed a funny thing to find there.'

He smirked, staring at it for a moment as he poured some more wine. 'Maybe the Night Hag dropped it as she was fleeing the scene?' he joked.

Kate grinned back. 'Hardly — unless *she* was a transvestite dressed in a dress suit and black tie.' She sighed and became serious. 'But I wonder whether it could have been someone who had been secretly seeing Johnson, may have decided to end an affair they were having and chose an OD as an ideal way of doing it.'

He grunted. 'Well, if that is the case, it is likely he was a prize hypocrite.'

'How do you make that out?'

'The cufflink is in the shape of a fish.'

'What's a fish got to do with anything?'

'The fish, which is derived from the Greek word, *ichthus*, while also representing abundance and fertility, has also long been regarded as a key symbol of Christianity worn or displayed by dedicated members of the faith. So, it is probable that whoever lost the cufflink was a so-called Christian, preaching goodness, mercy and all that jazz at the same time as he was doing the business with Johnson, which would hardly fit in with the Christian ethos . . . Can I have a look at it?'

She handed the cufflink to him, and he peered at it closely for a moment before handing it back. 'I see there's a monogram of three initials on one side — *AGT*, is it?'

'I thought it was *AGJ*.'

'No, definitely *AGT*. And obviously the owner liked it enough to have it engraved. Pity someone stood on it, or maybe even drove over it.'

She nodded. 'That's what I thought. The track on which Indi found it runs along the back of Johnson's property through a small wood, which is accessed by a gate at the bottom of her garden, and there were also tyre tracks in the wet ground from what looked like a heavy vehicle.'

'Which could have been made by a driver pulling in there to walk his dog or someone stopping to relieve themselves.'

'I can see that. But I'm uneasy about this whole thing. Something tells me there's more to Johnson's death than at first appears.'

He sighed, returning the cufflink to her. 'Something tells you . . . ? That old intuition thing of yours. But you have no evidence to indicate Johnson's death was anything but a suicide. Not doing a Don Quixote again, are you? You know, tilting at windmills?'

Her mouth tightened. 'I thought you'd say something like that.'

'Well, you do have a bit of history there, don't you?'

'That's as maybe, but my suspicions have nearly always proved to be right in the end.'

He got up to put more logs on the fire. 'Yes, but on this occasion, I'd suggest you leave things as they are. From what you told me, the police surgeon was quite satisfied that Johnson simply overdosed, and you have nothing that says otherwise, so why rock the boat? You'll only give yourself unnecessary aggro.'

She stretched and yawned. 'Perhaps you're right. But for now, I think I'm going to take a shower and then have an early night.'

Her hand slid along his thigh and squeezed it. 'You look tired, Hayd,' she added, a telltale gleam in her eyes, 'so maybe you should do the same . . .'

Immediately she felt him tense and there was a look of alarm in his eyes at the blatant hint, his near genophobic hang-up surfacing in a rush. 'E–early night,' he mumbled. 'No, I–I thought I'd watch a film.'

She treated him to a mischievous smile. 'Oh, I think there's something we can do that's a lot better than watching a film, don't you?' she replied.

* * *

Julian Grey had had a particularly busy week. As a financial adviser, his client base had grown so large now that he had had to employ a secretary and three full-time staff for his financial services business in Bridgwater. Even then, it was a regular nine-to-ten-hour day, six days a week, for himself alone, visiting the well-heeled corporate customers on his books at their homes all over the south-west and advising them on the various investment portfolios available to them. Still, he had to admit, all the years of graft had been well worthwhile. He had made a great deal of money since he had started his business. He now owned a string of rental properties in the south-west and a small yacht in the marina at Plymouth, as well as a number of lucrative offshore investments through a bank in Guernsey.

Sunday was normally his only day of rest, but for a change, he had decided to give himself a well-earned break and take the following week off. Starting as he meant to go on, he had spent his idea of a holy day nowhere near a church but relaxing in the gym and sauna at his big Georgian-style house set back off the Causeway at Mark village, and he had made sure something very special was lined up for the evening — and, if it suited him, hopefully for a few days more. Unmarried, but with a string of occasional paid-for "girlfriends" supplied by a classy escort agency in Bristol, he was looking forward to bedding the one who had just arrived for dinner when the phone rang.

Bob Chalmers sounded shot-away. 'It's Lizzie,' he said. 'Had the police round to my flat. She's–she's dead, Jules.'

Grey's grip on his whisky glass tightened. 'Dead? What do you mean?'

'What I say. D-E-A-D — like in dead.'

'Bloody hell, how?'

'Drug overdose, they think. She was apparently found in bed this morning by her cleaner. I–I've been asked to go and ID her body at the local mortuary tomorrow morning, and they say there's going to be an inquest.'

Grey glanced at the open doorway, conscious of the fact that his sexy guest was in the bathroom across the hall, freshening up. 'Shit! That's all we need with everything else that's been happening at Pagan's Clump.'

There was a sharp retort. 'Thanks for your sympathy.'

Grey grimaced and took a gulp of his whisky. 'Sorry, old man. I didn't mean it like that. I'm, you know, shocked.'

'How do you think *I* feel? She used to be my wife.'

'Did the police say whether they think it was an accident or suicide?'

'They don't know. Copper who delivered the message didn't have much info. Said the coroner's officer would be able to tell me more in the morning.'

'What do you think?'

'I can't see it being an accident. She may have been flaky, but she wasn't stupid.'

'So, suicide then, but why?'

'How should I know? We–we had one hell of a row after you left on Friday, and I walked out on her. Maybe that was it. She *kept* going on about this Night Hag thing of hers, so could be she flipped.'

'What did she say to the police when they came on Friday?'

'That her intruder must have been a bad dream.'

'Do you think they swallowed it?'

'Seemed to, but she said a bit too much, in my opinion. Told them about seeing a ghost or something on the stairs.'

Grey tensed. 'Didn't say anything about Pagan's Clump, did she?'

'Definitely not.'

'Well, that's something anyway . . .'

'You don't seem very shocked or upset over Lizzie's death.'

Grey glanced quickly at the open doorway again as he heard the click of the bathroom door.

'That's not true, old chap,' he said. 'She was one of us and of course I'm upset. I'm trying to be practical, that's all. Hang in there, and let me know what happens tomorrow . . . Oh, and you'd better tell Danny and Jenny the bad news.'

'You, er, don't think there's anything in this revenge thing Lizzie talked about, do you? This Night Hag business?'

Grey gave a disparaging snort. 'No more than I believe in bloody fairies and Father Christmas. Don't you go weird on the rest of us like Lizzie did, Bob.'

''Course not.'

'Relieved to hear it.' Grey cut off.

CHAPTER 11

The DCI was in the DI's office with Charlie Woo again when Kate and Hayden reported for duty Monday morning, and she inwardly groaned.

'Sergeant!' Ricketts called sharply, as she tried to slip in behind her desk without being seen.

'What's this I hear about you turning out for duty yesterday when you were supposed to be on rest day?' he snapped when she joined him in the office.

'DC Purewal rang me regarding the apparent suicide of a woman we had been interviewing on Friday,' she replied. 'As I was involved in the original interview, I thought I should attend.'

'An interview about what?'

'A suspected burglary, sir.'

'And . . . ?'

'She withdrew her complaint when we got there. Said it had obviously been a bad dream.'

'Then why did you need to attend the later incident? I am quite sure DC Purewal was competent enough to deal with it on her own.'

'I thought it was a bit strange that she should kill herself just two days later, sir.'

Ricketts frowned heavily. 'Why? Were there suspicious circumstances?'

'Er, not exactly, sir. But it didn't seem right to me somehow.'

Ricketts snorted. 'Didn't seem right? That's typical of you, Sergeant, isn't it? Reading something into everything you deal with. What some might call tilting at windmills.'

Kate's mouth tightened, as she remembered Hayden's dig about that. But before she could say anything, the DCI said, 'Well, let me remind you, Sergeant, that your day off was covered by a perfectly capable DS at Bridgwater, as per the rota system. There was no need for you to attend and, understandably, DS Walters is quite put out that you did so. In future if you are detailed as rest day, you will stay on rest day unless specifically authorised to report back on duty. Is that clear?'

Kate glimpsed Woo sending her warning messages with his eyes from behind his boss and forced herself to put up with the dressing-down for a change. 'Yes, sir,' she replied.

'Good, and don't even think of using police regulations to claim payment for being called out on less than eight days' notice. In fact, you will be allocated another day off in lieu of Sunday, with no extra payment for the hours you worked.'

'Thank you very much, sir,' Kate replied, and before Ricketts could say anything else, she about-turned and strode to her desk, leaving him staring after her in astonishment.

Kate deliberately avoided looking up from her desk when Ricketts finally stalked out of the office, and she started when a hand carefully placed a mug of coffee in front of her.

'Sounds as though you had a really good weekend off?' Charlie Woo commented innocently.

Kate sat back in her chair. Hayden had disappeared once again, no doubt in the direction of the canteen, and there was no one else in the general office at that moment.

'Couldn't have been better,' she replied, 'and it's nice to know that I am held in such high esteem.'

He gave her a crooked grin. 'What did you expect? A medal? Anyway, I have some good news. The team at Pagan's

Clump decided to dig a little deeper and they've found what they think is an ankle bracelet. It probably detached itself from the bones over time, and it is engraved with the name "Annie". Ring any bells?'

Kate shook her head. 'Doesn't mean anything to me.'

'Nor me, and evidently a check on misper records has proved negative.'

'So, another dead end then—?' Kate broke off, adding, 'Sorry, pun not intended.'

Woo winced. 'At least it might mean that the team have stumbled upon a likely birth name, which in the long run could prove to be a small step forward in identifying the dead woman. A clue maybe that may unlock the puzzle later.'

She took a sip of her coffee. 'So, what's happening now?'

'Well, a press conference is being arranged for later today and they're hoping that by putting the name "Annie" out there in the public domain, together with a pic of the bracelet, it might stir some memories, particularly among our elderly residents still living in the surrounding villages.'

Kate looked dubious. 'Could work, I suppose.'

'But that's not all. They've finally found a use for all of us on Highbridge CID. Isn't that brilliant? Now they have actually dug up a possible name, they've asked if we can feed that information personally to any local contacts we might have and see what comes up. That's why the DCI was over here.'

Kate forced a pout. 'And here was I thinking he came over here to see little ol' me. *Je suis inconsolable*.'

He laughed outright. 'You can't enjoy his attention all the time, Kate. He does have other people to torment, you know, even if you *are* his favourite.'

* * *

Robert Chalmers was not normally a nervous man. Driven by ambition and quite ruthless in a cowardly, back-stabbing sort of way, he had stepped on more than enough people to get where he was on the board of the big IT firm he was working for. Few things fazed him in life, and he was quick to take advantage of any situation that was likely to benefit him, regardless of the damage it might cause someone else. As far as he was concerned, people who played by the rules were weak losers who asked for all they got and he reserved a particular kind of contempt for those who failed to succeed in life, whether socially or in their chosen careers. He knew he wasn't liked, but he didn't care, as long as he got what he wanted.

But Chalmers was well out of his comfort zone when the police coroner's officer led him into the cold, bare room at the mortuary where the corpse had been carefully laid out on a steel table, under a plain white sheet.

To his shame, he was trembling as the officer gently pulled back part of the sheet and he found himself staring with a sort of horrible fascination at his ex-wife's pallid face. He was unaware of the voice of the coroner's officer asking him the crucial question until it had been asked several times, and then his own voice sounded distant and disembodied even to him when he finally responded with a whispered, 'Yes, that's Lizzie.'

Out in the fresh air, blinking in the fragile sunlight, he stood there for a few moments, swaying unsteadily.

'You okay, sir?' the coroner's officer asked him quietly.

He cleared his throat to try and mask his near loss of control. 'Rather a shock, that's all, thank you,' he replied. 'I've not had to do this sort of thing before.'

'Quite understandable, sir,' the other replied. 'I believe you were married to Ms Johnson at one time?'

'Some while ago, yes. It, er, didn't work out.'

'I'm very sorry to hear that, sir, and I fully appreciate how difficult this tragic affair must be for you, but I'm afraid I will still need to have a chat with you back at the station, if I may. Get a few necessary details about the deceased that we will need for the coroner. That okay?'

Chalmers nodded. 'I'll follow you there. I would just like to sit here quietly with my thoughts for a few minutes to try and reconcile myself to all that's happened.'

'No problem at all, sir. I'll see you shortly then.'

Chalmers watched him drive away, then walked slowly to his own parked car and sat for several minutes behind the wheel, turning things over in his mind. Things that he had been unable to address without sticking his head above the parapet by asking the coroner's officer directly, the one key question: did the police think Lizzie's death had been an accident, suicide, or something more sinister. An approach he had avoided, since it would only have risked arousing unwanted interest in the question itself and have perhaps set a hare running. So, he had kept quiet and put up with the officer's earlier noncommittal description of the incident as "a tragic sudden death that would require a post-mortem and a possible inquest in due course".

To be honest, he didn't feel any real sense of loss over Lizzie's death, even though, for show, he had made a point of taking Grey to task the day before for his seemingly unsympathetic response to the news of her passing. He suffered no pricks to his conscience for the way he felt. Essentially because he didn't have a conscience to begin with. He had never had one. Instead, his feelings were of relief. Relief that the complication, which had always been Lizzie Johnson, with her neurotic behaviour and loose mouth, no longer posed a risk to himself or the others.

So, he had once been married to her and he must have felt something for the poor bitch at one time. But whatever that had been, it had drained away long ago. Now, his only focus was on making sure her death did not lead to a worse scenario — a police investigation, which inadvertently turned over so many stones that it established a link between Lizzie and what had happened to Annie Evans all those years ago. Okay, that was pretty unlikely, but in his heightened state of anxiety, anything seemed possible.

He was still dwelling on that when his mobile bleeped. It was Julian Grey.

'Well, have you seen her?' his friend asked.

'Yes, it was Lizzie.'

'I didn't expect it to be otherwise. What are the police saying?'

'They're not saying anything. Just going through what must be the usual procedures. You know, formal identification, filling in forms, that sort of thing.'

'But do they think it was an accident, suicide or what?'

'No idea and I don't want to ask too many questions in case they get suspicious.'

'H'm, good point. Anyway, how are you holding up?'

'I'm fine.'

'You don't sound like it. After what you asked me yesterday re the possibility that there could be something in Lizzie's fears about being stalked, I was concerned you might be going doolally like her.'

Chalmers stiffened. 'Not a chance.'

'Glad to hear it. We all need to stick together. Can't have any doubters in the camp, can we? That could be fatal. Anyway, at least now, with poor old Lizzie brown bread, there's no risk of her dropping us all in it, so we only have to keep schtum like we all agreed at the start.'

'Agreed. Have you told the others what's happened, or do you want me to do it?'

'No, they're aware now, and I've suggested we meet up tonight for a powwow. Jenny has offered her place, and seven thirty seems about right. Okay for you?'

'Yeah, I can make that.'

'See you there then. Oh, and careful what you say to Old Bill, eh?'

'Do you think I'm an idiot?'

Grey didn't answer the question one way or the other.

* * *

Kate was on her way out to the CID car in the rear yard of Highbridge police station when her police mobile rang. It was the control room.

'Got a Reverend Taylor on the blower, skipper,' the operator said. 'Wants to speak to you. Says it's important.'

Kate frowned. Taylor? What the hell did he want? Not to report another attempted break-in, surely? She wasn't in the mood for silly games. After what Woo had told her about making inquiries of local contacts regarding the Pagan's Clump job, she had been about to do exactly that — and Billy James had been first on her list for a re-visit. She was tempted to instruct Control to tell the annoying priest that she wasn't available and have done with it. But then something stopped her. Taylor was a long-term local resident, and it was conceivable that he might be someone who would remember the name "Annie". So, maybe he was as good a person to start with as any; Billy could come later.

'Tell him I'm out of the office, but I'll call by to see him in half an hour, if that's okay?' she said.

A few seconds later the operator was back again. 'Says that'll do fine,' he confirmed. 'He'll be at home all afternoon.'

Probably putting the pane of glass he broke back in his shed window, she thought cynically. But as it turned out, Taylor was nowhere near his shed, but indoors, nicely dressed in a dark jacket and flannels and sporting a dog collar.

'Nice of you to come by,' he said, showing her to the same library, as before, and waving a hand towards one of the two floral-patterned armchairs.

'Would you like some tea this time, Sergeant?' he asked. 'Perhaps a buttered scone too, eh?'

Kate relented and smiled. 'That would be very nice,' she said, 'but just tea please.'

While he was gone, she cast an eye curiously around the room, seeing it properly for the first time. Two walls were occupied by built-in bookcases, and an old-fashioned desk and bosun's type chair stood against the third outer wall beneath a leaded light window. The shelves of the bookcases appeared to be buckling in places under the weight of the rows of heavy-looking volumes they were supporting, and initially she assumed these would be religious tomes of some sort. But closer inspection proved her wrong. Some indeed related to ecclesiastical things, and there were a number of Bibles and prayer books in evidence, but the majority of the space seemed to be taken up with books on history, art and politics, and one section was devoted solely to classical novels.

'You are fond of books, Sergeant?' Taylor said, returning to the room so quietly that he made her jump.

'Not really,' she replied, a little embarrassed at being caught out, and she waited while he set a tray, holding a china teapot, milk jug and two cups on a coffee table between their two chairs before returning to her seat. 'I don't get a lot of time for serious reading, I'm afraid.'

'Ah,' he said, propping himself on the edge of the other chair while he poured the tea, 'police work is very much a full-time job, I would imagine? Unsocial hours and all that. I remember it was very much the same for me when I was the parish priest.'

'But you don't seem to have shed your responsibilities entirely. I see you are wearing your clerical collar today, even though you said when we spoke before that you had retired.'

He smiled. 'As a minister of the gospel, you never truly retire, only on paper. You remain in the service of God for life, and you can be called upon to support the work of the Church at any time.' He gave a short laugh. 'You don't give it all up after thirty years, as you do in the police. Due to the illness of the regular parish priest this morning, for example, I was asked to perform the Eucharist at the eight o'clock service today, which I was happy to do.'

Kate made a rueful grimace, aware she'd received a firm slap on the wrist, and tried to cover her discomfort by taking a sip of her tea.

'So, what did you want to see me about, Reverend?' she asked after an uncomfortable pause. 'I was told it was important?'

He nodded, ignored his tea, and sat forward in his chair, his fingertips steepled under his chin for a few moments.

'Yes,' he said finally, dropping his hands and staring fixedly at Kate, 'it's about one of my former parishioners, a young lady named Lizzie Johnson. I gather she passed away last weekend, and I believe you dealt with the tragic case.'

'How did you know about it, if you don't mind my asking?'

'In communities like this, Sergeant,' he said, 'as you must already know, word soon gets around, and I was naturally very shocked when I heard the news.'

'Did you know Lizzie personally then?'

'No, hardly at all. She was one of my parishioners when I was the parish priest, although I must confess, she wasn't a member of my congregation, and I cannot recall her ever attending any of the regular church services. But I did perform the blessing at her wedding some years ago, though sadly, she and her husband, Robert Chalmers — another of my parishioners — later parted.'

'Oh, I see. So, what is it you wished to ask me?'

'Well, rumours are circulating because of the involvement of the police, and I am naturally concerned as to how she died. Are you able to tell me what caused her death? I hear that the lady who cleaned for her, a Mrs Millie Rowlands, was the one who found her, and she has said it was a drug overdose.'

Kate shook her head. 'I'm afraid it will be up to the coroner to determine cause of death, sir. I am not authorised to comment.'

'But surely you can give me an indication, Sergeant? Mrs Rowlands has been telling everyone that a lot of empty tablet packaging was lying on the bed in which Lizzie died and there was a bottle of whisky nearby. Do you think she took her own life, or was it a tragic accident?'

Kate sighed. 'Sorry, Reverend, I really can't comment.'

The frustration on Taylor's face was obvious. 'Sergeant, I really need to know if it was suicide — if only for the sake of her soul. She was obviously a very troubled young lady and—'

He broke off when he saw Kate's brows knit in a frown, as if he realised he had said too much.

'How do you know she was troubled, Reverend?' Kate asked quietly. 'Had you been to see her recently? Perhaps provided her with spiritual guidance?'

'No, not at all,' he replied quickly. 'As I said, I hardly knew her. I had no idea where she went to live after her marriage until I heard about the tragedy and what Mrs Rowlands had been saying. But I assumed that for someone to commit suicide, they must have been suffering from some sort of serious mental or emotional problem.'

'I never told you she committed suicide, Reverend,' Kate persisted. 'I said I couldn't comment.'

'True, but as *I* have said, according to Mrs Rowlands, a lot of empty tablet packaging was lying on the bed and there was a bottle of whisky there too. That in itself would suggest to me that she must have overdosed, and it is unlikely that she would have taken the large number of tablets said to be involved accidentally.'

'But if you hardly knew her, why are you so curious about the cause of her death?'

He gave a short, slightly shaky laugh. 'Why do I feel as if I'm being interrogated, Sergeant? I am not curious about the cause, I am concerned, which is an entirely different matter. Naturally, as she was once one of my, er, flock, if I can put it that way, I felt obligated to inquire into the circumstances, if only to include her in my prayers to Almighty God and ask for her salvation.'

Kate nodded, then forced another smile. He couldn't have come up with a more unconvincing answer, but there was no profit in pursuing the subject any further, so she left it there. 'No interrogation intended, Reverend,' she said quietly. 'I'm sorry if it sounded that way. But I am sure you will understand that I have a duty to the coroner to be as thorough as possible in looking into the circumstances of every unexplained death. That's my job.'

He visibly relaxed. 'Of course, of course,' he agreed quickly. 'I didn't want you to think my interest was motivated by some sort of ghoulish preoccupation.'

'I never imagined it was,' she replied, 'and though I cannot give you the answers you need at the moment, I will let you know as soon as I am in a position to do so.'

He took a sip of his tea and nodded, his disappointment still apparent. 'That would be most helpful, Sergeant, thank you, and I am really grateful you have found the time to come out here to see me when you have so much else on your plate at the moment with the Pagan's Clump matter . . .' He hesitated, then said, 'I don't suppose the, er, remains have been identified yet, have they?'

Kate shook her head, pleased that he had raised the subject for her, so that it didn't look as though she'd had an ulterior motive for her visit.

'Not as yet, no, but maybe you can help us there.'

'Help you? But of course . . . if I can.'

'The thing is, it seems the investigation team have found a silver-coloured bangle at the scene, which they feel may have belonged to the deceased, and it is engraved with the name "Annie". They're about to put out a public appeal to see if anyone remembers a local woman with that name living in the area some twenty to thirty years ago. I thought perhaps that, as you were probably the local minister at the time, you might . . .'

To Kate's astonishment, Taylor's cup seemed to dissolve in his hand, splashing tea and fragments of bone china down his trousers as well as all over the carpet and part of the coffee table. As he shot to his feet with an irritable apology, she saw that his face had developed a greyish pallor and beads of perspiration had appeared on his forehead.

Setting her own cup down on the coffee table, Kate also scrambled to her feet and, grabbing a napkin from the tray, went over to help him. He was already sponging himself down with another napkin, muttering more apologies, but she could see that the front of his trousers was soaked through, and his right hand was cut and bleeding.

She handed him her own napkin and he quickly wrapped it around the hand. 'You ought to get a couple of plasters on that,' she said. 'Have you any here?'

He nodded. 'In–in the kitchen,' he replied. 'There's a first-aid cabinet and—'

But Kate was already on her way to the hall. She found the kitchen and a distinctive white box bearing a red cross on the wall and returned to the library with some first-aid essentials in a tin. She found him still standing there, looking dazed, with the napkin wound around his hand like a bandage. She gently unwound it, noting with some surprise that the soft material looked like fine linen.

She noted something else too, something that caused her heart to miss not just one, but several beats. There was a monogram in one corner of the napkin embroidered with three entwined letters, and she remembered only too well seeing that particular combination before, only then it had been engraved on the broken cufflink found on the track behind Lizzie Johnson's house; a cufflink, which she had yet to hand in and still resided in her coat pocket!

CHAPTER 12

For a second, Kate simply stared at the napkin with a sense of shock. *AGT*. The letters seemed to jump out at her and for a moment she froze. Then, suddenly conscious of the fact that Taylor was still standing there with his open palm out towards her, waiting for her to do something, she quickly handed the napkin back to him to hold with his other hand and set the first-aid tin down on the coffee table.

'I'm, er, afraid you've ruined your nice napkin,' she blurted by way of explanation, hoping he hadn't picked up on her distraction. She quickly tipped some disinfectant on to a piece of lint from the tin, before cleaning his hand and applying plasters to a couple of the cuts, which were fortunately only superficial. 'Looks good quality too and the monogram in the corner looks very impressive. What does it stand for?'

He sighed. 'Oh, that. It's my initials actually. Arthur George Taylor. I am very fond of personal monograms. They fascinate me and also, of course, they are useful in identifying personal property if it is lost. I think this particular monogram, and the way it has been designed, is unique. Not that the Church approves of such self-indulgence, which they see as flying in the face of the Christian teachings of humility and service.' He winced as the disinfectant found its way into the cuts on his hand. 'As for the stains, I expect they will soon wash out. But I can't understand how I managed to do what I've just done. The cup must have been cracked already and fine bone china can be so very brittle. I must have squeezed it too hard.'

'These things happen, unfortunately,' Kate sympathised, though her mind was on a lot more than a shattered bone china cup. 'But at least you escaped more serious injury.'

He nodded. 'Yes, that's something to be thankful for . . . Er, you were asking me about a name on a bangle. What was it again?'

She threw him a quick, wary glance, slightly caught off guard by the fact that he had resurrected the very question which seemed to have so unnerved him previously. Either the incident with the cup had been a total accident on his part, and — contrary to what she had assumed — had had nothing to do with her question, or he had deliberately referred to it again to give that impression now he had more or less recovered his composure.

'Oh . . . it was . . . *Annie*,' she said slowly, but with emphasis. 'I wondered whether you might recall anyone with that name who might have been living in your parish or visiting it during your time as the local priest?'

He pursed his lips, then shook his head. 'Can't say as I remember that name, no. But twenty-plus years is a rather long time ago and one's memory can become quite selective as one gets older.'

She treated him to a tight-lipped smile. 'No problem, Reverend. It was a long shot anyway.'

Finishing patching him up, she ignored his protests and got down on her hands and knees to pick up the broken pieces of crockery, while he hovered over her, looking shaky and embarrassed.

'Why don't you sit down, Reverend,' Kate said, climbing back on her feet. 'You look quite pale. I saw a wastebin in your kitchen, so I'll drop these broken pieces in there for you.'

He propped himself carefully on the edge of the seat. 'Thank you,' he acknowledged. 'You have been so very kind. But what about yourself? I'm afraid your trousers seem to be wet in places from kneeling on the floor. I do hope they're not spoiled.'

'I'm sure they'll be fine,' she replied. 'But if you don't mind, I would like to use your bathroom to wash my hands?' *And take a look around for that other cufflink too*, she thought.

Why she felt the need to check to see if the two monograms were identical, she had no real idea. Okay, it would confirm that the cufflink *was* Taylor's, which would mean he had dropped it on the track behind Lizzie Johnson's house, but so what? She was not investigating a murder and there was no suggestion that Lizzie Johnson had died from anything other than her own hand. Consequently, his presence there could have been purely down to coincidence. After all, Taylor's house was only a couple of miles from Johnson's and it was a wooded area, where he might easily have gone for an afternoon stroll like anyone else. But nevertheless, her curiosity needed to be satisfied.

'But of course,' he said. 'Please help yourself. It's upstairs. Second door on the right.'

She dropped the bits of broken porcelain in the wastebin and was at the top of the stairs, looking for the bathroom, when she heard him busying himself in the kitchen; by the sound of it, clearing away the rest of the tea things. Great. At least that told her where he was.

The bathroom visit was accomplished within a couple of minutes and, hands washed and dried, she ventured back out into the corridor. She could still hear clinking noises apparently coming from the direction of the kitchen and made the most of the opportunity for a nose round while he seemed to be fully occupied.

There were three other doors opening off the corridor. One accessed a sparsely furnished spare bedroom containing two unmade single beds. The second was being used as a boxroom, and was full of old tea chests, piles of books and clothes and some stacked wooden chairs. Next to that was the shabby but comfortable, fully carpeted main bedroom. This was furnished in an old-fashioned style, with a double bed and fitted overbed wardrobes, plus the usual dressing table and large chest of drawers. Heavy patterned curtains had been half-drawn across the triple-glazed window and a dark suit was hung neatly on a hanger from a hook on the back of the door.

Kate made straight for the dressing table, guided by her own, usually reliable intuition. There was a chipped china tray set on top of it between a pair of porcelain Dalmatian dogs littered with bits and bobs, including buttons, collar studs and an assortment of change, but no sign of any cufflinks. She checked the first of three narrow drawers beneath and discovered a pocket Bible, a diary and, surprisingly, a pack of tatty playing cards. The next drawer held an old offertory bag bearing an embroidered white cross, more loose change, but seemingly nothing else and she was about to close it again and check the last drawer when something rolled out from under the offertory bag. It was a single silver cufflink in the shape of a fish.

Picking it up, she rummaged around in her pocket and extracted the broken cufflink. Then, holding both cufflinks up in the light of the window, she studied them carefully. There was no doubt. They were identical, and both were engraved with the letters *AGT*. She smiled a grim smile of satisfaction.

So, here was the confirmation she was looking for. Taylor was indeed the person who had dropped the cufflink on the track behind Lizzie Johnson's house. But when and why had he been there? He apparently had no dog and though, as she had acknowledged to herself already, he could have been out for a walk at the time, maybe after driving his car to the spot and parking it there, it was all too much of a coincidence that he had picked the very wood which backed on to Johnson's house. And Kate Lewis did not believe in coincidences.

Yet where did this get her in the scheme of things? She was not investigating Taylor in connection with a crime.

True, his behaviour had been very strange ever since she had first made his acquaintance. First, previously fabricating the break-in at his home seemingly to get some information on the Pagan's Clump investigation, which technically was an offence of wasting police time. Second, on this particular visit, throwing a dramatic wobbly downstairs at the mere mention of a name that was engraved on a bracelet recovered at the inquiry scene. Third, as revealed by the broken cufflink, being in close proximity to the house where a vulnerable woman had suffered a fatal drug overdose. But strange behaviour, while questionable in certain circumstances, was not in itself a crime.

So, interrogating him further in relation to anything she had learned so far, because it struck her as odd, could not be justified. She couldn't even use his bogus attempted burglary complaint as an interview opportunity to kick things off, since by now the shed window would have been repaired and she had no evidence to back up her allegation. If only she hadn't ignored Hayden's advice at the time to tackle Taylor about the window, instead of dismissing the incident as too trivial to pursue.

It was too late for regrets now, though, and despite her feelings of frustration, she had no option but to take her leave of the priest shortly afterwards with her curiosity still not satisfied and the burning questions that were on the tip of her tongue never asked. But one thing she was very sure about. There was something about the Reverend Arthur George Taylor that was not right and, come hell or high water, she had every intention of finding out what it was.

* * *

Billy James was not at home when Kate turned up there after a quick bite of lunch at a wayside burger van. The little toerag's house was plainly deserted. Knowing him as she did, she guessed that if he wasn't at home, dossing in front of the television beside a crate of lager, gambling away his benefits, he was likely to be at one of his many regular haunts, dealing in drugs or negotiating the disposal of nicked property he was fencing for one of his disreputable clients.

It took her most of the afternoon to find him. Then, weary and almost on her last legs, she finally spotted him around four thirty in the snug of a grotty looking pub between Highbridge and Bridgwater, and, as it turned out, he was not up to his usual tricks at all, but something a lot more interesting. He was just visible, some twenty feet away from the door, sitting on a high-backed bench seat facing in her direction, but with his head turned inwards towards the wall, talking animatedly to someone Kate couldn't see, who was sitting on a similar seat opposite him across a long table.

Quickly stepping to one side before he caught sight of her, she dropped on to one of another pair of bench seats behind him and his mystery drinking partner and slid quietly along to the end. Tucked unobtrusively into the corner by the wall, she slowly sipped the half pint she had brought in with her and strained her ears in an effort to pick up on what James and his companion were discussing. But that was easier said than done. On the other side of the room, a couple of rough-labouring types were engaged in a lively argument about football and this, coupled with the piped music coming in from the bar, drowned much of what was being said.

She was about to give up and sit back and wait for either James or the other person with him to get up and leave, when the two labourers briefly stopped talking to concentrate on their pints and she heard James say a bit louder than he should have done, 'Pleasure to do business wiv' yer.'

There was a grunt and a woman's voice replied in a slightly more muted tone, 'Yeah, but after the bundle I've given you, Billy, this dead bitch better be who you say she is, or I'll have your balls on a platter.'

Something weighty scraped across the table and sensing the speaker was getting up, Kate shrank even further into her corner to avoid being seen. Moments later, a figure, dressed in black leathers and motorcycle jackboots and clutching a full-face crash helmet in one hand, clomped past her towards the door, looking neither left nor right, leaving her sitting there with a grim smile on her face.

A biker meeting up with Billy James in the back room of a local pub would not ordinarily have struck Kate as that significant. Being a drug dealer, James had many clients of both sexes and from all walks of life on his books. But that particular biker had definitely not been one of them. Even though Kate had only caught a glimpse of them as they went by, the green spiky hair had been enough on its own. Debbie Moreton, the former crime reporter for the *Bridgwater Clarion* certainly seemed to get around, and since her Triumph Bonneville had not been in evidence out front when Kate had arrived but must have been hidden around the back out of sight, it was pretty obvious that she had not been there on a social visit. As to what that visit had been about, Kate was determined to find out.

James's face was a picture when Kate appeared in front of him as he was climbing to his feet. If his jaw had dropped any further, it would have hit the floor. But to give him his due, he recovered a lot quicker than many of his compatriots would have done in similar circumstances, and he forced a lop-sided grin.

'Ah, Kate,' he said. 'What yer doin' 'ere then?'

She smiled without humour. 'I might as well ask you the same thing, Billy.'

'Just 'avin' a quick one. Me local boozer, see.'

'Debbie Moreton's too, is it?'

He affected a puzzled frown. 'Dunno what yer on abaht. Don't know no Debbie whatever name you said.'

'Sit down, Billy,' Kate said softly. 'You and me are going to have a little chat.'

She saw his Adam's apple give the telltale lurch, but he remained standing. 'Can't tonight, sarge,' he said, making to slip past her. 'Got fings to do.'

Kate glimpsed the two labourers glance across at them curiously as they got up and left. The room was now empty, except for Billy and herself.

'Sit *down*!' she snapped.

He licked his lips and dropped back on to his seat. She squeezed in beside him and forced him to slide back along the bench to the wall, effectively trapped there by the table in front of him.

She tapped the breast pocket of his half-open, tatty leather jacket. 'What you got there, Billy?' she asked. 'Bit late for a Christmas present from Santa, isn't it?'

Another swallow and he shrugged. 'Some dosh I were owed, that's all. No law against that, is there?'

She felt him stiffen as she slid her hand inside his jacket, but he made no attempt to stop her. She produced a bulky envelope and prised open the flap with her fingernail, leafing slowly through the bundle of notes inside.

'Well now, Billy,' she went on, returning the envelope to his pocket. 'That must have been a hell of a lot of dosh you were owed?'

He said nothing, but his eyes were on the move as she stared at him fixedly.

'So, let's cut to the chase, shall we? What was the info you gave Debbie Moreton?'

Even as he opened his mouth to reply, she waggled a finger at him and shook her head. 'Don't give me a load of old bollocks, Billy,' she warned. 'I was sitting on the bench behind you both—' she pointed —'and I heard you and Debbie having a right old chat. So, who was the "dead bitch" you told her about, eh? Wouldn't be the woman whose remains we found up at Pagan's Clump, would it? You know, the one we've put out on a public appeal?'

He grimaced. 'I–I ain't sayin' noffink, an' yer can't make me.'

Kate nodded. 'Quite right, Billy. You have your human rights, of course.' She leaned closer towards him. 'Trouble is, with the best will in the world, things sometimes get out anyway, however close-mouthed you are. I mean, look at us two here. What if one of your mates got to know, on the quiet like, that you were seen in your favourite boozer this afternoon, having a nice chat over a pint with that pushy DS from Highbridge? They might wonder what you were telling her. Especially if it also became known that you walked away with a nice fat wad in your pocket. How do you think they would react?'

The tongue was out, moistening his lips again and he glanced quickly around him. 'Yer . . . can't . . . Yer wouldn't. I'd be brown bread in less'n a week an' yer knows it.'

She shook her head. 'Oh, it would have nothing to do with me, of course. But in a small community like this, as you yourself said to me before, everyone knows everyone else and things soon get around. It happens. Hence the old wartime phrase "Loose lips sinks ships", meaning a careless word in the wrong ear can have lethal consequences . . .'

'All right, all right!' he said fiercely under his breath. 'I'll tell yer what I give Debbie. But yer gotta keep schtum abaht where yer got it.'

''Course, Billy. Soul of discretion, that's me.'

He treated her to a contemptuous sneer. 'Fing is, I never fought noffink about them bones you lot found at Pagan's Clump till I 'eard the name "Annie" mentioned on the radio a couple hours ago. Then it all come back to me—'

'And like the good, public-spirited citizen you are, you decided to come forward and tell everyone what you knew,' she finished for him sarcastically. 'Is that why you contacted the press instead of the police? Or was it something to do with newspapers having deeper pockets?'

He failed to meet her stare, and instead of answering her question, continued with what he had been saying. 'See, there–there were this ol' girl . . . Sort of dosser, yer know, down on 'er luck. Used to live in the woods an' out on the marshes round 'ere when all of us was kids. Everyone fought she were a witch and she frit us to deaf. Some said she crept into 'ouses at night an' sat on folks' chests so they couldn't breave, to punish 'em fer fings they'd done wrong—'

'The Night Hag,' Kate finished for him, as she remembered the entry in Lizzie Johnson's diary about the selfsame supernatural entity, seeing the words the dead woman had used — *Terrified she'll come back* — light up the inside of her head for a second.

James gave her a keen look. 'What? Yeah, that were it. That's what some of the old folk what believed in all that crap said she were, the Night 'Ag. Some sort of daft superstition. But us kids, we called 'er "Dark Annie".'

'How did you know her real name was Annie?'

'We didn't. But someone said that's what she called 'erself, so we done the same.'

Kate hesitated, shocked by this unexpected revelation, which seemed to point to some sort of connection between Lizzie Johnson and the Pagan's Clump incident. But she was unable to properly process the information right there and then.

'Do you remember the woman's surname?'

'Nah, as kids, we just used to call 'er "Dark Annie". But I remembers, she always used to wear this 'eavy lookin' army coat and an 'ead scarf. There was also somefink wrong wiv one leg an' she limped when she walked, like. Real creepy, I can tell yer. Never forgot 'er, I ain't. Used to dream abaht 'er even when I were in me teens.'

'I bet. Go on.'

'Well, she sort of disappeared one day an' no one ever saw 'er again. No one knowd what 'appened to 'er neiver. All of us kids was only pleased she were gone . . . All of us, 'cept the ol' vicar geezer, that is—'

'Vicar geezer? What vicar geezer?'

He shrugged again. 'Some daft ol' priest who ran the local church. 'E were right pissed off. Spent weeks wanderin' round lookin' fer 'er and asking folks about 'er. Forgot to tell Debbie abaht 'im—'

'Well don't, if you know what's good for you. This bit of info stays with you and me. Got it?'

He gave a reluctant nod.

'I mean it, Billy. If any of this about the priest gets out, remember what I said about loose lips . . .'

'All right, all right, I won't say noffink. Gospel.'

'Good. Now why was this priest pissed off?'

'Dunno. Kept clear of 'im, as I never went to church meself, see.'

'What a surprise. Do you know what his name was?'

He thought for a moment, then said, 'Can't remember. Long time ago. An' he ain't there now. Retired, I 'eard, an' moved out the parish. I only remembered Annie 'cause when I were a kid, me ol' man used to freaten that she would come and sit on me chest if I kept getting' up to dodgy fings, like.'

'Didn't have much effect on you, though, did it?' Kate said drily, then stood up. 'Anyway, nice talking to you, Billy. Let me know if Annie decides to pay you a visit, won't you? I'd really like to meet her. She sounds like a really interesting lady.'

Seeing how pale his face suddenly became, she had difficulty holding back a chuckle as she left the room.

Back in her car, she sat for several minutes in a more serious mood, thinking about James's revelations. The old woman he had called "Dark Annie" had evidently had another persona as the so-called Night Hag, which meant she had to be the woman with the bangle whose remains had been found at Pagan's Clump. It was too much of a coincidence to be otherwise. But why had Lizzie Johnson been so terrified of the so-called entity coming after her? What had she done wrong? Could she have been involved in what had happened to Annie all those years ago? Having met and talked to Johnson and witnessed her fragile state of mind, it didn't seem possible that she could have ever hurt anyone, let alone been responsible for their death. But from experience Kate knew that you could never be sure of anything where people were concerned.

And what of the priest James had referred to? It was, again, too much of a coincidence for that to be anyone other than the Reverend Arthur Taylor. But if that was the case, why had Taylor denied all knowledge of Annie that afternoon? What the hell was he up to? First, the bogus attempted burglary complaint to get talking to her about the bones unearthed at Pagan's Clump. Then the cufflink he must have dropped on the track behind the very house where Lizzie Johnson had been found dead in bed. Now, after denying knowing anyone by the name of Annie, the revelation that he most probably not only knew who she was but had personally searched for her around his old parish after she had disappeared. There were so many loose strands that needed to be joined up, yet the one thing that was absolutely clear to Kate was the fact that the incident at Pagan's Clump and the death of Lizzie Johnson were not separate issues, but definitely linked in some way. Furthermore, she was convinced that the only way she was going to get to the bottom of things was by a more forceful "little chat" with the enigmatic Reverend Arthur Taylor, who obviously knew a lot more than he was telling. But it seemed Fate had other ideas. Before she could put her idea into practice, her mobile phone shrilled. The caller was Charlie Woo.

'Where are you, Kate?' he queried.

'Out and about.'

'I think you'd better come back in pronto. Something really unexpected has come up.'

'Same here, guv,' she said grimly. 'See you in twenty.'

CHAPTER 13

Charlie Woo was sitting behind his desk, studying what looked like a lengthy report when Kate walked into his office. His face looked grave.

'Ah, Kate,' he greeted. 'Thanks for coming straight back. Get anywhere with the enquiries you were doing on this woman, Annie?'

'You could say that,' she replied, dropping into a chair in front of his desk. 'But not what I had expected.'

He nodded. 'Be interested to hear what you've got, but first things first.' He tapped the report in front of him. 'Doc Summers was in here a short time ago. Couldn't stay long, as she had another commitment. But she wanted to personally deliver her post-mortem report on the overdose of Lizzie Johnson, the case you and Indi were dealing with. It came as a bit of a bombshell too, I can tell you.'

He stared at her levelly. 'To put it simply, it seems that the PM has revealed what were found to be tiny bits of soft, transparent plastic trapped both in the dead woman's throat and between the upper teeth on one side of her face, towards the back of her mouth—'

'Plastic?'

'Precisely. The sort that supermarket shopping bags are made of. There was also an injury to the side of her mouth on the same side, believed to have been caused by her teeth biting into her cheek—'

'The police surgeon made no mention of this.'

'According to the pathologist, the plastic fragments were so small that it was most unlikely he would have spotted them with a cursory death scene examination, and, don't forget, the evidence available to him at the time had pointed to a fatal overdose anyway.'

Kate shook her head slowly. 'So, what are we saying? That she didn't take a fatal drugs overdose?'

'Not exactly. It seems that she certainly had enough of the benzodiazepine drug in her system to kill her, especially when downed with half a bottle of scotch, and Doc Summers is quite satisfied that the amount she ingested would ultimately have been fatal. But the forensic examination has revealed that the *actual* cause of death was not a drug overdose at all, but asphyxiation, and that she must have been helped on her way by someone else.'

'Shit!'

Woo nodded grimly. 'Precisely. And the expert opinion, based on the available forensic evidence, is that her death was achieved by the simple expedient of pulling a plastic bag over her head and cutting off her air supply.'

Kate grimaced. 'So, my unease at the scene was justified, even though I couldn't put my finger on it at the time. We're dealing with nothing less than murder, callous, cold-blooded murder?'

'It all points that way, yes. The logical hypothesis is that she was taking too long to die from her overdose, and her killer was in a hurry, so they moved to Plan B. But although Johnson would have been very weak from the effects of the tablets, she still tried to put up a struggle and in desperation tore at the bag with her teeth before eventually losing the fight — hence the traces of plastic that were found inside her.'

He sighed. 'There's more too. Apart from the evidence uncovered at the PM indicating that asphyxiation rather than an overdose was the cause of death, signs of bruising were also found on the body, suggesting that she was probably held down, with her assailant sitting on her chest trapping her arms under their knees while they did the business with the plastic bag—'

'Yet the police surgeon said he couldn't find any defensive marks.'

'No, but I'm told that bruises to a corpse are not always clearly visible during an initial death scene examination. They can often take time to fully emerge. Nevertheless, the fact that they were present in this case does tend to reinforce the hypothesis that's been put forward.'

'And I suppose the empty blister packs which were lying on the bed coverlet, were put there afterwards to convince everyone that she had taken her own life. Benzos were dissolved in the scotch, I assume?'

Another nod. 'Toxicology has now confirmed that fact.'

Kate looked puzzled. 'But how the hell did the killer manage to ensure that she would drink enough of the lethal cocktail to do the business? If they were there with her throughout — a friend perhaps, pretending to commiserate with her over whatever was troubling her — how would they have avoided sharing the same lethal cocktail?'

'They could have stuck to some other drink, say red or white wine, washing up their glass afterwards, so as not to leave any trace of their presence — they could even have been a teetotaller?'

Kate considered that last suggestion, and immediately the Reverend Taylor and his dropped cufflink came to mind. The Church didn't believe in alcohol, did it? Was the enigmatic priest a non-drinker perhaps? It was possible, and the cufflink certainly tied him into the scene. But could she really see that strange, rather homespun man of God as someone capable of such an awful crime? And what on earth could his motive have been?

'It's a plausible explanation,' she replied slowly, 'but in any case, the whole thing seems to have been pretty clumsy and amateurish. I mean, you'd think that anyone with a modicum of common sense who was planning something like this would have realised that the true cause of death was bound to be discovered at the PM.'

'*If* it was planned in the first place. It could have been a spontaneous act of desperation, prompted by something Johnson said or did. Anyway, I've sent Indrani Purewal to secure the scene with a couple of woodentops, and called for SOCO to attend. I'm also heading out there myself straight after this briefing to see what's what. All a bit late, I know. But we have to go through the motions until the DCI gets back from a force crime reduction conference he's attending at the "big house", and there's always the chance that we could turn up something of evidential value, now that our focus is on a criminal investigation rather than a suicide.'

He shook his head with sudden irritation. 'Heaven knows, we need to get a positive result on something. The Pagan's Clump investigation seems to have hit a brick wall and now there's this other bloody job, where we are so far behind the curve on things that the chances of regaining the initiative seem pretty damned hopeless.'

'Maybe not as hopeless as you think.'

He stiffened in his chair. 'What do you mean? What do you know that I don't?'

'Well, let's say that from what I've picked up this afternoon, it looks very much like the two cases are actually connected.'

'Connected? How?' He leaned forward in his chair and stared at her intently. 'I think you'd better explain.'

Kate stood up and turned towards the door. 'Shall I get two fresh coffees first?' she said.

* * *

School was over for the day and all the "little darlings" had been collected by their parents in the final hour's mayhem of abandoned cars and armies of gossiping mothers descending on the school playground for the reunion with their tired, irritable offspring. The last of the teachers had also gone and a rather strange, creepy silence had descended on the local primary school, broken only by the sound of the cleaners clearing up as usual in the empty classrooms, toilets and echoing corridors.

Jennifer Talbot returned to the head teacher's study and sank gratefully on to the swivel chair behind her desk, ruefully staring at the pile of reports, charts and stats forms in her in-tray. It would be another hour at least before she locked up and went home, but at least she could finish off some of her essential paperwork in peace and quiet.

She reached into the left-hand drawer of her desk and pulled out the large bottle of Coca Cola she kept there, wishing with a crooked grin that it was whisky instead. Taking a long pull on the bottle, she slowly screwed the top back on, her mind far away from the pile of paper in front of her.

She had received Julian Grey's phone call during the lunch break, telling her about Lizzie's death. She had always known Johnson to be a sandwich short of a picnic at times, and the assumption by Grey that she had taken her own life was a logical one, especially after the way her old friend had behaved during that last get-together at her house after news of the discovery at Pagan's Clump. She could only hope that the meeting Grey had arranged for that evening at her house would provide some much-needed reassurance about the police investigation.

It was a good fifteen minutes of staring at the wall in front of her, turning things over and over in her mind, before she snapped out of her disturbed reverie and got down to the work she should have been tackling. She remained thus absorbed for the next three-quarters of an hour and only realised the time when the cleaning supervisor poked her head round the door to wish her goodnight before trotting off with her husband to their car parked by the front door. It was already half past five.

Rising from her chair, she locked some confidential papers away in one of the drawers of her desk and stretched her aching back. Then, retrieving her briefcase from the top of an adjacent filing cabinet, she pulled on her short coat from the back of her chair and headed for the study door and a final tour of the building to make sure all doors and windows were secure.

She had checked her secretary's office and the staff room and was on her way through the swing doors to the toilets, school hall and half-dozen classrooms at the far end of the building when she heard the loud "bang" and stopped short with a frown. Surely the cleaners hadn't come back in, or she had missed one of the teachers working late?

The staff toilets were empty, all the cubicle doors standing wide open, and, checking further along the corridor, she soon satisfied herself that there was no one in any of the classrooms or the pupils' toilets. She was marching along the next corridor leading to the school hall, which served as an assembly room, dining room and sports hall all rolled into one, when she heard another "bang", much closer this time.

Pushing through double doors, she found the school hall was in darkness, but spotted a light in the kitchens at the far end through a partially open serving hatch. Running her fingers down the panel on one side of the double doors, she switched on all the hall lights, more as a comfort than anything else, and immediately saw the kitchen light go out.

Her heart was thumping now, and her mouth and throat had dried up. 'Who's there?' she said in what she had intended as an authoritative tone, but which came out as a little more than a rasp. There was no answer.

What to do now? Common sense dictated that she rang the police on the mobile in her pocket, but she baulked at the idea. What if one of the kitchen staff had left something behind after lunch and had come back for it? Or the noise had been made by a cupboard door which hadn't been closed properly and was swinging backwards and forwards in a draught? She had noticed a breeze getting up outside when the cleaners had stopped by to wish her goodnight, so it was a feasible explanation, especially if a window had been left open. She would look rather stupid if the police turned up to a false alarm like that. The level-headed, pragmatic head teacher who was never fazed by anything? She wouldn't live it down. No, she was determined to retain control of the situation, and, plainly, it was her duty to investigate the situation first. Anyway, it was barely six o'clock in the evening and hardly the sort of time someone would pick for a burglary.

The kitchen turned out to be clear of any intruder and everything appeared to be in order. But even as she breathed a sigh of relief, she stiffened. Out of the corner of her eye, she saw the rear door, which accessed the wastebin area, stir slightly, then abruptly swing open before slamming back against the frame again. Her eyes narrowed. That door should have been securely closed and locked before the kitchen staff went home. But then maybe it had been, and it was the cleaners who had left it open. She would have to have a word with someone about that in the morning — a very stern word.

She marched over to the door, held it open and peered out into the dusk. There was a hint of a breeze now and, looking past the half-dozen wheelie bins standing against the wall, she saw that the security lights around the fenced perimeter of the school and on the wall above her head were now on and in their powerful sodium glare, she was able to satisfy herself that there was no one lurking about in the vicinity.

Quickly slamming the door shut, she turned the key in the lock and shook it several times to make sure it was secure. Then, about to head back to the hall, she froze. What sounded like a rasping chuckle had come from outside the back door where the wheelie bins were drawn up against the wall. Yet she had already checked the area and there had been no one in sight. What the hell was going on? She swung round angrily, intending to reopen the door and challenge whoever was playing silly games. She had had a long day and was tired, hungry and in no mood for stupidity. But then she hesitated, remembering with a shiver Lizzie Johnson's warning about Annie Evans coming after them all to punish them. Swallowing hard, she shook her head fiercely to banish such ridiculous thoughts from her mind. Despite her avowed contempt for Johnson's paranoia, however, she didn't reopen the door, but instead marched back across the hall towards the front of the building, switching the lights off as she went.

Her silver BMW saloon was parked a few yards away, in her reserved space by the Portakabin they used as a storeroom, but after locking the front door, to her shame, she found herself carefully scanning the tarmacked forecourt to satisfy herself that she was alone before stepping out of the porch and making her way briskly towards the vehicle.

No one appeared from behind the Portakabin or from the small copse by the front gates, as she had feared. But she found herself fumbling clumsily for the keys in her pocket on the approach to the BMW. With an oath she ended up dropping them before she could activate the keyless entry button. Scrabbling around on the ground, looking for the keys, she heard the sound of footsteps approaching her across the forecourt. Footsteps that for some reason made her skin crawl. Footsteps that advanced with the slow "clomp", "scrape" of someone dragging one foot behind the other.

For the first time in her ordered life, she felt blind panic rising inside her, but forced herself not to look in the direction of the sounds, fearful as to what she might see. Then to her relief, her fingers brushed against the keys, which had skidded right under the car. Quickly grabbing hold of them, she scrambled to her feet and pressed the button on the fob to deactivate the electronic door locks. Hauling the driver's door open, she threw herself into her seat even as the two-way flashers illuminated.

She was only just in time. Within seconds of setting the electronic locks on all four doors, the bent figure of an old woman, dressed in a long dark coat and shawl and leaning on a stick, materialised at the side of the car. The next instant, she found herself staring at a hideous, witch-like face with gimlet eyes and a prominent hooked nose that pressed itself against the driver's window, thin lips curled into a malicious sneer.

In her terrified, numbed state, she had no recollection of starting the engine. She was only aware of it suddenly thundering into life. Then she had slammed the gearstick into "drive" and was pulling away with a screech of tyres, swinging across the forecourt towards the main gates. Her last sighting of the awful harridan was in her rear-view mirror, standing in the middle of the forecourt with one arm raised to shoulder height, pointing menacingly at her fast-disappearing tail-lights.

Talbot had little recollection of the short journey home. Her mind was still in shocked limbo after what had happened, and she was practically on autopilot the whole way. She was conscious only of having to peer more closely along the headlamp beams as she negotiated the narrow, winding lanes because of something splashed across her windscreen, partially obscuring her view of the road. It was not until she pulled up in a flurry of gravel in her driveway and stumbled unsteadily out of the car that she discovered what it was. The word was scrawled across the windscreen in big, red letters at least eight inches high, like a garage forecourt "For Sale" banner:

MURDERER!

* * *

Kate got the coffees, but she was denied the opportunity of unloading on Charlie Woo. As she was in the process of depositing two steaming mugs on his desk, he released a loud unnatural cough, and directed a warning look at the door behind her. At which point, DCI Ricketts swept into the room like a bad smell.

'What the devil's going on, Inspector?' the DCI snapped, almost pushing Kate aside as if she weren't there. 'The message you left on my answer phone said we've got another suspicious death.'

Kate obligingly moved to one side and sat down on a chair to the right of the door, quietly sipping her coffee.

Woo nodded. "'Fraid so, sir,' he replied. 'The pathologist's report on the death of Lizzie Johnson is now in and—'

'Yes,' Ricketts cut in. 'But the brief I received from you a few days ago was that it was a suicide.'

Woo shifted slightly in his seat and shook his head. 'No, sir,' he corrected. 'I said the indications were that it was a possible suicide from an overdose of benzodiazepine tablets, which is what the police surgeon told Detective Sergeant Lewis here.'

Ricketts swung round to glare at Kate. 'I might have known *you* would be involved in this one, Sergeant,' he sneered, 'and it looks like you've cocked up yet again, with any evidence that might have been present at the scene either gone or completely corrupted by now.'

Kate deliberately ignored him and continued sipping her coffee.

'There was no way Kate could have suspected the death was due to anything other than suicide,' Woo pointed out in her defence, 'and the police surgeon found no evidence of foul play either.'

'So, how is it, days after the event, we suddenly have a conclusion of murder?'

With exaggerated patience, Woo gave him the full facts and Ricketts cooled down a little and grunted. 'Then why aren't you down at the scene now, Sergeant,' he demanded, turning back towards Kate, 'instead of sitting on your backside in this office drinking coffee?'

'I have only just told Sergeant Lewis of this latest development,' Woo said before Kate could respond. 'DC Purewal is already down there, securing the property, and I have SOCO on their way there too.'

Ricketts released a short, derogatory laugh. 'Long after the proverbial horse has bolted, of course, Inspector,' he retorted. 'Bravo! I suggest you and the sergeant here forego your nice hot coffees and take yourselves down there PDQ to see what, if anything, can be salvaged from this badly mismanaged investigation.'

Woo stood up. 'That's exactly what we were about to do, sir,' he said. 'Will you be attending also? Presumably you will be leading on this case from now on?'

Ricketts looked as if all the wind had suddenly been knocked out of his sails. 'Er, no, not exactly. Maintaining a watching brief, I would think,' he said quickly, 'until an SIO can be appointed, of course . . . bearing in mind my already very busy workload. I will have to check with headquarters on the issue. Keep me informed as to what is happening in the meantime.'

At which point he swept out of the office again, this time as if the flames of Hell were pursuing him.

'Prat!' Kate muttered. 'He couldn't detect a fart in a storm!'

Woo grinned. 'Now, now, Kate,' he cautioned, 'I can't have you saying disrespectful things like that about our leader . . . And you didn't even offer him a coffee either. How churlish is that? Now, before we both head down to this "badly mismanaged" scene, what is it you were going to tell me?'

CHAPTER 14

The three friends stared in shocked silence at Jennifer Talbot's car, starkly illuminated in the light of the porch. She had made no effort to clean the message off the windscreen before they'd arrived. It was vital to her that they saw it for themselves, as absolute proof of what had happened. She was determined not to risk being subjected to the same sort of scorn Lizzie Johnson had endured over her fears about a vengeful stalker.

'Looks like lipstick was used again,' Chalmers blurted suddenly, forgetting that only he and Grey knew about the similar message they'd seen scrawled on Johnson's balcony doors on the Friday before her death. Grey had kept the full facts to himself when he had telephoned Talbot and Aldridge about the incident.

'What do you mean "again"?' Talbot snapped, her gaze cold and hard.

'Yeah,' Aldridge joined in. 'Are you saying it's happened before?'

Grey threw Chalmers an exasperated glance at his indiscretion. 'Er, Lizzie had a message like this scrawled across her balcony windows the night she claimed to have been burgled,' he said resignedly.

'And you didn't think to tell us about that?'

'It didn't seem relevant at the time, sorry.'

'Not relevant?' Aldridge exclaimed derisively. 'The silly bitch was found dead two days later!'

'She committed suicide, for heaven's sake. She wasn't murdered.'

Talbot looked exasperated. 'How do you know that? When Bob rang us about her death, he said the police wouldn't say how she died.'

'It was an overdose, according to the cleaning lady who found her,' Chalmers cut in. 'There were empty tablet blister packs everywhere apparently. You know how het up she was over the bones thing. Something obviously snapped and she killed herself.'

'There's no "obvious" about it,' Talbot said. 'And this scrawl on my windscreen proves it. There's something else too.'

'Like what?'

Talbot glanced quickly around her and nodded towards the front door. 'Can we talk inside? I have no near neighbours, but you never know who could be listening.'

With the four of them sitting comfortably in her living room, drinks in their hands, Talbot told them what had happened at the school in as even a tone as she could manage.

Her words met with total silence. Seeing Chalmers cast an alarmed sideways glance at Grey, immediately she homed in on him.

'Okay,' she said tersely, 'what are the pair of you keeping back from Danny and me?'

Grey grimaced and gulped some of his whisky. 'Lizzie told us she saw an old woman like that peering in at her from her balcony the night of her burglary,' he replied. 'We–we thought she was imagining things or had simply made it up.'

Talbot shook her head in disbelief. 'And you said nothing? This gets worse. So now we know that Lizzie *was* right all along.'

'Oh, do me a favour,' Grey snorted. 'You're not seriously suggesting Annie Evans has risen from the grave or that there *is* some sort of malignant ghost after us? I never thought you'd come up with something as daft as that.'

'I wasn't talking about bloody ghosts, and you know it. I'm worried that there could be someone out there who has found out what we did all those years ago and is now seeking vengeance.'

'It's more likely that the woman you saw was some nutty old biddy with arthritis who was out for a walk and wanted to chat to someone.'

'Except that the school is miles from anywhere and, as you've now revealed, Lizzie also previously said she saw her.'

'But–but an old woman with a stick?' Grey's voice was even more incredulous. 'What's she going to do? Beat us to death with the stick? Or maybe she had an Armalite stuck up her sleeve, eh?'

Aldridge released a sneering guffaw. 'Yeah, could be she's a geriatric hitwoman hired by the local WI on a termination contract. We should get police protection!'

'This isn't funny, Danny,' Talbot expostulated. 'You know I rarely get worked up about anything, but I'm willing to admit that what happened to me tonight really shook me.'

Aldridge suddenly stood up. 'Well, frankly, Jen, I don't give a shit one way or the other! I've got enough on my plate with my business going down the toilet without worrying about a centenarian stalker . . . If she turns up at my place, maybe I'll run her over, like I did her mate, Annie!'

Then he gave a little mocking wave and walked out, leaving the others gaping after him, shocked into a stunned silence by what he had said. Before anyone could say anything further, they heard a car start up outside, signifying he had driven off.

'What a prize arsehole?' Chalmers breathed. 'I never realised it before. So, what do we do now?'

Grey shrugged. 'What can we do? He isn't bound to stick with us. He's a free agent.'

'But it's because of what he did that we're in this mess,' Talbot said. 'He killed that poor old woman and, as he admitted, he doesn't give a shit about it.'

Grey nodded. 'I don't think he meant it like that. He's got serious financial problems and he's very bitter about the way his business is going.'

'But if he's not going to play ball over the Pagan's Clump business, he could become a serious risk to us all. It only needs a careless word to be picked up by the wrong ear to drop us all in it.'

Grey sighed and, downing the rest of his drink, stood up. 'Okay, I'll pay him a visit, probably tomorrow, and have a chat with him. It might be I can suggest some revenue streams that could help his cash flow and see him over his present problems.'

'And what do we do about this bloody old crone in the meantime?' Chalmers asked.

'We sit tight, and we watch, and we wait to see what happens. She can't have anything definite on us or we would have heard by now. She's probably some elderly opportunist who was living in one of the villages at the time Annie Evans went missing and now that the grave has been found, is on a fishing expedition. So, we need to keep our nerve and play her at her own game. Sooner or later, she's going to have to pack in all the stupid, theatrical nonsense and declare her hand. Then we'll know what she's after.'

Talbot grimaced. 'And I have a nasty feeling we won't like that hand when she does,' she said soberly.

In the moonlit shadows on the terrace at the rear of the cottage, the bent figure of an old woman, wearing a shawl and a long dark coat moved away from the curtained patio door where she had been crouched listening intently to the lively conversation in the room on the other side through a convenient air vent in the wall. Then, descending the worn stone steps to the lawn, leaning on her stick, she limped across the springy turf and disappeared altogether into the dusk as if she had never existed . . .

* * *

There was a long pause after Kate finished briefing Charlie Woo, and his face wore a heavy frown as he digested the information. Then he sat back in his chair with a sharp exhalation. 'I believe you might have opened Pandora's box with all this, Kate,' he said, 'and it will be interesting to see if the cufflink DC Purewal found leads to anything in the end.'

Kate had given him all the information she had so far extracted from Billy James, without divulging his name, but she had deliberately left out any mention of the Reverend Arthur Taylor's involvement in things or the link to him through the cufflink Indrani Purewal had found. She was not yet clear where the churchman fitted into everything, and she wanted to pursue this avenue quietly on her own, until she had something more concrete to report.

'To recap on what you've told me then,' Woo went on, 'Johnson seems to have nursed obsessive fears about some sort of supernatural stalker, which the diary entry she made refers to as the so-called Night Hag. Your informant has backed this up with his own childhood memories of a scary old woman with the same nickname who wore what sounds like the sort of army greatcoat we think our Jane Doe, who was living rough in the woods and marshes at the time, was wearing. A dosser he and his friends nicknamed "Dark Annie". Almost certainly, I would think the same Annie who ended up in an unmarked grave at Pagan's Clump. It all suggests we have not two crimes, but one — perhaps with two victims.'

Kate nodded. 'In a nutshell, guv.'

He gave a crooked grin. 'The DCI *will* be pleased when I tell him. It means he can dump it all on the SIO already investigating the Pagan's Clump job and avoid taking on the responsibility of managing the new investigation.' His grin faded, to be replaced by a worried look. 'But what are we going to do about this bloody interfering journalist, Debbie Moreton? She's bound to be filing copy as we speak on her conversation with your informant. It will be all over one of the papers in the morning.'

Kate shrugged. 'Not much we can do. I would think she'll offer it around to the highest bidder and if her old boss at the *Bridgwater Clarion* doesn't get it, someone else will. But when you think about it, what has she really got? All she knows is that Annie was possibly an old dosser who lived rough in the area and was reputed by superstitious locals to be some sort of mythical demon, and that she disappeared one day, never to be seen again. The plus side is that if this info is published, it might stir the memories of some older members of the community and encourage them to come forward, which is exactly what we want, isn't it?'

He still looked dubious. 'True, and I hope someone does, because, as a journalist, Moreton is unlikely to reveal her source — something I know you won't do either. That means we've got nothing to verify any of the information. We still don't have a full name for Annie, so in reality, we're not much further forward.'

Kate nodded. 'I realise that and I'm working on it.'

'H'm, I don't like the sound of that. Not up to your old "go it alone" tricks, Kate, I hope?'

She shook her head. 'No, but I was on my way to see someone when you called me up. That will have to wait until tomorrow now. By the time we've been to the Johnson crime scene tonight to liaise with SOCO and the others, it will be too late in the evening for me to do anything else.'

'And who would this mysterious person be who you were on your way to see?'

'Sorry, I'd rather keep it to myself for the time being.'

He thought about that for a moment and stared at her fixedly. 'As your boss, I could insist that you tell me.'

She shrugged. 'Best of luck with that one, guv. But really, when I have something definite, you'll be the first to know.'

Pulling his coat off the back of his chair, Woo shook his head gloomily. 'Why don't I feel reassured by that?'

* * *

Indrani Purewal met Charlie Woo and Kate, as they ducked under the security tape drawn across the entrance to Lizzie

Johnson's property. She made a rueful face at Kate as he walked off ahead of them. 'It seems I was wrong, and your suspicions were right. It wasn't suicide then?'

Kate gave a thin smile and followed Woo's example by pulling on a pair of blue crime-scene booties that Purewal was already wearing, at the same time wondering why she was even bothering to protect the scene, as it had already been well and truly compromised.

'Anything but, according to the pathologist,' she replied. 'But there was nothing to indicate foul play when we attended, so we're no more to blame for the oversight than the police surgeon. He didn't spot anything either.'

'But that cufflink I found on the track and the diary you recovered could now be relevant to the murder investigation?'

Kate felt her insides stir slightly. That bloody cufflink! She had forgotten that it was Purewal who had found the thing, and it put her on the spot. She didn't want to cut her colleague out of her follow-up inquiries, as Purewal had been the original officer in the case and she had a right to know what was going on, but at the same time, she was reluctant to reveal what she had learned about the Reverend Arthur Taylor, until she was absolutely sure of her ground. There was no way she wanted to risk being sneered at and accused of tilting at windmills yet again. That still rankled with her more than she cared to admit.

'Maybe,' she acknowledged, 'but on their own, neither tells us a lot.'

'What about trying for some DNA off the cufflink?'

Kate shook her head, doing her best not to look guilty. She was acutely conscious of the cufflink still loose in her pocket, which she had resolved to hand in to the appropriate police property store once she had interviewed Taylor. 'Bit late for that now,' she replied. 'Don't forget, when you found it, it was covered in wet mud, and you then wiped it clean, because neither of us knew we were dealing with anything other than a suicide at the time. I doubt whether we'd get anything of value off it now.'

Purewal sighed her frustration. 'I can't see that we're going to get anything from the crime scene itself now either. All this seems a total waste of time to me.'

Kate gave a faint smile. 'You never know,' she said, 'miracles do happen.'

But as it turned out, there were no miracles this time. An intensive search of the property produced nothing of real interest, save a few small plastic packets of what was plainly cannabis, and a couple containing white powder, which was probably cocaine. It clearly indicated that Lizzie Johnson had been no stranger to the use of illegal drugs. Purewal also came across an assorted bundle of papers held in a box file on a bookshelf in the living room, which included miscellaneous correspondence and what looked at first sight like banking statements. Kate reluctantly took possession of the file and said she would go through it later, in case it contained anything that might be relevant to the inquiry.

The SOCO team also did their professional best, carrying out what was essentially a forensic examination of the bedroom, the kitchen and stair banister rail. But it was clear to everyone involved that the whole thing amounted to not much more than what the DI had himself previously termed "going through the motions".

Understandably, as a consequence, what little enthusiasm was motivating Woo and his colleagues soon started to wane and, finally calling it a day, the DI grabbed the CID car in which he and Kate had driven to the scene, and headed back to Highbridge police station to phone the DCI and fill him in on the current situation, leaving Kate and Indrani Purewal to finish off at the house and return in Purewal's car.

This gave Kate the opportunity she had been waiting for. She buttonholed Purewal in the kitchen while SOCO were packing up their gear and taking it out to their van.

She didn't beat about the bush. It was very late in the evening, and she was too tired to try softening the likely impact of her words on her colleague. She came straight to the point, in a frank, concise style, which lacked any sort of embellishment, and she wasn't surprised to see Purewal's expression harden as she listened to what she had to say.

'So, the same old "Go It Alone Kate" is back, it seems,' Purewal commented bitterly when she had finished. 'Giving everyone else the old mushroom treatment, "keeping us in the dark and feeding us on bullshit".'

Kate ignored the insubordinate tone of her response, knowing full well that her colleague's reaction was understandable in the circumstances.

'It wasn't like that at all, Indi,' Kate replied wearily. 'I only tumbled to the fact that the cufflink you found belonged to the Rev Taylor purely by accident after I called to see him at his own request this morning and then made the match in one of his bedrooms. As for the probability that Taylor knew the identity of the dead woman, Annie, despite his denial, that was only something I picked up from one of my sources a few hours ago. What chance did I have to share that info with you in the time available?'

'You could have called me up on my mobile to tell me.'

'You think so, with all the stuff that's been happening? Get real, Indi. Anyway, I'm telling you now, aren't I?'

Purewal made a rueful grimace, then gave a reluctant nod. 'Okay, sorry I lost it, but it all came as a bit of a shock . . . Is the DI in the picture?'

'I briefed him on everything except the Taylor connection.'

'Why keep him out of the loop on that? Bit deceitful, isn't it?'

'Not really. He's aware that I'm following up on something else, which I've said I wanted to keep to myself for the moment, but that's all. If I'd told him about Taylor, he would have had to pass that info on to the DCI with the rest of the stuff. With Ricketts's heavy-footed approach to everything and his hostility towards me, I knew that that would have cocked up everything, especially what I'm planning to do.'

'And what *are* you planning to do?'

'Obviously, to confront our wily clergyman to find out how he fits into this business and see where it takes me.'

'But how are you going to do that? You've told me that you only found the matching cufflink by unlawfully searching a bedroom at his home. That sort of evidence would be inadmissible in a court of law, as you well know, and it could give him grounds for legal action against you if you were unwise enough to admit to it.'

'I realise that. But the initials on the cufflink speak for themselves.'

'How do they? They could be anyone.'

'Not quite. Taylor himself not only admitted to me that he had a fascination for monograms but said that this particular monogram design was unique to him. Furthermore, it's a bit of a bloody coincidence, isn't it? I mean, a cufflink in the shape of a fish, which is in itself regarded as a symbol of Christianity and happens to be engraved with the initials of a former priest, found behind the home of a murdered woman who used to be one of his parishioners?'

'Yeah, but the evidence is still pretty thin, isn't it? And what about Annie? It's only your assumption that Taylor was the priest your informant said went looking for her when she disappeared; you weren't given a name. You don't even know for certain that what you were told was the truth anyway.'

'So why would my snout come up with a story like that in the first place? How would he have known that the involvement of a priest could be relevant to the current investigation?'

Purewal thought about that for a few seconds, then shrugged. 'Okay, point taken. And I assume the reason you've told me about all this is because you want me to tag along with you to see this dodgy priest?'

Kate shook her head. 'That's not entirely true. I unloaded on you in the first place because I felt that, as this was your case originally, it was only right that you should be made aware of what was happening. As for "tagging along", I would certainly be delighted to have you with me, but you would need to understand that I could well end up in hot water by interviewing a potential murder suspect without first consulting the lead investigator. If you are involved, you are likely to find yourself in the same firing line as myself were it all to go pear-shaped.'

Purewal's face twisted into a brief cynical smile. 'Then it's up to us to make sure it doesn't go pear-shaped, isn't it?' she said. 'When do we do this?'

'Tomorrow morning, first thing.'

'I'll make sure I put on clean drawers, just in case!'

CHAPTER 15

Kate guessed that the DI was at "morning prayers" — the regular morning meeting with the DCI and the superintendent — when she and Indrani Purewal met up at Highbridge police station the next day, since Woo's office was empty. She quickly scribbled him a note, telling him they were following up some inquiries on the Johnson case, as per the day before, and left the note on his desk, hoping that this would keep him off their backs for a while at least. Two of their other colleagues were already in the general office when they walked in, heads down at their desks, working through bundles of files, but they hardly seemed to notice them arrive, let alone show any interest in what they were up to when they left again after grabbing the keys to one of the CID cars from a hook by the door.

As for Kate's other half, he had disappeared in the direction of the canteen as soon as they'd driven into the police station car park, and she knew he was unlikely to be in the least bit interested in where she had gone after a belly-full of cooked breakfast. Nevertheless, she made sure he couldn't escape making a contribution to the investigation. Dropping the bundle of papers Purewal had found in Lizzie Johnson's bedroom on his desk, she left him a note, instructing him to go through them to see if anything of possible significance jumped out at him, if and when he finally deigned to wander upstairs to the office.

She didn't think there would be anything, but if there were, she was confident he would find it. Hayden may have been one of the laziest, work-shy characters she had ever known — and he certainly wasn't going to be impressed at being lumbered with the file of papers she had left for him — but his outward persona belied the fact that he was also one of the sharpest knives in the drawer, with a keen analytical mind that missed very little. He just needed a kick up the backside from time to time, Kate thought with a wry smile as she climbed behind the wheel of the car, and this was one of them . . .

The Reverend Taylor appeared to be at home when Kate and her colleague pulled up outside his house, and it looked as if he might even still be in bed. The blinds were drawn, and there were no obvious signs of life, despite the fact that it was well after nine. *Tough titty*, Kate thought grimly as she cut the engine. Whether he liked it or not, his lie-in was about to be rudely interrupted.

The air was cold and damp as she and Purewal climbed out of the car, the chill of the marsh seeping into their bones and their breath condensing in the cold air as they walked up the path to the front door. Kate felt her stomach muscles tighten with a mixture of excitement and trepidation as she rang the bell, acutely aware of the potential difficulties of the interview she and Purewal were about to carry out with very little real evidence to justify it at the forefront of her mind. To her surprise, the door opened almost straight away, and Taylor peered out at them a little myopically. He was still dressed in his pyjamas and dressing gown.

'Gracious, Sergeant Lewis,' he exclaimed, eyeing first Kate and then Purewal. 'You're up early. What can I do for you? Do please, come in. It's bitter out there.'

The hall smelled of toast and coffee, and he led the way into the library, as he had on the previous visit.

'Coffee? Tea?' he asked hospitably.

Conscious of the reason for their visit, Kate gave a tight smile and shook her head. 'No thanks, Reverend,' she said. 'We're fine, really.'

He shrugged and waved them to the same two armchairs before pulling out the bosun's swivel chair tucked under the desk, which he wheeled over to them both. 'Right,' he said, sitting down and leaning forward with his knees almost touching the end of the coffee table, 'how can I help you this time?'

'May I introduce Detective Constable Indrani Purewal,' Kate said, nodding towards her colleague. 'She's working with me on the Lizzie Johnson case.'

Taylor raised his eyebrows. 'Lizzie Johnson again? Is that why you're here? I would have thought you had asked all the questions you needed to ask about her when you were here yesterday, Sergeant? I hardly knew the poor woman, as I told you.'

Kate shook her head. 'I know, but the thing is, there's been another rather surprising development, which we feel you may be able to help us with.'

'Oh? And what on earth is that?'

'This, Reverend,' Kate replied in a sharper tone and tossed the broken cufflink dramatically across the coffee table, to land in his lap. 'We believe it belongs to you.'

The move was quick, deliberate and intended to shake him, and it certainly succeeded — even surprising Purewal, who tensed in her seat, plainly unprepared for what Kate had decided to do. For at least a couple of seconds the priest simply sat there gaping in absolute astonishment at the piece of broken jewellery lying in the folds of his dressing gown. Then, like someone presented with a lethal object that could explode at any minute, he gingerly picked it up and turned it over in his hand.

'Where on earth did you get this?' he breathed.

'My colleague here found it on a woodland track,' Kate replied. 'You should recognise it, as it is engraved with your initials?'

Taylor was no fool and Kate could almost hear the cogs spinning in his brain, putting two and two together.

'What track?' he asked, obviously knowing the answer even before she told him.

'The track behind Lizzie Johnson's house, Reverend,' she replied, 'and we were wondering how it could have got there?'

Pulling out her pocketbook, she sat back in her chair and waited for him to answer, watching him gnawing at his lip, with eyes that flicked one way and another as he tried to think of a way out. Finally, with a heavy sigh, he simply gave up.

'It must have fallen out of my shirt cuff,' he said. 'I didn't realise I had lost it until later and I couldn't think where that could have happened.'

'Which begs the question, what you were doing in that precise spot in the first place?' Purewal put in impatiently.

He threw her an agonised, trapped look and began wringing his hands. 'What can I say?' he replied. 'I was obviously visiting Lizzie.'

'When was this?'

'Er, several weeks ago. She–she asked to see me because of something that was worrying her, and I gave her some spiritual guidance—'

'And left the crucifix with her, which we found in her bedroom?'

He nodded. 'It often helps in such cases. Reassurance, you know. Something solid to hold on to.'

Kate reached forward to retrieve the cufflink from his lap and return it to her pocket, ignoring the look he gave her. 'Is that when you also carried out the exorcism?' she resumed before he could protest.

His eyes widened. 'How do you know about that?'

'Let's say I have my sources. So, was it?'

He appeared to gag several times, as if suffering from indigestion. 'I–I didn't do a proper exorcism,' he went on eventually. 'I merely went through the motions to satisfy her.'

He took a deep breath. 'But please, you must not tell anyone about that. I would be in a lot of trouble if you did. You have to understand that exorcisms in the Anglican Church are controversial and very rare. They– they have to be performed by a deliverance team who are specifically trained in psychiatry and exorcism, and permission has first to be obtained from the diocesan bishop—'

'Permission I assume you didn't have?' Purewal summarised.

He shook his head helplessly. 'I did what I thought was right by trying to help a terrified, vulnerable woman, who was nearly out of her mind with fear, but in my position, I am not allowed to conduct such a rite, and I would be in very serious trouble if what I did got to the ears of the bishop, even though I am ostensibly retired. Who–who told you about this?'

'That's irrelevant,' Kate continued. 'Let's get down to brass tacks, shall we? Why did you tell me yesterday that you hardly knew Lizzie and didn't even know where she lived when that was completely false? Hardly the sort of behaviour you would expect from a member of the clergy, is it?'

He slumped forward, covered his face with his hands and rested his elbows on his thighs. 'God help me,' he choked, 'what have I done?'

'That's what we'd like to know, Reverend,' Kate persisted ruthlessly. 'What *have* you done?'

She saw his body tense. Then he slowly removed his hands from his face and straightened in the chair again.

'Whatever do you mean?' he exclaimed. 'Are you suggesting I am responsible for that poor woman's suicide? That–that I drove her to it? That's not fair. I tried to help her.'

'We aren't talking about suicide, Reverend,' Kate said grimly. 'The fact is, Lizzie Johnson didn't kill herself. She was murdered!'

'She was what?' He lurched forward in the chair and almost toppled it. '*Murdered?*'

He stared first at Purewal and then at Kate, fear in his eyes now, as the possible implications dawned on him. 'You don't think I—' He broke off and hauled himself to his feet, his face now angry and reddening by the second. 'This is disgraceful. You're accusing me of–of murder? On what grounds? And–and why have I been singled out? Okay, so I fibbed, I admit it, but that, or the fact that I visited Lizzie and dropped a cufflink outside her house, doesn't make me a murderer.' He gagged again and carried on in a quicker, more desperate tone. 'Lizzie had lots of other people visit her too, you–you have to understand that. The crowd she used to go around with in her youth still live locally, and she told me that they all got together at her place from time to time. Robert Chalmers, her ex-husband, was often there—'

Kate held up both hands in a soothing gesture. 'No one is accusing you of anything, sir,' she said. 'But you have told us a series of blatant lies, so you have rather brought this on yourself. Now would you please sit down and control yourself?'

It was touch and go. The elderly man was plainly furious and his hands clenched into tight balls. But under the hard, unsympathetic stares of the two detectives, he seemed to wilt slightly and, grasping the arms of the swivel chair, he sank back on to it, mopping his forehead with a large handkerchief.

'I am a man of God,' he said in a strained voice. 'There is no way I would hurt anyone, let alone a defenceless woman.'

Kate waited for him to recover fully from his outburst, then she said, 'What was it Lizzie Johnson was so frightened of?'

He grimaced. 'A demon,' he replied simply. 'She was convinced that she was being stalked by some mythical creature living out on the marshes, which the superstitious locals called the Night Hag, and that it was intent on doing her harm.'

'Why?'

'What do you mean?'

'Well, why would this, er, Night Hag want to do her harm? Did she think she had offended it in some way?'

'I have no idea. Lizzie wasn't well, mentally. She had all sorts of funny ideas from dabbling in the occult.'

'Are you sure there wasn't more to it than that?'

'Sorry?'

'Isn't it the case that there was an old homeless woman living out on the marshes when you were the resident parish priest in the area, who had earned that reputation for herself because of her strange looks and behaviour?'

'I–I couldn't say.'

'Couldn't you, Reverend? Couldn't you, really? I would like you to think about your answer for a moment. You see, we have it on good authority that you knew this old woman very well — to the extent that when she suddenly disappeared, you went searching for her.'

'I don't know who you mean.'

'I think you do. I believe the kids called her "Dark Annie". Ring a bell?'

Taylor's face was an unhealthy shade of grey now and he seemed to have difficulty finding his voice.

'I have to remind you,' Kate went on, 'that we are investigating what looks like a double murder inquiry here. If you fail to cooperate with us, we can always continue this conversation down the police station.'

Taylor shook his head quickly and held up one hand in a gesture of capitulation. 'No, please, I have done nothing wrong. I'll tell you all I know.' He took a deep breath, then carried on in a rush. 'It's true, I did know Annie. When–when I first arrived in the parish, I heard about her from the verger and went to see her in the corrugated iron shack in which she was then living out on the marshes. She–she was reluctant to talk to me and was actually quite offensive at first. But bit by bit, over several weeks, I earned her trust and eventually she came to see me at the church. I later managed to persuade her to help out, doing some basic cleaning and sorting out the hymn books after the services. In return, I gave her food and, regrettably, cans of beer to satisfy her alcoholism. Then one day she simply vanished. I–I had no idea where she had gone so, yes, I did search for her for some time, but I never found out what had happened to her and assumed she had probably left the area.'

'Didn't you report her disappearance to the police?' Purewal asked.

For a moment he looked incredulous at the question. 'She was a vagrant, what you people call a dosser. She didn't have a regular address and could have gone anywhere. What would have been the point in reporting that she had vacated her tin shack? As it was, she was feared and loathed in equal measure by many of the suspicious villagers and I knew they were relieved that she had gone—'

'So, you let it drop? Forgot all about it?'

He glared at Purewal. 'No, I didn't drop it, officer. I spent weeks searching but got nowhere. What else was I expected to do? I knew very little about Annie; where she had come from or where she might have gone. I had no information on her at all.'

'Did you know her surname?' Kate asked, studying his haggard-looking face intently.

He shook his head. 'I never asked her. It wasn't my business to.'

Kate made a grimace. 'Well, it looks like we know where she ended up, dumped in an unmarked grave near where she used to live. What we don't know is how she got there and exactly what happened to her.'

Taylor shook his head mournfully. 'Well, I couldn't tell you, and that's the absolute truth.'

'So, why have you been lying to us so far? You could have told us what you knew before.'

'I–I was scared. Originally, when I thought Lizzie's death might have been suicide, I was worried that I could somehow be blamed for it; you know, giving the wrong advice to a vulnerable middle-aged woman with mental health issues. That's why I asked to see you yesterday. I needed to know whether her death was suicide or due to an accident, if only to ease my conscience. I had no idea it was a murder.'

'And Annie? Why did you deny knowing her?'

'For much the same reason. I was quite shocked when you came out with her name. Up until then, it hadn't occurred to me that the bones found at Pagan's Clump could be Annie's. After all, it was over thirty years ago that I last had any dealings with her, and a lot of water has passed under the bridge since then. I panicked when you asked me about her. I didn't want to get sucked into your inquiries and have the past all raked up again.'

He took another deep breath. 'Now, if you're going to arrest me, would you please let me at least get dressed?'

To his surprise, and apparently that of Purewal too, Kate shook her head and stood up. 'Not today, Reverend, but we might be back if further evidence comes to light, or it turns out that you are still hiding things from us. I trust you're not planning on leaving the country any time soon, are you?'

Indrani Purewal could hardly contain herself until she and Kate got back to the CID car. Once inside, she turned on her excitedly. 'With respect, Sarge, what are you doing? He should have been arrested on sus.'

Kate stared across at her for a second, then said, 'On what grounds, Indi? Yesterday you were criticising me for going ahead on this without sufficient evidence. Now today you're saying the opposite.'

'But he has now *admitted* calling to see Lizzie Johnson and we also have his cufflink to prove it. Also, he has been lying to us from the start, not only about knowing Johnson, but the woman, Annie, too.'

'So what? How does that make him a double murderer? A lot of people lie to the police, usually through fear of us and the powers we have, and it's not a crime anyway.'

'But he is linked to both incidents.'

'Yes, but by very tenuous means. As he himself pointed out, visiting Johnson and dropping his cufflink where he did doesn't make him a murderer and, as for Annie, so he did know her. Again, so what? He insisted that he went out of his way to help her, which cannot be proved, of course, but it cannot be disproved either, and the very fact that he is known to have searched for her when she went missing is hardly the act of a killer.'

'That could have been a ploy — you know, make a big show of searching for her to convince everyone he had nothing to do with her disappearance.'

'Why bother? No one, it seems, lost any sleep over her disappearance, so who would he have had to prove that to? And finally, what could his motive be for killing two people of completely different ages, station and type thirty years apart? Gain? Revenge? Rejection? Passion? Power? I can't see a fit anywhere.'

'So, you think that despite all Taylor's lies and his connection to both Annie and Johnson, he is totally innocent of any crime, and everything is a complete coincidence?'

'I never said that. I am simply saying we haven't got enough to arrest him on sus. Things have changed and, whereas in the old days we might have chanced our arm and given it a whirl under the unofficial "Ways and Means Act", today we have to be very careful about bringing people in on a fishing expedition. Think about it. We nick him, take him in and stick him in the pokey. He gets a lawyer and under interview he continues to deny committing any criminal offence. What do we do then? We release him without charge, of course, simply because we have nothing — forensic or otherwise — to charge him *with*. Then the press get hold of it and the world and his wife are demanding to know why an elderly, well respected man of God, who has served his community faithfully and selflessly for thirty-odd years was arrested in the first place. Am I getting through?'

Purewal made a face. 'Loud and clear, skip. So, what was the point in bothering to question him in the first place if we're not going to do anything with what we've got anyway? It was a total waste of time.'

Kate started the engine and pulled away. 'That's not true, Indi. Okay, maybe we haven't managed to solve a possible double murder, but we have succeeded in clearing up some loose ends and confirming a number of what were ambiguities before. Nevertheless, like you, I am not at all happy about the Reverend Arthur Taylor. I am convinced he knows a whole lot more than he is saying. But for the moment we have no alternative but to bide our time until we have the evidence we need to pull him in . . . and that will come in time, believe me, it always does. At least we've made a start.'

'So, what's next on the agenda?'

'I think we'll pick up on Taylor's cue. He made the point that Lizzie Johnson received visits from lots of other people apart from himself and that Johnson often got together with the friends she used to mix with when she was young. I think it might be a good idea if we paid a visit to each of them in turn to see what they have to say for themselves.'

'Do we know who they are and where they live?'

'Very much so. If you remember, I noted the details in my pocketbook from Lizzie Johnson's diary when we went through the house that first time.'

'Do you think we ought to brief Charlie Woo about the Reverend Taylor first, though?'

'No need yet. I was asked to carry out local inquiries following the release of the public appeal, and that's exactly what we'll be doing.'

'But it's unlikely any of Lizzie Johnson's friends will know anything about Annie.'

Kate swerved slightly to miss a deer streaking across the road. 'Don't you be so sure,' she said. 'I think there is a lot more to this business than even we realise.'

CHAPTER 16

Kate and Indrani Purewal did not head back to Highbridge police station after leaving the Reverend Taylor's home. Kate was concerned that they could run into Charlie Woo or, even worse, DCI Ricketts if they did so, which could have resulted in them being subjected to an unwanted grilling and jeopardise any chance they might have had of pursuing the inquiries Kate had in mind. To cover their continued absence from the station, the wily skipper made a quick call to the department's office manager, Ajeet Singh, and left a message for Charlie Woo, rather than phoning him direct, explaining that they were still tied up on the same job and would report back as soon as they could. This enabled them to stay well out of harm's way, and, following a brief stop at a roadside café, where Kate treated Purewal to a light snack and a coffee, they pressed on across the Levels to their first target.

Julian Grey lived in a big, Georgian-style house set back off the Causeway outside the small village of Mark. There was a red Porsche Kate remembered previously seeing outside Lizzie Johnson's house parked in the driveway and beside it, a green Morgan sports car, which from the dated number plate Kate guessed was a vintage model. She smiled to herself, thinking that it was a good job Hayden wasn't with her instead of Indrani. His love of classic cars was almost an obsession. He would have positively drooled over the Morgan and probably ended up forgetting why he was there.

Deep down, neither of the two detectives really expected to find Grey at home in the middle of the day, assuming that, like most professional people, he would most probably be at work. They were therefore resigned to the fact that their visit could become nothing more than a reconnoitre. Sight of the two cars parked out front came as a welcome surprise. At least it suggested someone was at home, and that turned out to be the case. A tall, dark-haired man with a Mediterranean tan and a gold stud in his left ear answered the door on the second ring, looking more than a little uncomfortable in his white towelling robe.

'Julian Grey?' Kate asked, giving her best smile.

'What of it?' he retorted sourly.

Taking that as confirmation, Kate produced her warrant card and introduced them both.

'Police?' Grey exclaimed. 'What on earth is this about?'

'We're making some routine inquiries into the death of a Ms Lizzie Johnson,' she replied. 'We gather you were a friend of hers?'

He grimaced, casting a brief glance behind him. 'Not exactly the best timing, Sergeant, but, er, you'd better come in.'

A willowy blonde in an identical robe appeared from one of the rooms on their left as they stepped into the hall and, wiggling across in front of them, disappeared up an imposing staircase opposite, throwing them a mischievous glance over her shoulder at the same time.

'My, er, girlfriend,' Grey explained. 'Staying a few days. We had, um, a late breakfast.'

Kate glanced at her watch, which registered eleven forty-five, and smiled knowingly. 'Very nice, too, sir,' she said.

He gave a short, embarrassed cough in response, but made no further comment, showing them into a large, opulent sitting room, boasting matching ultra-modern furniture, a cocktail bar and what appeared to be a very expensive Bose sound system. Still looking far from happy, he waved them to a pair of deep armchairs, frowning as Kate pulled out her pocketbook and pen and set them on her knee.

'Not working today then, sir?' she said as an opener.

'I have my own business as a financial adviser, so I can come and go as I please, Sergeant,' he replied, dropping into a third chair facing them and glancing suspiciously at her pocketbook. 'I have an office in Bridgwater, but most of my time is spent out and about seeing clients.'

'Right,' Kate acknowledged with a little glint in her eye. 'That can be quite tiring at times, I should think.'

His eyes narrowed, obviously unsure as to whether her remark was intended as a polite observation or carried a more pointed meaning.

'So, what can I do for you, Sergeant?' he said rather more coldly, glancing again at her pocketbook as she opened it up. 'You say you're here about poor Lizzie. To answer your earlier question, yes, she and I were very good friends; had been since we were at primary school together. Her suicide has come as quite a shock, I can tell you.'

Kate stared at him fixedly. 'Unfortunately, sir, I have to tell you that her death was not due to suicide or even an accident.'

For a moment, Grey gaped at her in the same way as Taylor had done. 'You're not saying she was–was *murdered*?' he echoed. 'That cannot be.'

Kate began making notes. 'Why do you say that, Mr Grey? Why couldn't it be?'

He shook his head irritably. 'Why are you writing things down, Sergeant? Should I be calling my lawyer?'

Kate shook her head. 'No need, Mr Grey, you're not under arrest. We are only seeking information from people who knew Lizzie Johnson, to help us with our inquiries. Now you were saying . . .'

He nodded but looked more than a little shocked by Kate's revelation about Johnson's death. 'Yes, well, Lizzie was such a harmless soul — batty, but totally harmless — and I was given to understand that she had died from a drug overdose of some sort. How can that be murder?'

'Who told you she died of a drug overdose, sir?'

'A–another friend of mine, Robert Chalmers, her former husband. He telephoned me with the bad news.'

'When was this?'

'The day after it happened — Sunday night, I believe. The police had called to see him at his flat in Bristol to tell him Lizzie was dead.'

'I know you said Lizzie was harmless, but can you think of anyone who might have had an axe to grind where she was concerned? Someone she had offended by her behaviour or had otherwise upset? You did say she was what you called "batty", after all.'

'Absolutely not. I can't think of anyone who would want her dead. As for her being batty, I just meant she had some wacky ideas. She believed in ghosts and things that, er, go bump in the night and had been delving into the supernatural for years. It had become quite an obsession with her—'

This was Purewal's cue under the detectives' previously agreed strategy and she jumped straight in with the objective of what Kate had earlier described to her as "shaking his tree".

'Was the Night Hag part of that obsession?' she asked bluntly.

Thrown for a moment by the question directed at him out of the blue by Kate's partner, Grey visibly started and seemed to be having trouble collecting his thoughts.

'Night Hag?' he blurted. 'I don't know what you're talking about.'

'Lizzie was apparently living in fear of some sort of supernatural entity,' Purewal continued. 'She made reference to it in a diary we found at her house. Said it was coming after her. Surely, as a friend, she must have discussed this with you?'

Grey had recovered his composure now and was back in control. 'Not me personally, no,' he said with a manufactured laugh. 'I expect it was one of her many fanciful notions.'

'Would she have discussed her fears with anyone else? One of her other friends perhaps? We understand that, apart from yourself, there were several people she grew up with who are still living and working in this area.'

'That's true enough,' he agreed, without offering any names. 'But I can't imagine Lizzie speaking to any of them about it.'

'What about her ex-husband, Robert Chalmers. Do you think she would have mentioned it to him?'

'I've no idea. Perhaps you should ask him. You must know where to reach him, as I gather he was asked by the police to identify her body.'

Kate came in again with another low ball. 'Did Lizzie not bring up the subject of her fears at the meeting you and her other friends had at her house shortly before her death?'

He didn't bat an eyelid. 'Meeting? Oh, you mean the little social she organised for a few of us. Hardly. We were only there for the booze.'

Kate consulted her pocketbook. 'In her diary she said, *The bitch is free. God Help us!* Do you know what she meant by that and who she was referring to?'

'Sorry. As I have already explained, Lizzie had a lot of fanciful notions.'

'But from the way the entry was made, it looks as if the meeting itself was arranged to discuss this person, and in her diary, Lizzie then goes on to say that you all came to a *unanimous decision to keep schtum about it*. Keep schtum about what?'

'I haven't the faintest idea. By the time the evening was over, I'd had so much to drink, that I had little recollection of anything.'

Convenient, Kate thought, then went on. 'Lizzie also seemed annoyed with someone named Danny. She said, apparently in relation to the matter that was allegedly discussed, and I quote again, he was *not interested one way or the other. Incredible, when it was all his fault in the first place*, and she called him a bastard. What was that about and what was Danny supposed to have done?'

'Couldn't say. Danny Aldridge is an old friend of all of us, but he can be a bit of an arsehole at times, and he had probably said something she objected to. Drink can soon wind people up, you know.'

Kate's eyes narrowed. Grey was obviously not about to volunteer any information unless he had to. She abruptly changed tack.

'You said you've known Lizzie ever since you went to primary school with her, so presumably you were born around here?'

He nodded, looking wary as if wondering what was coming next. 'Yes, my father was a local councillor. He died a while back, and I decided to stay on in the area, sold the family home and moved to this place, setting up my present business in Bridgwater.' He smiled suddenly. 'You know, close enough to get to work, yet not on top of it.'

Kate didn't respond to the smile. For some reason his self-assured manner irritated her. 'When you were a child,' she went on, 'did you ever hear about an old vagrant woman living out on the Levels who some of the local people considered to be a witch?'

'Not that I recall, no.'

'I understand the children were frightened of her and they called her "Dark Annie".'

She saw a barely perceptible jerk of his eyelids, but it was gone in a moment. Then he affected a deep frown.

'Annie? Wasn't that the name of the woman the police have given out in their public appeal this afternoon? I picked it up on the radio around half an hour ago. Something to do with a body found in an unmarked grave at some place called Pagan's Clump?'

So, he had already heard the appeal, had he? she mused. He must have found a spare few minutes to listen to the radio when he wasn't knocking off his so-called girlfriend.

'That's the one, yes,' she confirmed drily. 'Do you remember the old woman? We're told she was quite well-known in the surrounding villages back in the day. Interestingly, Dark

Annie and the Night Hag, whom Lizzie referred to in her diary, are said to have been one and the same.'

''Fraid I can't help you there.' He laughed again. 'Let's be honest, the Somerset Levels abounds in myth and legend. Glastonbury is only down the road, and we have always had a plethora of witches, ghostly monks and spectral dogs on the prowl. I can't be expected to remember the names of all of them. Furthermore, if you're talking about when I was at primary school, hell, that must be more than forty-five years ago, which is bound to stretch the memory a bit.'

Kate shook her head. 'We're talking more about the time you were in your late teens or early twenties. which would have been when she disappeared—'

'Disappeared, did she? Well, that's very sad. But—' he shrugged —'I have no knowledge of any Annie, alive or, er, disappearing. Sorry.'

'When did you last see Lizzie?'

He puckered his brows in thought. 'I think it was the Friday before she died. I met up with Bob Chalmers at her place for a drink and she said she thought she had been burgled.'

'Had she?'

'Bob and I couldn't find any evidence of that, and I stayed long enough to help settle her down, then left Bob with her. After all, she was his ex, so he was better placed to do that than me.'

'She didn't mention anything about this Night Hag or Dark Annie then?'

'Nope. In the end, she seemed to accept that she had simply had a bad dream.'

He looked suddenly annoyed. 'Look, Sergeant, I realise you have a job to do, but really, I can't help you with any of this, and I do have a–a guest with me at the moment, so . . .'

Kate stood up, returning her pocketbook back to her pocket. 'Fully understand, sir,' she acknowledged. 'One last thing, though. Can you remember where you were last Saturday night?'

He seemed unsurprised by the question and treated her to a little smirk. 'Yes, I was here — with my girlfriend, whom you've already met.'

'Thank you for your time, sir.'

'Sorry I couldn't be of more help.'

'Smooth, arrogant prick!' Purewal commented the second he closed the front door behind them, almost as if she secretly wanted him to hear what she said.

'An arrogant prick, who, like our homespun Reverend Taylor, appears to be lying through his teeth,' Kate murmured thoughtfully, as they both climbed into the CID car. 'I wonder what he's got to hide?'

* * *

Kate would have been even more curious about Grey had she been aware of his reaction to their visit the moment they left the house.

Shouting up the stairs to his blonde guest, he waited, impatiently tapping the banister rail with one hand until she rejoined him in the hall.

'I'm afraid you're going to have to leave,' he said, his face tense.

She looked astonished. 'Leave?' she echoed. 'Whatever for? Did I disappoint?'

He gave an irritable grimace. 'No, not at all. Something's come up, that's all.'

'To do with those two coppers, is it?'

'Yes, they were here to tell me about a close friend who's died,' he lied glibly. 'There's some issues I have to deal with right now.'

She pouted. 'Sorry about your friend, but you did engage my services for five days. I could have lost out on another client because of this.'

'I appreciate that, but these things happen, I'm afraid. Now, please, get dressed and packed. Soon as you can.'

For a moment it appeared that she was going to argue the point. But then she simply snapped, 'Suit yourself, sweetheart. The agency will still charge you for the five days, so it will cost you anyway.'

He nodded, his impatience with the delay showing. 'Fine. Fine. They have my card details, don't they?'

Then he was striding away from her, back down the hallway, jerking his mobile phone from his pocket as he went and disappearing into another room two doors down from the sitting room, which she knew to be his study. The door then slammed shut, and it was the last she saw of him.

Twenty minutes later she was behind the wheel of her tasty Morgan sports car, pulling away from the front door of the house, making sure that the wheels of the vehicle deliberately churned up the loose shingle of the driveway and left deep furrows in their wake to clearly register her feelings about the ignominious treatment she had received at the hands of her latest well-heeled client. Not that Grey would have cared one way or the other even if he had been aware of her departure in the first place. Closeted in his study, he had far more serious worries on his mind — like trying to prevent a thirty-year-old secret becoming the catalyst for bringing his comfortable, secure world crashing down about his ears due to a single unguarded comment made by one of his remaining three friends.

Ashen-faced, and restlessly pacing the room, he repeatedly tried to raise Aldridge, Talbot and Chalmers on their mobiles. He had to alert them to the fact that not only had the death of Lizzie Johnson now become a police murder investigation, but that detectives were already on their way to interview them, and it was essential that they were all saying the same thing. But he was out of luck. Incredibly, all he got from each of the mobiles was the same infuriating automated messages, telling him that the person he was calling was unavailable and to "please leave a message after the tone"!

For the next twenty minutes, with a growing sense of panic that was totally alien to "Mr Cool", he prowled the study with his mobile clamped firmly against his ear, dialling the three numbers in turn repeatedly, but with the same result each time. In desperation, he even resorted to ringing their home numbers, but yet again, the automated voice kicked in. He could hardly believe it. Not one of them contactable. Okay, at this time of the day they would probably be at work, but surely at least one of them would be able to pick up, and it was far too risky ringing them on their business numbers, as he couldn't be sure who might be listening in on the call.

After a further fifteen minutes trying, between gulps of whisky from the cut-glass decanter on his desk, he was about to give up altogether, when his persistence was finally rewarded. He received a call back. It was Robert Chalmers.

'You wanted me?' Chalmers said. 'Got your number in my missed calls.'

Grey took a deep breath. 'Been trying to get you for nearly an hour,' he replied.

Chalmers was unapologetic 'Yeah, well, I was with a client, so tough titty. What's up? World War Three?'

'Almost. I've had a visit from two police detectives. Lizzie's death is being treated as a murder.'

There was a gasp from the other end. 'What? You're joking?'

'I wish I was.'

'But who'd want to kill Lizzie?'

'Well, someone obviously did, and the worrying thing is, they seem to suspect a link between Lizzie and that bloody vagrant woman, Annie.'

'Shit!'

'Exactly. Furthermore, this Detective Sergeant Kate Lewis has got hold of all of our names and addresses from some diary she found at Lizzie's place. They're bound to be interviewing the four of us and it's vital everyone is singing from the same hymn sheet. So, pin your ears back and I'll give you the party line.'

Chalmers listened to what Grey had to say without interruption and when his friend had finished, Chalmers's tone of voice sounded a lot more subdued than before.

'Have you told the others?' he asked.

Grey snorted. 'That's what I've been trying to do. Like you, they've both been on answerphone.'

'Well, best of luck with Danny. He rang me earlier this afternoon in one of his depressive moods, rambling on about his rotten life. He was almost incoherent at times and, as usual lately, he sounded as pissed as a newt.'

Grey's mouth tightened into a hard line. 'That's all we need. He could let something slip and drop us all in it.'

Chalmers gave a short unamused laugh. 'I wouldn't think so. If I know Danny, by the time the police get to him, he'll be paralytic and in no state to talk to anyone about anything.'

Grey was not reassured, and he rang Aldridge the moment he'd finished talking to Chalmers, but as before, there was no response. Now regretting the amount of time he'd spent on the phone to Chalmers, he tried Jennifer Talbot again. To his relief, she answered straight away.

'Sorry, Jules,' she said. 'I was at a staff meeting when you rang and I'm not long home. I was going to ring you later.'

He was still smarting at the hassle he had been put through and couldn't resist making his feelings known. 'I've spent half the day trying to contact you, Jen,' he replied. 'I needed to speak to you urgently. It's not on, it really isn't.'

'Well, slap my wrist!' she snapped back sarcastically. 'I didn't realise your telephone calls had priority over everything else in my life.'

He scowled but was unrepentant. 'Never mind that,' he retorted. 'Listen to me. Something important has come up and—'

But that was as far as he got.

'Sorry again, Jules,' she cut in. 'Have to go. Someone at the door.'

'*No!*' he shouted, hit by a premonition as to who her caller might be. 'Don't answer it. Hear me out first.'

'Ring you back in a minute,' she replied, then she was gone.

CHAPTER 17

Jennifer Talbot stared at the two women standing on her doorstep, her eyes focusing on the distinctive wallet one was holding out in front of her.

'Miss Jennifer Talbot?' the woman asked. 'Detective Sergeant Kate Lewis and Detective Constable Indrani Purewal, Highbridge CID.'

Talbot felt her stomach muscles start to knot but forced herself to remain calm. 'How can I help you?' she replied.

'Could we come in for a few moments?' Kate said. 'We are carrying out some inquiries into the death of a Ms Lizzie Johnson. We understand you knew her quite well?'

Talbot stepped back and motioned them inside. 'Yes, Lizzie and I grew up together,' she replied, showing them both to a couple of country-style armchairs in her immaculate living room.

Sitting on the edge of a deep settee, facing them across a similarly deep-pile carpet, she smiled, and added, 'We went to the same local primary school . . . Ironically, I'm now head of the same school.'

'Congratulations,' Kate acknowledged. 'Funny how things turn out, isn't it?'

'Certainly is . . . Lizzie's suicide came as quite a shock, I must admit.'

'I'm sure it did. But I have to tell you, her death was not in fact suicide. We are now conducting a murder investigation.'

Talbot's face paled and Kate saw her hands clench briefly in her lap before she recovered her composure. 'How dreadful,' she exclaimed. 'Poor Lizzie. Do we know why . . . ?'

Kate shook her head. 'Not as yet, no. That's why we are here, and it would be helpful to us if we could ask you a few questions about her, as she was such a close personal friend.'

'Of course. Fire away.'

'Do you mind if I take a few notes?'

'Not at all. I have nothing to hide.'

Kate immediately picked up on the response. Why would Talbot be quite content to answer questions verbally, yet feel bound to emphasise that she had nothing to hide when it came to things being written down? It was a small point, but Kate had been trained to notice the small points, and she was surprised that, unlike Julian Grey, Talbot had not actually queried the reason for notes being taken. In fact, after the initial surprise she had exhibited on their arrival, and her brief shock at the revelation about her close friend's death being murder, she seemed quite unperturbed by their visit.

As an experienced police detective, Kate was well versed in assessing people and this thin, middle-aged woman, with the short, grey hair, pale, lined face and the sharp, perceptive gaze behind the tinted blue spectacles, came across as not only calm and self-controlled, but from her body language, also noticeably cold and unemotional. It was not difficult to visualise her striding into a classroom and by her very presence commanding immediate attention from pupils and teachers alike. The absence of a wedding ring on her fingers or any other jewellery, and her rather old-fashioned neat blue suit and sensible shoes suggested that she was probably a spinster. Maybe, Kate mused, someone who had put a successful professional career ahead of any matrimonial opportunities and, in doing so, now nursed a deep, bitter resentment for all the wasted years and the rapidly approaching prospect of a lonely old age. Unlike Julian Grey's desperate attempt to hang on to his long-lost youth and the wild, Jack the Lad image he had no doubt enjoyed among his peers when in his thirties, this one seemed to be a logical, practical realist with few illusions about life and death and little emotional attachment to anything, either past or present.

Kate's opinion of her was reinforced by the way she continued to answer questions thereafter, all of which were like little echoes from Julian Grey's own interview; almost identical in content and delivered in a matter-of-fact way that provided few legitimate grounds for further scrutiny. It was pretty obvious to Kate that the woman was well briefed, and she suspected that Talbot and Grey had previously got their heads together in preparation for such an interview — even down to claiming that the last time she had seen Johnson was at the so-called get-together several weeks prior to her death. It was predictable that the same sort of negative responses would be given by the rest of the little gang when they were eventually questioned too.

Overall, it was beginning to feel as if the whole interview process was becoming nothing more than a complete waste of time and she was on the verge of giving up altogether and calling it a day, when, purely as a last resort, she decided to try for a breakthrough one last time by adopting a bit of police "ways and means" subterfuge.

'When I asked you a moment ago about an old vagrant woman living out on the marshes at the time, whom the kids called Dark Annie,' she said, 'you told me you had never heard of her. But before we leave you in peace, can we return to Annie for a moment? You see, the thing is, I put the same questions about her to your friend, Julian Grey, when we spoke to him before we came here and I must admit, I am quite puzzled, following my chat with you.'

For the very first time, Talbot looked concerned, and she stiffened in her chair. 'How do you mean?' she asked, and her tone had a sharp edge to it.

'Well, as I've already told you, we have turned up a local source who was born in this area and has been living here continuously for the same period as you and your friends, and he well remembers Annie. This was something I also put to Mr Grey, and he was quite candid in what he said about her. Are you sure you have no recollection whatsoever of this old woman, either as a child at primary school or during your teens and twenties when she apparently disappeared? It would be very helpful to our inquiries.'

For a moment Talbot said nothing, and behind the tinted lenses, her gaze seemed to lock on to something over Kate's shoulder, as if she were seeking inspiration from the far wall.

Kate tried to ignore Purewal's eyes boring into her with laser-like intensity from the adjacent chair.

'It–it was a long time ago,' Talbot said suddenly, 'and I was only very young, but on reflection, yes, like Jules, I do seem to remember talk of an old witch woman, who used to wander the marshes. But–but I can't remember much else about her. It's only a vague memory I have, which must have been sitting there in my subconscious all this time. I didn't give too much thought to your question when you first asked it.'

'Would her name have been Annie, do you think?' Kate went on gently, trying to control her excitement and not spook her.

'It–it could well have been something like that. I can't remember.'

'We understand she disappeared one day. Can you recall anyone saying anything about that?'

Talbot quickly shook her head. 'No idea, sorry. I can't remember anything else. Was Jules able to help you anymore?'

'Unfortunately, no. But we believe that the bones found at Pagan's Clump may be Annie's.'

'Pagan's Clump?' Talbot's pretended innocence was commendable, but it was too late.

You've already shot your bolt, love, Kate thought to herself.

'Did you not hear the police appeal for information this afternoon?' Kate asked.

'No, I'm afraid not. I've been in school all day. No time to listen to the radio or anything.'

Kate didn't try and pursue things any further. There was no point, and it would have aroused her suspicions about exactly how much Grey had really revealed.

'Well, we'll leave you to it then,' she said, climbing to her feet. 'Thanks for your cooperation.'

* * *

There was a dankness to the air when the two detectives returned to their car and telltale smoke-like wisps were beginning to drift across the driveway in front of them. Sensing the fact that her subterfuge with Talbot had not gone down well with her colleague, Kate made an effort to create a distraction.

'Looks like we're heading for a murky evening,' she commented. 'Mist is already drifting in. Let's hope it doesn't get too thick before we're done for the day.'

Purewal ignored her. 'That was a bit naughty of you in there,' she said instead.

Kate paused with her hand on the door handle. 'Oh? What was?' she replied, knowing full well what her colleague meant.

'Telling her an outright lie that Grey had admitted remembering Annie when he hadn't. If she was subsequently interviewed as a suspect, but denied knowing Annie, and was then reminded of the reply she gave to us today, she could allege you falsified information to trick her into saying something she didn't intend to say.'

Kate raised an eyebrow. 'Nonsense. I did no such thing.'

'But you said—'

Kate opened the door and slipped into her seat, as Purewal climbed in beside her.

'I *said*,' she continued with emphasis, turning to face her, as she buckled up, 'that Grey was "quite candid about

Annie when we were talking about her". So he was. He said he couldn't remember her at all. You couldn't be more candid than that.'

'But you gave Talbot the impression—'

'Talbot took from my comment what she wanted to take. It's not my fault that she misunderstood what I was saying, is it? And anyway, she only admitted to something she knew about already. She wouldn't have admitted to remembering Annie if she hadn't remembered her.'

'It was sailing bloody close to the wind, though, wasn't it? The CPS wouldn't like it one little bit and the powers-that-be would have your hide for breakfast.'

Kate smiled grimly. 'The tactic was perfectly in order, Indi, trust me, and at least it took us a bit closer to the truth.'

'Yeah, and where did that get *us*?'

'Grounds for reinterviewing that lying bastard, Grey, again and finally establishing what he and the others actually know about Annie and why they've been doing their level best to hide what they know all this time.'

'We going back to see Grey now then?'

Kate shook her head, glancing at her watch. 'No, I think Glastonbury calls.'

'Glastonbury?'

'Yep, it's where another of the little gang, Danny Aldridge, lives and, hopefully, by the time we get there, he'll be home from work.'

'Maybe we won't get the chance,' Purewal commented, displaying an apparent gift of clairvoyance, as Kate's personal mobile bleeped.

Kate pulled over and interrogated her texts. There was a message from her colleague, DC Jamie Foster, and it read:

Don't know where you are, or what you're up to, but Big Bad Wolf on the prowl about to blow your house down!

Kate grimaced and showed Purewal the message.
'Big Bad Wolf?' Purewal queried.

'Must mean the DCI,' Kate replied sourly. 'Aren't we the lucky ones?'

At which point, her police radio blasted her call-sign. 'From DCI. Return Base immediately,' the metallic voice instructed.

'As I thought,' Kate said sourly. 'Looks like our charming Mr Ricketts is on our case at last.'

'So, that's peed on your fireworks, hasn't it?'

Kate shrugged and cast her a brief smirk. 'You know what they say,' she said. 'There's always tomorrow.'

* * *

Julian Grey was finally rewarded by a return call from Jennifer Talbot, but his relief that she had come back to him was to turn out to be short-lived.

'Okay, so what's up?' she asked a little cautiously. 'Problem?'

'What's up?' he echoed in almost a snarl. 'I had the Old Bill here, that's what.'

'So did I,' she replied. 'Two women detectives.'

His stomach sank. 'Shit! I knew it would be them. I tried to warn you. What did they ask you?'

'They told me Lizzie's death was not suicide but was being treated as murder, and asked if I knew of anyone who might have had it in for her. Then they went on about her fears and her obsession with the so-called Night Hag, mentioning also that meeting we'd all had with Lizzie before she died . . . Oh yes, and they referred to some diary they'd found in Lizzie's bedroom and some of the things she'd written in it about us keeping — I think the word was schtum — about everything—'

'Much the same with me. What did you tell them?'

'Only what we'd all agreed.'

'Good girl. They were obviously on a fishing expedition. Did they say anything about Annie?'

'Yes, they said a public appeal for information had gone out about bones found at Pagan's Clump, which were believed to be the remains of someone called Annie and that she and Lizzie's Night Hag were thought to be one and the same person. They asked me if I remembered an old vagrant woman living rough on the marshes when I was a child.'

He grunted. 'The bastards are gradually putting things together, but thankfully, it appears that they've a way to go yet.' His tone sharpened. 'What did you tell them?'

'The same as you, that I'd only heard of an old woman a lot of the children were scared of, but I didn't confirm her name was Annie.'

He released his breath in an explosive gasp. 'You told them *that*? I thought we'd all agreed to deny any knowledge of Annie?'

'I only repeated what you'd already said.'

'For your information, I didn't say anything. I claimed I knew nothing at all about her.'

Talbot faltered. 'But–but they led me to believe you remembered her.'

'The devious, two-faced arseholes!' he almost spat. 'No, I never admitted to that at all — quite the opposite — and now the cat's well and truly out of the bag, which means they'll be back to question me again. What a bloody mess!'

'So, what do we do now?'

He gave a humourless laugh. 'I could say pray, but it would hardly be appropriate under the circumstances, would it?'

CHAPTER 18

Kate and Indrani Purewal walked into an empty office when they got back to Highbridge police station. There wasn't a soul about. But there was a note on the large whiteboard by the double doors, which read, *Incident Room Upstairs*. They found the clubroom and bar on the upper floor was getting a makeover, with lines of desks being dragged into position by a mix of uniformed and plain-clothed personnel. Computers, printers and other kit was in the process of being plugged into dedicated sockets in the walls. It was a scenario Kate had witnessed before. The club often doubled as a major incident room when a serious crime investigation was underway, and she guessed things had moved up a notch since they had left the station in the morning, with the Pagan's Clump inquiry now being centred here instead of at the more restrictive mobile incident room previously parked at the scene.

There was a glass-panelled office, similar to the DI's inner sanctum in CID, at the far end of the room, which was specifically set aside for the use of the senior investigation officer, and she and Purewal threaded their way between the desks towards the office's open door, where Charlie Woo could be seen standing talking to the DCI and a short, heavily built man bulging out of a light-grey suit, whom she didn't recognise.

Woo and the stranger had their backs to them, but the DCI was facing down the room and she saw his head jerk up the moment he spotted the two detectives, his gaze homing in on her, like a predatory animal which had spotted its next lunch. At the same moment the other two men seemed to pick up on the change in his body language and turned towards the new arrivals.

Woo looked strained and rattled, and Kate guessed Ricketts had been giving him a hard time, as usual — no doubt on account of her and what she had been doing — while the stranger's stare was of such unwavering intensity that she felt as if she were being mentally stripped naked in front of everyone.

The man himself was quite an eccentric looking character, with collar-length auburn hair, thinning on top and a matching beard that needed a trim. His grey suit was noticeably rumpled and the brogues he was wearing were badly scuffed. But there was something about him that arrested her attention. At first sight, the rather coarse, rubicund features and heavy jowls gave him a somewhat Falstaffian appearance but there was a no-nonsense set to his jaw and a noticeable keenness in the pale blue eyes that suggested this was not a man to be trifled with or underestimated. He was in every way a complete antithesis of Toby Ricketts.

'Ah, Kate. Indrani,' Woo said, stepping forward and extending a hand towards the stranger, 'this is Detective Superintendent Jack Wilson. He's taking over the Pagan's Clump investigation from Detective Chief Inspector Maurice Skindle, including the Lizzie Johnson murder inquiry, and the incident room is being moved up here because of the latest complex developments—'

'No need for you to remain,' Ricketts snapped at Purewal, cutting Woo off in mid-stream. 'We only need the sergeant here now.'

Plainly taken aback by his rude, peremptory dismissal, Purewal didn't bother to reply, but treating him to a cold, hostile stare, promptly turned on her heel and stalked back into the general office.

There was a brief awkward silence afterwards and although no one said anything to Ricketts, the embarrassment in the air was almost tangible as they all trooped into the little office.

Kate's eyes were on Wilson, who was obviously taking everything in, and though he'd not said anything, she sensed he had been far from impressed by Ricketts's treatment of one of his detective constables. But he gave nothing away and, dropping into the swivel chair behind the worn, wooden desk he had now inherited as SIO, he waited while the others seated themselves in the plastic chairs provided in front of him.

For a few moments he said nothing, but stared into space with a heavy frown, as if thinking about what he wanted to say. Then abruptly his gaze took in the three detectives facing him and he leaned forward, hairy meat-hooks resting on the desktop, with the fingers splayed.

'From the briefing I've received from the DI here,' he said in a rough London accent, 'it seems a connection has been established between the two jobs — the remains buried at Pagan's Clump, which may or may not belong to this dosser, Annie something or other, and the murder of Lizzie Johnson.'

No one said anything and he stared at each face in turn with raised eyebrows. 'Well, is that it or not?'

Ricketts gave a little cough. 'It's what I — we — believe to be the case, sir,' he replied. 'DI Woo and myself, that is. It's based on the quite exhaustive inquiries I initiated and the forensic evidence that was recovered at the scene of the Lizzie Johnson murder as a result. This might have escaped attention had my suspicions not been aroused — suspicions that were later backed up by the post-mortem examination, of course.'

Kate stared at him in astonishment. The gall of the man, when all along he had done his level best to poo-poo every suggestion she had come up with and "cuff" — or shut-down — everything he could. Lightly shaking her head, she couldn't hold back on the cynical smirk she directed at the floor.

Her reaction didn't go unnoticed by Wilson and he shook his head with apparent impatience, though Kate could tell he was deliberately winding Ricketts up by putting him on the spot. Punishment for the way he had treated Purewal perhaps, she thought.

'Yeah, that's all very well,' he said, 'but it doesn't answer my question. What I want clarified is how the connection between Johnson's death and the remains found at Pagan's Clump was made. What's your take on things, Sergeant Lewis? I believe much of what has been uncovered so far is down to you?'

Ricketts couldn't let that go. 'That's not quite true, sir,' he blurted. 'The fact is, Sergeant Lewis is merely one of the team and she has only recently returned to her role here after a year away on a sabbatical. She is still, er, finding her feet and—'

'I would nevertheless like to hear what she has to say,' Wilson cut in, the stare he directed at Ricketts one of barely concealed contempt. 'So, Sergeant, what have you got to tell me?'

Casting a guilty glance at Charlie Woo, Kate unloaded everything and in a moment she had a captive audience.

* * *

Predictably, Ricketts was the first one to speak when Kate had finished what she had to say, and his face registered outrage.

'Do you mean to tell us that you have been carrying out your own private investigation into this affair all this time without any reference to anyone of senior rank?' he exclaimed hotly and turned slightly to throw a critical glance at the DI. 'Did you know about all this, Inspector Woo?'

Kate spared the DI any embarrassment by cutting in quickly. 'I was initially following up inquiries into Lizzie Johnson's alleged suicide,' she replied, 'but I then came across some things I wasn't happy with, which led to extending those inquiries into other areas. I didn't go looking for links to the Pagan's Clump investigation. They found me.'

Ricketts snorted. 'What absolute balderdash,' he said, forgetting in his furious tirade that he was dangerously close to accusations of overbearing conduct. 'So, not content with failing to investigate the Johnson case properly, you compounded your negligence by resorting to your usual practice of renegade behaviour.' He took a breath. 'And on top of it all, you actually carried out a totally unlawful search of this clergyman's bedroom without a warrant. You do realise that the evidence you obtained this way, linking him to Johnson, would be inadmissible in a court of law, don't you?'

Wilson, who had been sitting there, quietly listening to his outburst, cleared his throat loudly.

'This is getting us nowhere, Mr Ricketts,' he said. 'While the sergeant here may have sailed a lot closer to the wind than she should have done, I think we have to accept that at least she has managed to unearth more information on this complicated business than anyone else.'

For a second Ricketts looked lost for words. Then shaking his head angrily, he said, 'This has to be a discipline matter, sir. She has done this sort of thing once too often.'

Wilson grimaced. 'Enough, Mr Ricketts!' he snapped. 'This is neither the time nor the place to be openly discussing another officer's professional conduct. Furthermore, in case it has escaped your notice, I am currently heading a potential double murder investigation that is devouring time, resources and money every day. Lots of it! I have no interest in the process of dotting of is and crossing of ts. I am into results, and it seems to me that Sergeant Lewis is our best chance of getting them.'

Turning his hard, uncompromising stare on Kate, he said, 'So, Sergeant, you stand bollocked. Don't do it again. Agreed?'

Kate tried not to look at Ricketts, but out of the corner of her eye she saw that he looked about ready to implode. 'Yes, sir,' she said.

'Good. Now, what about these four former friends of Lizzie Johnson? You've said you've interviewed two of them and suspect they know a lot more about what happened to Lizzie Johnson than they have admitted. What about the other two?'

'DC Purewal and I were on our way to see one of them — a man named Danny Aldridge — when we were called back here.'

Wilson glanced at his watch. 'Fancy putting in a bit more time to try and see him? I know it's getting late in the evening but it's probably the best time to catch your man at home if he's working during the day.'

Kate nodded. 'I'm sure DC Purewal would be up for that, sir,' she said.

'Excellent. Shake the truth out of him if you have to . . .' Wilson coughed again. 'I'm, er, speaking metaphorically, of course.'

Kate permitted herself a little smile. 'He'll be metaphorically shaken *and* stirred, sir,' she replied, putting on her best James Bond.

Wilson stood up, pushing his chair back. 'Then there's nothing left to discuss, is there?' he said. 'Let me know how you get on.'

Purewal was still angry over her peremptory dismissal by the DCI and Kate found her in the Ladies' hiding behind a dense cloud of cigarette smoke and coughing loudly.

'I didn't think you smoked,' Kate said.

'I don't!' Purewal replied. 'I borrowed one from Danny Ferris, as he was going off.'

'How do you fancy staying on for a bit?' Kate asked.

'Why should I?'

'We'd be off to interview Danny Aldridge — detective super's ask — and it will annoy Mr Ricketts if we do it.'

Purewal strolled across to a cubicle to drop the still smoking butt down the toilet.

'That's reason enough for me,' she replied with a tight smile. 'But it will also cost you a burger from the chip shop on the way.'

Kate frowned. 'I bought you a snack earlier.'

'You can afford it.'
'What sort of burger?'
'Something like a Big Mac.'
'That's a bit greedy.'
'I'm a growing girl and I need my vittles.'

Giving her thin, shapely figure the once-over, Kate treated her to a faint smile. 'And there was me thinking you were living on air,' she said enviously.

CHAPTER 19

Danny Aldridge was drunk and that was far from unusual. In fact, in the last few days he had been out of it by early afternoon. He couldn't remember when he had last checked in at his office in Wedmore and he'd left most of the routine day-to-day running of his failing estate agency to his long-suffering secretary and the only sales representative the firm had, who had been in post for about three months and looked twelve years old. Aldridge knew he had ruined the business, blaming market forces instead of his alcoholism for all that had happened, and in his sober moments he did feel guilty as to what his late father would have said if he'd still been there to see what was happening. But instead of doing something to solve the problem, he took refuge in the nearest available bottle and conveniently forgot about it.

He had been vaguely aware of the repeated ringing of his mobile in the afternoon when Julian Grey had been trying to contact him in a panic about the visit of the police, but he rarely bothered to answer phone calls, digital or otherwise, and this time he had not been in a fit enough state to comprehend what the sound actually was. So, he simply ignored it and allowed himself to sink back into the safe, comforting darkness of his inebriated stupor.

When he finally awoke, it was early evening, and the uncurtained windows of his living room were black, moonless squares streaked with the familiar tendrils of white mist that often drifted in off the surrounding marshes at night. Hauling himself to his feet, he had managed to switch on the light and stumble to the downstairs toilet to be violently sick when he heard the strange tapping on the frosted window pane. At first, he was far too absorbed in "talking into the white telephone" to pay much attention to the sounds, but as his retching and stomach convulsions grew less and less, and the tapping on the window became sharper and more insistent, he found himself left with no alternative but to investigate.

Holding his throbbing head on with one hand, he returned unsteadily to the living room, flicked on the outside security lights and peered with one eye through the full-length, glass patio doors — only to stagger back again with a cry of shock as a nightmare figure suddenly lunged out of the mist now choking the patio and crashed into the glass, shaking the whole door violently within its double-glazed steel frame.

The old, bent woman was dressed in a long, dark coat and shawl and clutched a walking stick in one hand. Her hideous, leering face, with its large, hooked nose and thin, twisted lips, was reminiscent of some horrific storybook witch, and her expression radiated pure malice, as she pressed her wrinkled flesh against the glass.

As Aldridge's horrified gaze locked on to the frightening visitant, he found almost instant sobriety, and he shrank slowly back from the patio, feeling behind him for the hall door in a desperate attempt to get out of the room and find somewhere to hide. But deep down, he knew that there was no escape. The nemesis that had been waiting for him in the shadows for thirty years had finally come for him and there was nothing he could do about it.

* * *

The mist that Kate had previously referred to as the detectives were leaving Jennifer Talbot's home had thickened considerably by the time they left the police station and joined the main road to Glastonbury. It reduced visibility to a point that made driving a real challenge, despite the powerful dipped halogen headlights and twin fog lamps with which the car was equipped. Leaning forward as close as possible to the windscreen, Kate peered intently into the clouds of drifting nothingness in an effort to catch even the slightest glimpse of the road. At the same time she tried to ignore the false breaks and the mirage-like shapes that repeatedly formed, vanished and reformed again within the curling white skeins, seemingly in an effort to confuse and mislead.

Indrani Purewal sitting tensely beside her had the front passenger window down and her eyes were glued to what she could see of the roadside and the treacherous rhynes and bogs, which she knew lay in wait feet away.

To their relief, the mist thinned appreciably when they got to the outskirts of Glastonbury, at which point the satnav took them off the main road into a narrower lane. Though visibility was still poor, they were at least able to spot the hazy outlines of hedgerows and drystone walls and, more importantly, the willow-lined bank of the rhyne that bordered their left-hand side all the way along.

Malacca House, as Aldridge's place was apparently called, turned out to be directly in front of them, on the far side of a T junction they were approaching — or, as the satnav described it, "two hundred yards ahead" — but they had no trouble spotting the place well in advance. The glowing red bud had appeared suddenly in front of them, as if to guide them in, and as they stared at it, it increased rapidly in size and intensity, like a giant rose throwing open its petals to celebrate its beauty to the world. But there was nothing beautiful about this particular "rose". As a pair of tall, stone pillars materialised in the car's headlights on the far side of the T junction, the rose seemed to erupt into a massive boiling glare within the pillars that seemed to dissolve the mist before it and reach far up into the night sky like a giant Olympic torch, accompanied by a series of massive explosions.

Malacca House was ablaze . . .

* * *

The long driveway to the house was like a tunnel formed by overhanging trees and Kate drove straight between the pillars without slackening speed, the inferno into which they were heading burning off the mist as it reached out for them with curling, fiery fingers. Dense clouds of noxious black smoke, lit up from within like some glowing paranormal essence, had already begun to exit the blazing building through some of the windows and part of the roof and the crackle of blazing timbers, punctuated by the "crack" of breaking glass, could be heard well before they got to the building itself.

Then the car had skidded to a halt on the forecourt in a shower of gravel. Grabbing torches from the back seat, the detectives threw open their doors without a second's thought for their own safety and raced towards the front door of the house, Kate shouting into her radio for fire and ambulance support as she ran. But the heat that met them was already intense. They immediately found themselves recoiling from it, coughing up their insides on the smoke that quickly enveloped them, as they struggled on, with burning, streaming eyes that prevented them seeing much of anything.

One thing that did stand out in the beams of their torches, however, was the silver-coloured Mercedes car parked a few yards away. 'We need to get inside,' Kate shouted. 'Chances are Aldridge is probably still in there.'

The front door was of the heavy, solid oak kind that no doubt harked back to the Victorian era, which they later learned was when the house had been built, and it was locked or bolted on the inside, denying anything but battering-ram access.

'I'll try the back,' Purewal volunteered close to Kate's ear. 'There must be another door.'

Then, turning on her heel, she displayed her superior fitness by taking off like a deer, in spite of the choking fumes, vanishing into the smoke within seconds.

A tile from the roof narrowly missed Kate's head as she went after her and there was no sign of her colleague when she stumbled upon the open gateway at the side of the house, which seemed to lead to the rear of the premises. Wooden rose arches loomed at regular intervals along a paved path, and she felt several vicious stabs on her face and hands from the still prominent thorns on the dormant climbers before she reached the end — only to find Purewal had completely disappeared.

The fire looked to be confined more to the other side of the house, a visible part of which was encased in scaffolding, and the mist around her was rapidly thinning under the radiating heat, as the clouds of black smoke obliterated more and more of the huge, rambling building. A few feet back from where she stood, the swirling white tide was now steadily retreating across a wide expanse of lawn, but it was still impossible to see the further extremities of the property. Peering into the murk, she thought for a moment that she saw a dark figure moving away from her and, thinking it was her colleague, yet wondering where she was going, she called out loudly, 'Indi?'

But there was no response and the next second the figure broke up into fragments and vanished. Obviously, another trick of the mist . . .

A few feet further on along the path, she spotted an open door — the last thing that was needed, as open doors only added oxygen to a fire, helping it to spread. But the damage was done, and she stumbled towards it, forcing herself into the smoke which was now pouring out through the opening.

She nearly tripped over Purewal. The detective was lying just inside what seemed to be a kitchen. She bent over her and heard her groan, 'Bastard hit me.' But there was no time for explanations. Grabbing her by her coat collar, she literally dragged her across the tiled floor and back out through the door. Then unexpectedly, strong hands were reaching down to help her, and a flashlight was blazing in her face. Several uniformed figures were gathered by the door, and a voice barked at her urgently, 'Get yourself out of here, love. The whole place is going up.'

As Purewal was physically taken from her by a couple of burly figures and hauled away to safety, her colleague's weak voice drifted back to her. 'Ran off across lawn . . .'

That information was enough for Kate. After what had happened to her friend and colleague, she was driven by a reckless determination to lay hands on the perpetrator at any cost, and she immediately swung towards a short flight of steps leading up on to the lawn.

The grass was soft, wet and springy and she felt her shoes sinking into it like a sponge the moment she plunged into the gloom, slowing her down and turning her feet to ice inside her sodden shoes.

Had she thought about what she was doing, she would have recognised the futility of it. The chances of finding whoever had attacked Purewal were virtually nil in the thick, smoke-tainted mist, even if she was in fact heading in the right direction. But Kate had always been impulsive and hanging back and considering the options first — as cool, logical-thinking Hayden would have done — was not her way. Something had to be done and whatever the likelihood of success and the possible risks involved, she was hell-bent on doing it.

She reached a line of trees, which seemed to mark the edge of a strip of wider woodland and, after a moment's hesitation, she pushed through, finding herself deep in rotting, clinging vegetation and trees dripping with moisture. Her passage disturbed something — she thought it might have been a bat — which skimmed her hair, as it flashed over her head, and a short distance away, the cry of an owl announced its presence with a loud, unearthly screech.

She stopped for a moment to listen. But a heavy silence now greeted her, as if the wood were holding its breath, and within the smoky gloom the phantasmal creatures produced by the mist seemed to crowd around her with a persistent curiosity in the course of changing from one grotesque shape to another.

She shivered and swept her torch around her in a half-circle, but the beam merely seemed to bounce back at her, as if warded away by an invisible entity. Feeling resigned to the fact that she had lost her quarry, she was about to turn round and head back out of the wood, when she heard furtive movement, seemingly coming from somewhere over to her right.

She swung round, peering intently along the beam of her torch, but her smarting eyes saw nothing but shifting white vapour, which parted briefly to reveal the sentinel-like boughs of the trees, before closing up again.

'Who's there?' she snapped, trying to control the tremor in her voice.

There was no reply, but she thought she detected the sound of heavy breathing close by, followed almost immediately by a series of grunts.

Gripping the torch more tightly in her hand, she pushed into the undergrowth in that direction, her heart pounding and her skin pricking unpleasantly. Then suddenly the hunched figure was there, right in front of her, rising up out of the undergrowth with a vicious snarl, its claw-like hands reaching out for her, like some spectral abomination.

With an involuntary gasp of shock, she staggered backwards, almost losing her balance in the process. But even as she steeled herself against the attack that she felt sure was coming, her assailant simply fell to their knees in front of her, as if giving up on the whole thing. Then in the naked blaze of the torch, she saw why. Their legs and the lower part of the long dark coat they were wearing had become hopelessly entangled in a lethal mix of brambles and stands of fencing wire, which they had plainly walked into in the gloom.

Kate had had no real preconceptions as to what sort of villain she would be facing were she ever to catch up with them. She had learned a long time ago that criminals came in all types, shapes and sizes. But she would not have been surprised to find her quarry was some brutish, opportunist thug armed with a knife or a psychotic, sexual pervert who got off on the thrill of torching buildings. But in fact, this one was neither. Instead, the hideous pox-ridden face with its tiny, gleaming eyes and large, hooked nose, which leered malevolently at her from under a lop-sided shawl, might easily have stepped out of the pages of a nightmare fairytale: the archetypal witch of ancient myth and fevered imagination that haunted childhood dreams and provided the writers of gothic fiction with an endless supply of scary material. Kate didn't need to be told that she was face to face with none other than Lizzie Johnson's "terrifying" visitant — the so-called Night Hag!

'Well, I'll be damned!' she said grimly. 'If it isn't the Wicked Witch of the South-West. Now, if I were to free you from those nasty thorns, Esmerelda, would I get a magical wish, do you think — like in the storybooks?'

'Get me out of this,' the Reverend Arthur Taylor snarled, tearing off the rubber mask and talon-like witches' gloves he was wearing, 'I'm cut to pieces, and I've also twisted my gammy leg.'

Kate tutted as she pulled out her radio. 'Not much going for you at the moment, Reverend, is there?' she mocked. 'Looks like Lucifer, your real master, has abandoned you and cluttered off back to his fire pit.'

* * *

Two uniformed police officers quickly located Kate after her radio call for assistance. They turned out to be the same two officers — part of the neighbourhood policing team sent to the scene as backup by the control room — who had grabbed Purewal off her after she had dragged her injured colleague from the smoke-filled kitchen. This time they had come equipped with strong wire cutters provided by the fire service commander and it took them no more than fifteen minutes, working by torchlight in the gloom, to free Taylor from the clutches of the tangle of brambles and old fencing wire.

The mammoth blaze was close to being extinguished under the force of the firefighters' powerful hoses by the time they all returned to the front of the building, and they found two newly arrived ambulances, parked there, facing down the driveway with their doors open. Complaining vociferously about lacerations to his arms, hands and legs, coupled with the alleged damage to an old gammy ankle injury, Taylor demanded to be taken to hospital for treatment and was promptly whisked away in one of the ambulances under police escort.

Kate didn't even watch him go. She didn't really care if he bled to death. In her book, it was what he deserved after what he had done. More importantly, she had spotted Indrani Purewal in the back of the second ambulance, and she ran over to her as they were closing the doors.

The once pretty young woman was lying on a stretcher, and she was barely conscious. In the glare of the interior light, she looked dreadful. There was a large, bloodied wound to one side of her head, closing her eye and reducing the area around it to a mauve-red mess. A paramedic was in the process of treating her, and the detective's face was drawn and almost corpse-like.

'She'll be fine,' the paramedic reassured. 'Wound will mend, but she's likely suffering from concussion, so we need to get her to the hospital to be checked out.'

Purewal's sound eye suddenly flickered open. 'Sorry, Kate,' she said in a soft, slurred voice over the paramedic's shoulder. 'Need new partner now . . .'

'Don't you worry about that,' Kate replied. 'Get yourself sorted. Did you see who attacked you?'

Purewal managed a weak, rueful smile. 'No . . . All a blur . . . Got clobbered with something hard . . . Couldn't see what.'

'Well, it looks like we've got him now anyway,' Kate said. 'And it's all down to you.'

But Purewal said nothing further. Her sound eye was already closing and almost immediately she lost consciousness completely.

Moments later Kate watched the ambulance gently pull away, heading back up the driveway, and she muttered a quick prayer for her plucky colleague as the vehicle's flashing beacon faded into the mist like the gyrating blue light of Dr Who's Tardis.

A big BMW saloon 4x4 drove on to the forecourt minutes later and she was almost immediately joined by Jack Wilson and Charlie Woo.

'Hi, Kate,' Woo greeted. 'Bit of a rough do, eh? Hear Indrani copped a nasty one. How is she?'

She grimaced. 'Not brilliant. She's already en route to hospital with a nasty head wound and, according to the paramedic, probably suffering concussion from whatever she was hit with. I hope she'll be okay, but only time will tell.'

His face hardened. 'And I gather your damned priest was responsible?'

Kate ran the palms of both hands up and down her face a couple of times in a weary gesture. 'I don't know. Indi couldn't ID her assailant and although I have the walking stick he was using, it doesn't appear to have any blood on it. I frisked him when I nicked him, and he wasn't carrying any other weapon—'

'He could have chucked it.'

'Agreed, and we won't be able to carry out a proper search of the grounds until the morning — that's *if* the mist lifts. As for Taylor himself, he's en route to hospital as well, complaining about leg injuries. So, it'll be a while before he can be interviewed.'

Wilson grunted. 'That can't come soon enough as far as I'm concerned. What about this man, Danny Aldridge, you came here to see. Has he been located yet?'

She shook her head and gnawed her lip for a second. 'It's possible that that's Aldridge's Merc over there, which would suggest he could have been at home when the place went up. But the fire service won't be able to get into the house to check the place over until it's safe for them to do so. Could be some time yet.'

Wilson grunted. 'Well, we can get an ANPR check done on the Merc right away to see if the motor is registered to him. But for the rest of it, it's got to be a waiting game. So, it looks like being a long night.'

In fact, as it turned out, the night was not as long as Wilson had predicted, and a fire service team wearing breathing apparatus went into the gutted building an hour later. But the search they carried out brought no satisfaction. Twenty minutes after that, partially cremated human remains were located in the part of the building that had been enclosed by the scaffolding. When Kate and her senior colleagues were finally given the okay to enter the building themselves, it was with a sense of grim resignation, and they left again after viewing a blackened, contorted cadaver, that was still ripe and displaying some erupting internal organs, with the horrific image indelibly imprinted on their memories.

'Well, ANPR check says the Merc was definitely registered to Aldridge,' Woo said, looking badly shaken. 'So, I would say it's ninety-nine-percent certain that the stiff is our man.'

'And yet another bloody murder for the books,' Wilson finished. 'Let's hope that, with your arrest of the "drag queen" priest, Sergeant, it will be the last.'

Kate nodded, but deep inside her, that familiar little worm of doubt was once more beginning to stir uneasily.

CHAPTER 20

It was after midnight when Kate got home. She had only left the crime scene because she had been ordered to do so by Jack Wilson. Both he and Charlie Woo had seen how tired and fraught she was after all that had happened, and it was apparent that she was no good to them in that state. 'I want you bright and bushy-tailed tomorrow,' Wilson had said, 'so that you are on top form for the interview of your cross-dressing vicar when he comes out of hospital. DI Woo and myself will handle things here from now on. So go home, get a bloody shower — and go to bed.'

That was exactly what Kate intended doing when she pulled up in the driveway of her cottage in Burtle village. But seeing the lights were on in the living room, she guessed Hayden was still up and would no doubt be burning with questions, which she would have to answer.

In fact, as it turned out, he wasn't burning with anything. Exactly the opposite. He was slumped in his armchair by the extinct fire with his mouth hanging open, fast asleep. An empty wine bottle was standing on the hearth beside him, and the wine glass that was held loosely between his curled fingers had tilted over, spilling its contents into his lap and creating a haemorrhage-like stain.

She shook her head, for some irrational reason, irritated by the sight of him sitting there asleep in the chair after all she had been through, and carefully prised the glass free before setting it on the coffee table. Then, leaning close to his ear, she shouted with a sudden burst of malicious energy, 'Chair's on fire!'

Hayden erupted from the seat like a rocket, knocking over the bottle and nearly pitching over the coffee table.

Regaining his balance with difficulty, he stood there for a moment, swaying unsteadily, and scowling at her, his face flushed and angry. 'I suppose you think that was funny,' he snapped, plainly unimpressed.

'A bit,' she replied coldly.

He studied her smoke-grimed face and dirty, matted hair. 'Well, you don't look so brilliant yourself,' he said. 'What time is it?'

'A little after midnight.'

'Midnight?' he echoed, turning his head quickly to look at the grandfather clock in the corner. 'What the hell have you been up to until this time? You look as though you've been dragged through a hedge backwards.'

'Glad you noticed,' she snapped back, now even more irritated by the fact that he seemed more interested in how she looked than what might have happened to her. 'I can see why you're a bloody detective.'

His scowl deepened. 'Well, you're too late for a nightcap anyway,' he declared with obvious satisfaction. 'I've already finished the last bottle of red.'

'So I see,' she retorted, determined to have the last word. 'Most of it in your lap by the look of it.'

At once the dinner and emotional closeness they had enjoyed together the previous Sunday was forgotten and, in the ups and downs of their tempestuous relationship, it was back to the usual bickering and sniping.

He glanced down quickly at his trousers and winced, then abruptly dropped back into his chair, as if to hide the stained cushions from her.

'Bit–bit of an accident, that's all,' he muttered in embarrassment. 'Fell asleep . . .'

But she was too tired to care, or to continue the unnecessary squabbling that she had started. Dumping her coat over the arm of the settee, she threw herself on to it and kicked off her shoes, drawing her feet up under her.

'Indrani Purewal was attacked tonight,' she said soberly, running both hands through her hair.

His jaw dropped. 'Indi?' he exclaimed, his mood abruptly changing.

'She's in hospital,' Kate went on, 'suffering from concussion and a nasty head wound.'

'Good Lord. Will she be okay? I mean, how on earth did that happen?'

Kate yawned, realising how tired she was. 'Get me a double scotch and I might manage to keep awake long enough to tell you,' she said.

Twenty minutes later, with the single malt coursing through her like molten lava, Kate told him everything, and he didn't ask a single question — essentially because she was fast asleep almost as soon as she finished.

* * *

Hayden must have put her to bed. Carried her upstairs and dumped her under the sheets, still dirty and reeking of smoke. She awoke after a deep, dreamless sleep at seven thirty to the smell of a fry-up, which drew even closer as Hayden walked into the bedroom carrying a tray laden with bacon, eggs, fried bread and a mug of steaming hot coffee.

'You've been on the news,' he announced. 'BBC. Well, not you in person, of course, but a story about your fire and the suspect murder of the local estate agent, "who cannot be named until formal identification has been carried out".'

'That'll be a bit of a job,' Kate retorted, wriggling up into a sitting position with her back against the pillows. 'There wasn't a lot left of him . . . Oh, thanks for the breakfast, by the way. Nice thought . . . Sorry about my shitty behaviour last night.'

He looked her over critically, then sniffed. 'All forgotten. I was as bad. But without wishing to be rude, I'm afraid to say you smell like an expired bonfire, so I think a shower should be next on your agenda, with the bedclothes consigned to the dirty linen basket.'

She grinned. 'You say the sweetest things, Hayd,' she complimented through a mouthful of bacon.

He half turned for the door, then stopped again when she called out after him, 'Oh, by the way, did you enjoy the stimulating read I left on your desk?'

He gave her an old-fashioned look, and said sarcastically, 'Oh, that huge wad of *War and Peace* you brought back from Lizzie Johnson's place, you mean? Loved every minute of wading through it. Nice to see you were thinking of me.'

'You know you're always in my thoughts, Hayd,' she chuckled.

He grunted. 'Yeah, well, I was a bit curious as to what you expected me to find, especially as I didn't know what I was supposed to be looking for. Anyway, most of the stuff consisted of "love letters" to and from some accountancy firm from what I could see.'

'Love letters?'

'Yeah. Mostly statements. Fascinating stuff if you're suffering from insomnia. All about some long-term tontine investment she and a few others had taken out, which seemed to be earning them all quite a bit of dosh on interest.'

'Tontine? What the hell's that when it's at home?'

'I haven't a clue. I majored in philosophy and ancient history during my time at uni. Finance was never my bag.'

'Didn't you think of looking it up?'

'I didn't see a relevance between Night Hags, things that go bump in the night and financial investments,' he said pompously. 'Funny, that.'

'Well, perhaps you'll find the time to do it when we go in later?' she said acidly.

He smirked. 'I'll do my best to fit it into my busy work schedule.'

She chose to ignore the quip. 'And you found nothing else?'

'Only some divorce papers, including settlement details, and a couple of recent press cuttings about the discovery of the bones dug up at Pagan's Clump.'

'Pagan's Clump?'

'Yeah, with a handwritten note pinned to them, saying the one word, *Annie*, followed by three exclamation marks.'

'Is that right? So, more evidence of a connection between Lizzie Johnson and our pile of bones. I think we are getting very close to some answers now.'

He made a grimace. 'Maybe *we* are. But before you jump for joy, I suggest you finish your breakfast and head for the shower before you stink the whole place out.'

* * *

Charlie Woo was sitting drinking coffee in his office when Kate arrived at work with Hayden a couple of hours later. Kate was relieved to see that the DI was on his own and, in particular, that DCI Ricketts was nowhere to be seen, which had to be a plus. Hopefully it would stay that way, she mused, walking briskly towards the glass-panelled inner sanctum and leaving Hayden to return to his desk.

'Sleep well?' Woo asked her, as she walked in and sat down in front of his desk.

'As a log,' she replied. 'Any news on Indi?'

A shadow passed over his face. ''Fraid so,' he said. 'Dunno what she was hit with, but she's evidently had a brain bleed and they're operating on her as we speak.'

Kate felt sick. 'God help her!' she breathed.

He made a face. 'Hopefully, she'll pull through okay. Hospital said they would ring me when they knew more.'

He took a deep breath. 'Thing is, with Indi, er, off the inquiry for the immediate future, you will need a new partner, as Mr Wilson is apparently very keen on you staying on the team—'

'Hayden,' she cut in quickly. 'He was in at the start, so it's only right he should come back in. He's been fully briefed on everything.'

He nodded slowly. 'I thought you'd say that.'

'So, what's happening with Taylor?' she went on abruptly. 'Is he still in hospital?'

He shook his head. 'Discharged this morning. Cuts and bruises and a bandage round his gammy ankle, which they say he sprained. Not much sympathy for him, I have to say. The guv'nor has the interview set up for ten. He'll join us downstairs in interview room one then.'

'Solicitor?'

He shrugged. 'He doesn't want one. Says he's innocent and the Lord knows it, which is the only thing that matters. All he seemed concerned about when Uniform collected him from the hospital was the whereabouts of his bloody car, which we found incidentally parked in a lay-by behind the property.'

'Anything of interest in the car to connect him to the fire?'

He shook his head. 'Remarkably clean. Fire service investigators do suspect that the fire was started deliberately with some form of accelerant, but it's early stages in the investigation, and samples they have taken from what they believe was the seat of the fire will have to be sent for lab analysis to confirm the fact one way or another and determine what sort of substance may have been used. They also believe that it started in the part of the house supported by the scaffolding. They say the place was obviously under some sort of renovation and the remains of gas bottles and other containers of flammable materials were found inside, some of which had exploded, adding to the speed and ferocity of the blaze.'

Kate nodded, remembering the explosions she had heard on their approach to the burning building.

'Any trace of the sort of weapon that could have been used on Indi?'

'Nothing. Loads of debris and some smoke damage in the kitchen, but nothing like that. We've got matey's walking stick, but it carries no obvious traces of what could be blood, only mud from his fall in the wood. It's also a fairly light, old-fashioned walking stick with a crook for a handle. Not the sort of thing that would have caused Indi's injuries, though we'll get it checked out forensically anyway of course.'

'So, we have nothing to positively tie Taylor to the blaze?'

'Not really, no. But he was found close to the scene and evidently ran away when the house went up. He was hardly paying a social visit either dressed as a witch and wearing a rubber mask and fake "witches" hands with nice long nails.'

Kate looked dubious. 'But what we have is still way out on the very edge of circumstantial, isn't it?'

He scoffed. 'Oh, come on, Kate, you going soft in your old age? Why the hell was he out there in the dark, miles from anywhere, if not to burn the house down? There can be no other rational explanation.'

She chewed her lip for a second. 'The thing is, if you were intending to kill someone by setting fire to their house, would you go to all the trouble of dressing up in Hallowe'en costume beforehand? It would be far more likely you would do that if you were there to frighten them, rather than burn them alive.'

'Well, maybe he didn't intend to kill anyone, but to set fire to the first house he came across and that he got off on the witch bit? Heaven knows, we've both seen enough crazies with weird, perverted fetishes like that since we've been doing this job.'

'Maybe, but I don't see him as someone in that category. I think he was there for an entirely different purpose.'

'What purpose?'

'I've no idea.'

He glanced at his watch and stood up. 'Well, you'll get to ask him in about twenty minutes, but before you do, you might want to see this.'

He picked up the newspaper he had been looking at and tossed it into her lap.

'Seems your favourite reporter has been at it again,' he said. 'Front page of several of the nationals are evidently carrying her handiwork this morning. This is the local rag version. Spooky stories obviously attract readers.'

Kate raised her eyebrows at the headline shouting at her from the front page of the *Bridgwater Clarion*:

Resurrection At Pagan's Clump.

She made a disparaging snort. 'The bitch didn't forget her old rag after all then,' she commented bitterly.

As she read on, the litany of dramatic phrases in the piece jumped out at her.

Ancient superstition of Night Hag stalker . . . Murder from the grave . . . Witch woman, Annie, on the loose . . . One innocent victim. How many more? . . . Panic in surrounding villages . . . Fears of possible serial killer? Keystone Cops baffled, as usual . . . Pity we can't bring in Sherlock Holmes . . .

'What a cow,' Kate said. 'Talk about poetic licence.'

'Certainly hasn't done us any favours,' he agreed. 'ACC Ops has already been on to the guv'nor about it, and understandably, Mr Wilson's not a happy bunny at the moment. In fact, you could say he's more than keen on getting this business done and dusted as quickly as possible, now we have Taylor in custody.' He stared at her. 'A word to the wise . . . It might not be the best time to suggest to him that we might have the wrong man!'

CHAPTER 21

The Reverend Taylor looked white-faced and dishevelled in the chair behind the interview room table. He was dressed in a long white coat provided by the scenes-of-crime department. His own clothes had been seized to be examined for anything of evidential significance linking him directly to the fire or the assault on Indrani Purewal. He gave Kate a weary, helpless look when she followed Detective Superintendent Wilson into the room, as if, incredibly, he actually imagined after all that had happened that there might be some sort of affinity between the two of them.

At the short pre-interview briefing, Wilson had set out his strategy and said he would lead on things, but Kate was to come in whenever she thought it was appropriate. Not really knowing the man or his style of approach, Kate felt more than a little trepidation over how that would play out, but she decided she could only give it her best shot and hope it worked out.

As it was, Wilson jumped straight in as soon as the tape recorder had been switched on and the formal legal preliminaries and personal introductions had been completed.

Reminding the churchman he was under caution, Wilson asked, 'Reverend Taylor, may I call you Arthur?'

'Of course. That's my name,' Taylor replied sullenly.

'You know why you were arrested and why we are interviewing you today, don't you, Arthur?'

'I have sinned,' Taylor muttered.

'How do you mean you have sinned?'

'I took it upon myself to inflict punishment on some wayward souls for their wrongdoing, which was arrogant and against the very Christian teachings I had once upheld.'

'Was one of those wrongdoers Danny Aldridge?'

'Yes.'

'And Lizzie Johnson?'

He nodded and looked genuinely regretful. 'Poor Lizzie too.'

'Well, I have to tell you that, following the fire at Malacca House, a body has been found at the scene, which we believe may be that of Danny Aldridge.'

Taylor closed his eyes tightly for a second and tried to make the sign of the cross with both cuffed hands.

'May his soul find peace,' he said.

Wilson ignored his response. 'So, are you saying you killed them both?' he asked.

If the detective had been expecting the quick confession he was seeking, he was disappointed. Taylor had been staring dolefully down at the desktop, but his head now shot up and he stared at him in horror. '*Killed* them?' he almost choked, and he half rose in his chair, causing the uniformed constable sitting in the corner to tense in his seat. 'I didn't kill them. I haven't killed anyone. I am a man of God.'

Wilson didn't move a muscle. 'Sit down, Reverend,' he said calmly, and waited until the priest had slumped back in his seat before resuming. 'You told us a minute ago that you took it on yourself to punish them. How did you intend doing that if not by killing them?'

'By–by frightening them, of course—'

'What, you mean dressing up in a Hallowe'en costume and doing a trick-or-treat routine? You don't seriously expect us to believe that, do you? Lizzie Johnson and Danny

Aldridge weren't impressionable tiny tots, they were adults in their fifties.'

'But–but it's the truth. I wanted to make them understand the dreadful sin they had committed and to confess to what they had done for their own salvation.'

'I thought it says in the Bible that vengeance is the province of God?'

Taylor looked down at the table. 'So it does, but sometimes the Lord needs a little help.'

'And what was it these people had done?' Kate found herself asking quietly. 'What was this dreadful sin you're talking about.'

He turned towards her, almost eagerly. 'Killing Annie, of course — Annie Evans. They knocked her down, then buried her body at Pagan's Clump so no one would find out.'

Wilson stiffened and leaned forward in his seat. 'How do you know that?'

'Because I saw them there after it must have happened. It was thirty-odd years ago, but I still remember it as if it were today.'

'I think you had better explain,' Kate said.

Taylor took a deep, trembling breath. 'There were five of them,' he went on. 'A close-knit little group of what you might call "Hooray Henrys and Henriettas". Privileged young people with rich, influential parents who all lived locally. The parents were respectable enough, but weak and over-protective towards their children, letting them do more or less what they liked. The youngsters were well-known for their wild parties, heavy drinking and drug-taking.'

'Go on.'

'I had been out one night with my verger to a local public house near Pagan's Clump, sorting out arrangements for the funeral of the licensee's mother, when they turned up already under the influence, celebrating leaving university and taking out some sort of big investment. The licensee promptly sent them packing and I thought that was the last we would see of them. But when we left, we came across them again, stopped on the side of the road at Pagan's Clump. It was obvious that they had lost control of their car and we stopped to see if anyone was hurt. My verger was in the front passenger seat, as I was driving, and he asked them if anyone was hurt. But they insisted they were okay, blaming a fox, which they said had run out in front of them.'

He shook his head dismally. 'I–I thought no more about it until I heard of those human remains being found at Pagan's Clump the other day and, remembering the incident all those years ago, I put two and two together.'

'So why would you necessarily assume that the accident involving these five youngsters and the body that had been buried at Pagan's Clump were connected?' Kate persisted. 'After all, thirty years is a long time ago and anything could have happened during that period.'

He nodded again. 'Then thing is, the tin shack in which Annie was then living, now long gone, of course, was in the woods at Pagan's Clump, so the fact that that accident had happened there struck me as much too much of a coincidence, and inevitably, I began to suspect the youngster's car had not hit a fox at all, but the unfortunate old woman, whom I knew had habitually walked the lanes collecting fallen branches for her fire from the verges.'

'Which prompted you to make your complaint about the bogus burglary so you could pump me for information,' Kate cut in.

He nodded again. 'Very deceitful of me and I can only apologise,' he replied, 'but you see, I needed to know whether my suspicions were justified.'

'And when you heard about the anklet being found in the grave, with the name *Annie* engraved on it, you believed they were and decided to punish those responsible by killing each one in turn,' Wilson accused sharply.

'That's not true,' Taylor shouted, thumping the table with the palm of his hand and literally bursting into tears. 'I'm innocent, I tell you. Aldridge was–was alive when I got there yesterday and–and when he saw me through the patio doors he–he ran back into the house. I never saw him again and it was as I was leaving and heading across the lawn to get to my car that the house suddenly caught fire behind me—'

'What "whoosh", like that?' Wilson mocked.

'Yes,' Taylor retorted, wiping away his tears awkwardly with the back of one cuffed hand. 'Just like that!'

'Was that before or after you hit Detective Constable Purewal across the head? You do know she's in a critical condition in hospital, don't you?'

'No, I didn't. But I didn't hit her. I had nothing to do with any of it and I wasn't even aware that it had happened until now.'

'And you saw no one else in the vicinity of the house while you were there?' Kate asked.

He shook his head. 'Not until you found me after I had fallen over in the wood.'

'And what about Lizzie Johnson?' Wilson came in again. 'I understand you have accepted that a cufflink found on the track behind her house following her death was one of yours?'

'Yes, I have already admitted to Sergeant Lewis that it is one of mine. I must have dropped it during one of my welfare visits to Lizzie.'

'Welfare or murder, Reverend, that's the issue here.'

'There *is* no issue as far as I am concerned, Superintendent. As I told Sergeant Lewis before, Lizzie was in a fragile mental state and she asked for my spiritual guidance, as a result of which I carried out an exorcism of her house for her as a favour.'

'Why did she approach you instead of the current parish priest?'

'A few weeks ago, I ran a sort of two-day seminar at the church hall about spiritualism and the evil of Satanism. Lizzie came along and took part in a rather passive, back-room way and afterwards she asked me to go and see her to give her some advice, which I did.'

'Bit hypocritical doing that at the same time as you were trying to put the fear of God into her, wasn't it? Not much Christianity there, was there?'

Kate saw Taylor's hands clench inside the handcuffs, but he didn't lose control this time. It was apparent to Kate that Wilson was deliberately trying to wind him up even more than he had already, as a means of getting to the truth, but the priest seemed to have cottoned on to the tactic now and was plainly not going to bite anymore.

'I have already admitted my sinful behaviour in trying to frighten her into a confession, as I did with Danny Aldridge, Superintendent,' he replied. 'I will also admit to doing the same thing to another of the group, Jennifer Talbot, and I had fully intended repeating the performance in due course with the remaining two, Julian Grey and Robert Chalmers. But whatever sins I have committed, they did not include murdering Danny Aldridge or Lizzie Johnson, and the last time I saw Lizzie was in the early hours of the Friday preceding the weekend in which she died, which was when I carried out the very first of the three manifestations I have performed so far.'

'And how did you do that?' Kate asked.

Shame was written all over his pale face and he stared down at the tabletop again. 'Lizzie had told me she kept a spare key to the back door under a mat outside and I used that to enter the house and frighten her, dressed as an old crone. But she barricaded herself in her bedroom, so, before I left, I showed myself on her balcony and scrawled the word *Murderer* on the glass door.'

'Rather childish behaviour, wasn't it?'

'Don't you think I don't know that? I'm disgusted with myself.'

'So, where were you on the weekend she died?' Wilson continued.

'At home, doing some gardening.'

'Can anyone verify that.'

'I'm afraid not.'

'So, you could easily have nipped over to her house, done the deed, and returned home without anyone being the wiser.'

'If I knew exactly what the "deed" was, yes, perhaps I could, but I didn't, any more than I set fire to Danny Aldridges's house.'

Having found a new confidence, Taylor went one stage further. 'Now, can you tell me whether you are going to charge me with something or not? I would rather like to go home and get some proper clothes on.'

* * *

'Well,' Wilson asked Kate over coffee in his office, 'that was a bloody waste of time. The only thing we seem to have got out of that interview is the surname of the woman, Annie — if that *is* legit, of course.' He stared at her fixedly. 'So, what did you think of our only suspect? A good actor and an accomplished liar or simply a misunderstood pain in the arse?'

Kate frowned. 'I don't think he was lying, sir. I believe he was telling the truth. I have to say that I don't see him as a cold-blooded killer either.'

She expected an immediate, angry put-down after what Charlie Woo had said earlier, but instead, he screwed up his face in what seemed like an expression of frustration.

'I have to agree with you,' he said and, reaching into his jacket pocket, he produced a silver-coloured hip flask and tipped some of the contents into his coffee.

Kate shook her head when he placed the flask on the desk in front of her, and he retrieved it with an understanding smile and returned it to his pocket.

'So, what now?' he growled. 'That's the point.'

Kate pursed her lips for a few seconds. 'Well, sir, in my opinion we haven't got enough to charge him with anything.'

'Right, then talk to me.'

'Well, it's beyond doubt that he was in the vicinity of Malacca House when the fire broke out and it's almost certain the fire service will ultimately confirm that the fire was down to arson, but I checked his custody record on the way in. He wasn't carrying so much as a box of matches on him, his car was clean and unless Forensics find Indrani Purewal's blood or traces of some sort of accelerant on his clothing, we can't actually tie him into the fire. Furthermore, as I said to the DI earlier, if you were going to kill someone, it's hardly likely that you would go to the extent of dressing up in a Hallowe'en costume beforehand, is it? What would be the point? But if you were out to frighten them, as Taylor claimed, the fact that he was dressed as a witch to fit the part would make perfect sense.

'As for Lizzie Johnson's murder, we did find one of his cufflinks on the track behind her house. But as well as going there to, as he put it, "frighten her into a confession", he freely admits he visited the place otherwise at her invitation, and also carried out an exorcism on the premises for her. So, the fact that he was in the house is not in dispute, and it proves nothing in so far as her murder is concerned. True, he has no alibi for the night she was killed, but with respect, I don't have to tell you that the onus is on us to prove he committed the crime, not the other way about.'

He gave a crooked, humourless grin. 'Thanks for setting me right on the legal issues, Sergeant,' he said with lightly delivered sarcasm. 'But yes, I agree, that at this stage we have absolutely nothing for CPS to get their teeth into, except maybe a case of wasting police time or a very thin public nuisance offence. Which means we have no option but to grant him police bail in the vague hope that Forensics will turn up something in the meantime that will link him to one or both the murders.'

'And if they don't, sir?' Kate said quietly.

He drained his coffee and stood up. 'Then we are up shit creek without a paddle, if you'll pardon the expression.'

Kate shook her head. 'Not necessarily, sir,' she said. 'There is another possibility worth exploring.'

He stared at her quizzically. 'Which is?'

'That these murders have nothing to do with Pagan's Clump or Annie Evans, but something else a lot deeper.'

'What "something else"?'

'I don't know yet, but my gut tells me we've been on the wrong track from the start and that we need to widen our perspectives.'

He nodded slowly. 'Then I suggest you get stuck into that PDQ, Sergeant, and give me some reassurance that my fast-approaching retirement pension is still secure.'

CHAPTER 22

'How'd it go?' Charlie Woo asked when Kate returned to CID from the incident room.

She shook her head. 'Not good. We've got the wrong man.'

He raised an eyebrow. 'You didn't tell the guv'nor that?'

'I didn't have to. He agreed with me. Looks like we'll have to release Taylor on police bail.'

'Where does that leave us?'

'In schtook and looking for someone else.'

'So back to square one?'

'Not entirely. Mr Wilson has agreed for me to pursue some inquiries of my own.'

'Heaven help us!'

She grinned. 'If you're going to be rude, I shan't tell you anything.'

He gave a faint smile back, but there was the same shadow she had noticed before lurking behind it.

She sensed the reason. 'Any news on Indi?'

He made a face. 'Hospital rang. They said she lapsed into a coma after her op.'

'A coma? Bloody hell!' Kate closed her eyes tightly for a second. 'How could that be? She got a nasty bang on the head. But—'

'Apparently, she has an abnormally thin skull, and the blow did more damage than would be the case with most people. We can only wait and pray that she comes through it, but things are not looking good.'

Kate could feel tears beginning to form and quickly turned away from him, savagely wiping them with the back of one hand. She cleared her throat and glanced around the empty general office. 'Have you seen Hayden?' she asked in a voice that did not sound like her own.

Charlie Woo tried to sound cheerful. 'I'll let you guess on the probabilities,' he said.

Kate found him in the canteen, wrapped around a plate of pie and chips.

'Have you done what you said you'd do?' she demanded.

'Er, no,' he said, through a mouthful of pie, 'but it's in hand.'

'What do you mean "in hand"?' she practically snarled, still thinking about Indrani Purewal. 'You mean you haven't done anything, but you still have time to come down here and fill your gob.'

'Well, it *is* lunchtime and I have to have something inside me.'

The contempt on her face made him flinch. 'Is that all you can say? You're a total waste of a skin! I'm sorry I ever met you.'

Still brimming with tears, she turned away from him and marched back out of the canteen.

Her harsh reprimand evidently got to him, for he abandoned his dinner — probably the first time he had done that in living memory — and lumbered after her, catching up with her at the bottom of the stairs and grabbing her arm.

'You didn't mean that, Kate, did you?' he pleaded. 'Please, you didn't mean that?'

She tried to pull away, but he was too strong and holding her too tightly. In the end, she simply buried her face into his stained shirt and sobbed her heart away. A couple of uniformed policemen were coming through the door to the foyer and Hayden quickly steered her into the empty office of the local intelligence officer to save her embarrassment.

He waited until her sobs had died away, then raised her face to his and kissed her. 'Indi, is it?' he asked gently, guessing what had prompted her emotional outburst. 'I did hear.'

She nodded. 'It's all my fault, Hayd,' she whispered. 'I should never have allowed her to go to the back of that house on her own.'

'Now, you listen,' he said sternly, 'she's a copper, like you and me. We all take risks, that's what the job is about. You forget, I ended up in a similar state when I was clocked over the head by someone a few years ago, and you've had enough injuries yourself. Remember when you were shut in that car boot at the breaker's yard, shortly before the car was due to be dumped into the crusher? The only people to be blamed for what happens to us are the scum we have to deal with. Now get a grip before you go outside. I'm sorry I let you down — again. I know I'm a lazy slob, but I will do something about that from now on, and that's a promise.'

He hesitated. 'Er, you didn't really mean what you said, did you, about wishing you had never met me?'

She smiled weakly up at him, her eyes still glistening. Then she said mischievously, 'Only about you being a total waste of a skin, fat man.'

He frowned. 'I say, that's not a lot better. Especially after I saved you this.'

He delved into his pocket and handed her a twin packet of Mars Bars.

'Thanks,' she said, wiping her eyes with a handkerchief. 'I'll eat them on the way.'

'On the way? What do you mean?'

'We've got someone to see.'

'Oh?' he replied. 'What's happened then?'

'I'll tell you in the car.'

'And, er, where exactly are we going?'

'How about a nice trip to Bristol?'

* * *

Robert Chalmers lived in an upmarket area of Clifton, outside Bristol city. The balcony of his newly and tastefully renovated flat — or apartment, as he preferred to call it — overlooked a leafy square from the very top of the building and the double-glazing ensured he enjoyed a good night's sleep, despite the noise from the revellers who roamed the area after clubbing and partying well into the early hours. Greenleaf Mansions suited Chalmers admirably. It was as close as he wanted to be to the centre of Bristol and conveniently situated within a short drive of the huge monolithic premises of the IT company he worked for, where he was a junior board member. Like the other four members of the tight little group of friends he had belonged to since primary school days, he had done well in his life — mainly because of his now deceased parents whose money had bought friends and influence and had enabled him to build on that solid base after their deaths.

Now sitting on his balcony, waiting for the visitor he was expecting, he stared unseeing into the fragile sunlight of another winter's day. A large Havana cigar sprouted from one hand, its smoke curling round his head and into the living room behind him, as he thought about his life and his friends, and pondered dismally on the news he had received on his mobile from Julian Grey.

Danny Aldridge dead? Burned to death in a fire at his house? It didn't seem possible. He had only been speaking to him on the telephone the day before. Okay, so Danny had sounded depressed, as he had told Julian afterwards, and his slurred, at times unintelligible, speech had indicated he was drunk. But that hadn't been unusual. Danny was frequently drunk, and he was also depressed over the decline of his estate agency business. But surely, he hadn't topped himself? And what a horrible way to do it. Then he remembered Lizzie Johnson. They'd all thought she had committed suicide at first, hadn't they? But it had turned out to be murder. Maybe Danny's death was the same. Maybe someone had gone in there, slugged him and set his place alight for good measure.

But why? Who hated them enough to do something like that?

He drew more heavily on his cigar and went into a brief coughing fit, as he thought of the old vagrant woman, Annie Evans. Surely there couldn't be anything in Lizzie's claim that she was being stalked by some vengeful ghost? It was impossible. Those things were only products of fiction books by people like Stephen King and Dean Koontz, or horror films on the big screen. They didn't exist in real life. Start thinking otherwise, old son, he mused, and you'll end up in the funny farm. But what about Jenny Talbot? You couldn't get anyone more level-headed and cynical than Jenny Talbot, and yet she had told them all about the ugly old crone who had materialised in the school grounds, waving her stick at her — and someone had certainly scrawled the word *Murderer* on Lizzie's patio door and on Jenny's car windscreen. He'd seen it with his own eyes.

Wandering to the balcony wall and peering down into the street, he tried to expel thoughts of supernatural entities from his mind. *Total rubbish*, he told himself. *Only a bloody idiot would believe in something like that*. No, all this wasn't the work of a ghost, but someone of flesh and blood. Someone who was out to punish all of them for the death of Annie Evans all those years ago and that was the only possible answer. Yeah, but if that was the case, it was even more scary.

He shivered, feeling suddenly very cold. Then glancing at his watch, he frowned. The visitor he was expecting was late by twenty minutes, which was annoying, as he had taken the rest of the day off specifically to see them. Probably the damned traffic, as usual. But even as that thought occurred to him, there was a buzz from the steel box on the wall by his front door, which was connected to the communal access control system on the main street door. Lodging his cigar in an ashtray on the chair arm, he got up and went to answer it.

* * *

The satnav took Kate and Hayden straight to the apartment block in the square without a hitch and they were able to park the CID car a couple of spaces down from the gleaming brass sign on the wall, which bore the snooty name *Greenleaf Mansions*. There was a smart oblong plate on the inside wall of the porch, also made of highly polished brass, which carried an array of numbered call buttons, obviously wired to each of the twenty or so apartments. Hayden peered at it and made a face, before stepping back to the edge of the kerb, and shading his eyes with one hand to peer up at the top of the building.

'Lucky us,' he commented. 'Chalmers lives on the top floor. I jolly well hope there's a lift.'

Kate grinned. 'A posh place like this, Hayd?' she said. 'It would be a bit off if it didn't have one. But anyway, a nice climb would do you a power of good.'

'Give me a coronary,' he retorted as she pressed the button labelled *Apartment 20*.

There was a brief delay and then a voice Kate recognised as that of Robert Chalmers snapped, 'Yes? Who is it?'

'Police, Mr Chalmers,' Kate announced. 'Can we have a few words, please?'

'What about? I'm busy.'

'It won't take long, Mr Chalmers.'

'Okay, you'd better come up,' he sighed, and the big glass front door buzzed.

They found themselves in an expensive-looking lobby, with oak-panelled walls hung with gilt-framed paintings and a tiled floor. There was an internal door with a central glass panel to their left in the corner, no doubt giving access to the ground-floor apartments, and a lift with double doors adjacent to a stone staircase to their right.

Kate had her finger on the button to the top floor when the blood-curdling scream came, apparently from directly outside the building, followed by shouting and pounding feet.

'What the hell . . . ?' Kate began and, swinging round, raced back out the main door to the street, with Hayden puffing along behind her.

A crowd had collected to the right-hand side of the building and a young woman was crouched over on the kerb, vomiting into the gutter, while an elderly man was cuddling an older woman whose face was buried in his chest, sobbing.

The cause was clearly visible. The man in the dark suit was lying face down in the middle of the road, where a taxi had slammed to a halt only feet from where he lay. At first Kate assumed there had been a road accident, but seeing a young couple standing a few yards away pointing up to the top of the Greenleaf Mansions tower block, the horrific realisation dawned on her.

Pushing her way through the knot of onlookers which had now gathered out of ghoulish interest, she bent over the prostrate body. She knew even as she approached it that the man was dead. He couldn't have been otherwise. One leg was bent right under him, an outflung arm had been partially torn off at the shoulder and his head was a bloodied, crushed mess, leaking a large pool of fluids, fragments of bone and what she recognised as whitish brain matter on to the tarmac.

Identification was virtually impossible, but Kate knew without being told who the dead man was. It was Robert Chalmers.

* * *

Straightening up, Kate held her warrant card out in front of the crowd. 'Police,' she said loudly above the hubbub. 'Back off, all of you. *NOW.*'

Someone appeared with a plastic sheet from somewhere and laid it over the corpse, and, as the crowd started to drift away, a thin, bespectacled man blurted in her ear, 'He jumped. I saw him suddenly fall.' He pointed up towards the top of Greenleaf Mansions. 'From up there.'

Kate pushed past him, another thought in her mind. 'Stay here and get witnesses' details,' she shouted at Hayden, as the distant sound of approaching sirens became audible. 'I've got to get up there. I'm probably already too late.'

'No way,' he threw back, sensing the reason. 'You don't know who's up there.'

'Do it!' she retorted. Then she was gone, streaking across the pavement and back into the lobby of Greenleaf Mansions, where an elderly woman, seemingly one of the residents, was standing just inside, with a small dog in her arms, holding the door open as she peered out.

'Police,' Kate rapped at her. 'Have you seen anyone come out of here?'

The woman looked pale and shocked, her mouth hanging open. She shook her head as if she was in a world of her own. Kate didn't bother to explain, but headed straight for the stairs.

She had hauled herself up perhaps six or seven of them when she heard the hollow "tap, tap, tap" of rapidly moving footsteps coming from below her. She swore as understanding dawned. In her reckless haste, she had not noticed that there were also stairs going down. There was a basement, and someone was heading down there at almost a gallop.

Stumbling back to the lobby, she turned left and took the descending stairs two at a time. Seconds later, she burst through a door at the bottom and found herself in a large, poorly lit underground car park, with several vehicles already parked there in numbered bays. The quick "tap, tap, tap" of footsteps, was magnified considerably within the concrete walls, but it was difficult to determine where the sounds were coming from. As she stopped for a moment, panting heavily, she tried to decide which direction to take, when she heard the footsteps suddenly stop and a heavy door slam. Whoever it was, they were now back outside on the street! She took a chance and headed left between two concrete pillars. She spotted the big, metal vehicle door right away. It was on the far side of the car park, with an illuminated sign above it bearing the word *EXIT*. The door was closed, but she recognised it as one of the automatic kind, which could only be operated by an infra-red key fob. But a few feet to one side of it, there was another much smaller pedestrian door, with the illuminated words *EMERGENCY EXIT* above it.

She knew it would be open when she reached it and she was right. The bar across the centre of the door had been pushed down and she could see daylight beyond. She stumbled through into a cul-de-sac, with a high wall to her right, sealing off the street and the automatic exit door to her left. Beyond the door, the cul-de-sac was walled on both sides and obviously connected to the main road at the front of the building. It was totally deserted. Whoever had been fleeing from Greenleaf Mansions had made good their escape.

Returning to the lobby, she saw through the front door of the building, which had now been wedged open, that there were two marked patrol cars directly outside in the street, blue lights still flashing. There was also an ambulance parked in the middle of the road, blocking it and her view of the corpse, which she guessed was still lying there.

'And who are you?' The rough voice spoke from right behind her. She hadn't heard the "ding" of the lift arriving, but he must have emerged from it.

She turned to face a short, muscular-looking man, with a droopy moustache and cold grey eyes, dressed in a black leather jacket and blue jeans. She flashed her warrant card.

He grunted, sounding slightly hostile. 'Highbridge CID, eh?' he said and introduced himself round a wad of gum. 'DS Harvey Wilcox, Bristol CID. And what might you be doing in *our* neck of the woods then, Sergeant Lewis?'

'Well, we were intending to have a chat with Robert Chalmers in connection with a double murder case we are investigating, but unfortunately, he seems to have taken a dive out of his apartment on the top floor.'

He gave a low whistle. 'That him out there?'

Kate smiled wryly. 'Bit difficult to say in his present state.'

He gave an understanding nod. 'Yeah. See your point. Jumper, d'ye reckon?'

'Difficult to say. All I know is that he fell from his apartment as we arrived. He could have committed suicide, accidentally fallen off his balcony or, er, even been pushed.'

He showed immediate interest. 'Pushed? By who?'

Kate was tempted to tell him about the person she had chased out of the building but decided against it. She had no evidence of anything and the last thing she needed was to get tied up in the investigation of what was now a Bristol case.

'No idea. I was listing the possibilities.'

He relaxed. 'My money's on a jumper, unless we turn something else up.'

She shrugged. 'Mind if I take a look around his apartment?'

'Why? You're not holding out on me, are you?'

'Not at all. Curious, that's all.'

'Then be my guest, and I shouldn't need to tell you not to touch anything.'

Kate gave a tight smile. 'No, you're quite right, you *don't* have to tell me that.'

Hayden joined her in the lobby as she and Wilcox were waiting for the lift, and further introductions were completed on the way up.

The door of Apartment 20 was wide open, and a uniformed policewoman was standing to one side of it. Wilcox led the way through a small hall into a plush, extravagantly furnished living room with double glass doors to a balcony on the far side. There was a deep-pile, blue carpet on the floor and what appeared to be original modern art paintings on the walls.

A woman in plainclothes was standing on the balcony, peering over the wall down into the street. Wilcox introduced her as Detective Constable Shu Chang, then explained who they were and why they were there.

'No sign of a struggle or anything to suggest foul play, that I can see,' Chang remarked.

'As I said to our two colleagues here,' Wilcox said, 'my money's on a jumper.'

Kate's gaze roved slowly around the room. 'Posh place,' she observed. 'Obviously a bit of money here. So why would Chalmers commit suicide?'

Chang turned her lips down in a deprecatory gesture. 'Why does anyone top themselves?' she replied. 'Perhaps his apparent wealth was superficial, and he had money troubles, or his wife had walked out on him—'

'He wasn't married. Divorced.'

'Well then, perhaps that had something to do with it. You know, things got on top of him, so over he went.'

Kate treated her to a cynical smile. 'Maybe you're right,' she agreed, her tone of voice expressing the opposite. 'And admittedly, the wall is not very high. I'm surprised the planning authorities accepted it. But it would still be a bit difficult to fall over it accidentally.'

She left the balcony and followed Hayden as he trundled round the room, casting a perceptive eye over everything.

'Two glasses,' he said suddenly.

'What do you mean?' Wilcox asked.

He pointed to a tray on an ornately carved wooden coffee table, then walked over to it and bent down to sniff one of the glasses. 'Scotch, I would think.'

'So?'

'*So*, it looks like Chalmers had company.' He wandered over to a sideboard standing against one wall and pointed again, this time at a tantalus, with its three cut-glass decanters standing at one end.

'From there obviously,' he added. 'Which suggests someone was in here moments before he went over the balcony.'

'Why moments before?' Wilcox queried. 'Those glasses could have been left there for several hours, days even.'

Hayden waved an arm around the room. 'Does Chalmers look like the sort of person who would leave unwashed glasses like that even for minutes, let alone hours or days? The apartment is spotless. Cushions plumped up, curtain tiebacks neatly in place, everywhere spick and span. I had a peep in the bedroom over there and the ensuite bathroom, and it's the same story. Bed neatly made, all clothes folded up and put away in the fitted wardrobe, shower spotless and smelling of some kind of lemon cleanser. Et cetera, et cetera. No, Chalmers had a visitor all right, and further evidence of this is in the ashtray out on the balcony and the smell of cigar smoke in here.'

'What do you mean about evidence in the ashtray. There's a cigar there all right, which he had obviously stubbed out, but that doesn't prove anything.'

'No? Well, if you look closely, you will see it's a large, expensive Havana cigar that is only half finished, and it's still smoking faintly. What smoker would stub out an expensive half-finished cigar and the next moment suddenly take it into his head to jump off his balcony and end it all? Doesn't seem logical somehow. My guess is, he stubbed it out when his visitor rang his apartment from down in the porch, found out who they were, then let them in. Which means he knew them. That's why he had a drink with them when they came up.'

'Go on, *Sherlock*,' Wilcox said.

Hayden grinned, obviously enjoying himself. 'But the visitor was spooked when we arrived, rang his apartment from downstairs, then announced who we were. So, they quickly gulped down their whisky, did the deed and scarpered while we were examining his body in the street.'

Chang gave him a slow handclap. 'All very Agatha Christie,' she said drily. 'But not a shred of evidence to back it up. All you've got is schoolboy supposition.'

Kate scowled. Chang was getting right up her nose. 'I think you should know that we are currently investigating the deaths of two of Chalmer's friends on our manor,' she said, 'both of which we believe to have been homicides. This one could be the third and, like the others, clumsily made to look like either an accident or suicide.'

Wilcox's eyes widened and his DC stood there, tight-lipped and obviously embarrassed.

'So,' Kate said, turning for the door, 'I suggest you get your SOCO team and the forensic pathologist here asap, to make sure you dot all the right i's and cross all the right t's. Oh, and it might be a good idea for your DCI to liaise with our SIO in the incident room at Highbridge nick when he has a moment!'

CHAPTER 23

Something had happened. Kate sensed it immediately she and Hayden walked back into Highbridge police station. There was a strange, tense atmosphere and colleagues they passed on their way in through the back door from the rear yard and then on the stairs to CID, looked away without a word, as if they were guilty of something. There was no one in their department, so they made their way up to the incident room, and it was only when they walked in and saw the stoney-faced teams sitting silently at their desks that Kate had an awful premonition.

Charlie Woo was with Jack Wilson in the SIO's office, and both looked up quickly in the middle of a low-voiced conversation when they saw them.

'What is it?' Kate asked as she entered the office. 'It's like a morgue in the nick this afternoon.'

Wilson threw a quick glance at Woo before he said anything, but deep down, Kate knew even before he came out with it.

'It's Indrani,' he said, the voice of the big, tough detective almost breaking up. 'The hospital rang . . . I'm afraid she didn't make it. She passed away an hour ago from a suspected embolism!'

Kate would have hit the floor as her legs gave way beneath her had Hayden not been behind her to grab her, and he steered her, sobbing and shaking, to the nearest chair.

'There was nothing they could do, Kate,' Woo said quietly. 'It happened so suddenly while she was in a coma. They've, er, sent their sincere regrets.'

Wilson produced his hip flask and, rightly or wrongly in her present state, he motioned to Hayden to pass it to her, with the little cup removed and in his other hand. This time she took it and drank straight from the flask. Then very gently Hayden prised the flask from her fingers and returned it to Wilson.

'Let it all out, sweetheart,' Hayden said close to her ear, his big paws on her shoulders. 'There's no hurry.'

For a long few minutes Kate sat there, her body racked with sobs, and no one said a word. Then, wiping her streaming, red-rimmed eyes on both sleeves, she reached for a handkerchief and blew her nose violently, before raising her head to stare directly at Wilson.

'This was my fault,' she whispered. 'I should have stopped her. She died because of me—'

'Balls!' Wilson responded unequivocally. 'She died because she was a courageous, no-holds-barred police officer, who was determined to do her duty, and, like so many others before her, lost her life because of it. This tragedy had nothing to do with you, Sergeant. This was down to Sod's Law and an evil, no-account scumbag we shall very soon put behind bars.

'Now, if you feel up to it, I want you to bring me up to speed on the incident at Clifton. I've already had a DCI Rumbold from Bristol on the blower, so I think I'm pretty well in the picture, but it would help to hear the facts from you and Hayden.'

He paused a second, then studied her narrowly. 'After that, Hayden can take you home and I'll see you both again in the morning, once you've had a good night's sleep.'

It was the second time in less than twenty-four hours that Kate had been ordered home to bed and her response was immediate and defiant. 'There is no way I'm butting out on things now, guv,' she said. 'I owe it to Indi to find the swine responsible for her death, and that's exactly what I am going to do.'

Wilson's expression was hard and uncompromising. 'You will *do* as you are told, Sergeant,' he said. 'You're no good to me as you are. I want you sharp and clear-headed for the job that has to be done, which means first getting your head down for a good night's sleep. Capisce?'

Kate opened her mouth to protest, but she was up against a brick wall.

'This is not a request,' Wilson said. 'It's an order and if you refuse to comply, I will have no option but to take you off the case altogether. So, what's it to be?'

Kate knew that there was only one possible answer she could give . . .

* * *

Sleep did not come easily to Kate that night, even after a hot shower and the light pasta meal Hayden prepared for her. She tossed and turned until the small hours, her mind plagued by nightmares in which she re-lived again and again a horrific, distorted version of the fire at Malacca House, and awoke, sweating and gasping for breath. Each dream was the same as the last. Her dead colleague appeared, walking away from her through thick, white mist towards a blazing light, deaf to her entreaties to turn back. Then suddenly she turned round with a hideous rictus grin, to reveal a massive hole in her head crawling with maggots, and pointed accusingly at Kate before vanishing into the ground.

Hayden was invariably a heavy sleeper, but her frenetic restlessness even awakened him, twice invoking irritable, unintelligible mutterings from him before he drifted off once more. Going by the clock on her bedside table, it was after three before she managed to sink into a deep, dreamless sleep and she was unaware of anything until she felt herself being firmly shaken by someone at what proved to be the unearthly hour of six in the morning.

She found Hayden standing by her bedside in his old-fashioned striped pyjamas, his mop of unruly blond hair like a wrecked haystack and his eyes shining with excitement.

She could hardly credit the sight. Unless he was on an early start, Hayden never got up before nine, and never before it was light if he could avoid it. Even then, it was always a struggle. He liked his "pit", as he called it, far too much.

'I think I have it,' he said to her, 'I really do.'

Shocked, but still half-asleep and bleary-eyed, she lay there for a few seconds, trying to comprehend what on earth could have got her husband out of bed at such an ungodly hour. Then, gradually coming round, she emitted a long groan, and slowly wriggled upright in the bed with her back against the pillows.

'What the hell are you doing up?' she asked in a slurred voice. 'War been declared?'

'Come downstairs,' he said. 'There's something I have to tell you.'

It took her a few minutes to rouse herself enough to drag her weary body out from under the sheets, and she immediately wished she hadn't when her waking brain reminded her with a knife-like stab to her gut of Indrani Purewal's tragic death and the fact that it was not simply a bad dream but cold, harsh reality.

Pulling on her dressing gown, she made her way slowly out of the room to the landing. She stumbled once on the steep, narrow stairs and Hayden rushed forward from the living room, fearing she would fall. But moments later she was dropping on to the settee and staring puzzledly at his laptop. It was open, and in standby mode, with an A5 pad of scribbled notes lying beside it.

Hayden sat down beside her and indicated the laptop with a wave of his hand. 'When you woke me up the second time last night,' he said, 'I couldn't get back to sleep, so eventually I came downstairs to do a bit of research on my laptop, and I think I've struck oil.'

Kate raised a hand to her throbbing head and pulled her dressing gown closer to her in the cold, unheated room. 'Hayd, will you please tell me what you're talking about,' she said, plainly irritated by his excitement.

'Tontines, old girl,' he enthused. 'Tontines, remember? You asked me to look up what they were after I found references to a tontine in Lizzie Johnson's bundle of papers. I have to say, I was surprised to find that there's quite a bit about them on the net.'

She sighed wearily. 'Tontines?' she exclaimed. 'You woke me to tell me about bloody tontines?'

'Yes, and it's fascinating stuff. For instance, I didn't realise that they originated in the seventeenth century and were named after a Neapolitan banker, Lorenzo di Tonti — Tonti, see? Tonti-ne? He's said to have invented the schemes, with a proposal to the French government, which was rejected, but the first tontine was actually started in the Netherlands and—'

'*STOP!*' Kate shouted, cutting him off in mid-stream. Her brain was swimming in a pool of confusion. Hayden had a clever analytical mind, but he was a typical academic, who got so carried away when researching something, that he often got distracted and lost sight of the kernel of what he was researching. Right at that moment she couldn't handle it.

'For pity's sake get to the bloody point, will you? It's now six twenty in the morning.'

He flushed. 'Oh, sorry. Well, the nub of it is that a tontine is a sort of mortality lottery, where a lump sum is paid into an investment scheme by a group of investors who are gambling on their longevity. Each receives incremental payouts during their lifetime and when an investor dies, his or her share is shared out among the rest, with the final survivor inheriting the lot.'

Kate frowned, curious in spite of her tired, depressed state. 'And if everyone dies before the end of the term, what then?'

'From what I can gather, the whole thing is simply wound up.'

'All a bit creepy, if you ask me.'

'Not if you become the sole surviving investor, it isn't,' he said, and his face was suddenly grim.

Kate fell in at once and she was now completely compos mentis, her eyes bright with understanding. 'But–but that could be the motive for all these killings,' she breathed. 'As we thought, Annie Evan's death all those years ago had nothing to do with it. These aren't revenge killings at all, but what you might call investment gains. Whoever is doing this stands to inherit everything.'

Hayden nodded. 'And unless there is another investor in this particular tontine that we know nothing about, only two now remain.'

'Which means one of those has to be the murderer—'

'Exactly, and one will shortly be the next victim — but which one?'

Kate snapped her fingers. 'Who set up this tontine scheme in the first place?'

'If I remember rightly from Lizzie Johnson's papers, the kingpin was Julian Grey. He's a financial adviser, isn't he? He would have known about things like that; how to do it legally and who to go through, moneywise.'

Kate whistled. 'It all adds up,' she exclaimed. 'This was probably his long-term plan from the start. Either that or he suddenly needed a large injection of cash and saw this as a way to get hold of it.'

She scrambled to her feet and stood there swaying unsteadily for a few seconds.

'And where the devil are *you* going?' Hayden asked sharply.

'To get dressed, you idiot,' she snapped. 'If we're right about all this, Jennifer Talbot could be in grave danger. We have to get to her before Grey does!'

He glanced at his watch. 'It's after seven. She's a headteacher, isn't she? She's probably already on her way to school.'

'Good point,' Kate agreed, and went across to the old-fashioned house telephone standing on a half-moon table by the stairs. 'We should ring the school first.' Then she stopped short with the telephone receiver in her hand. 'But we don't have the telephone number.'

Hayden snatched up his mobile from beside his laptop and his fingers were soon flying over the keys, searching the internet. A minute or so later he called the number out to her slowly, while she dialled. To her surprise, her call was answered immediately.

'Carla Jameson, school secretary?' a pleasant female voice said.

Kate quickly introduced herself. 'Is Miss Talbot in yet, please?' she asked. 'I need to speak to her. It's very important.'

'Sorry, Sergeant,' Jameson responded. 'But Miss Talbot has been off sick for the past two days. She suffers a lot from bad migraines. We're not expecting her back until tomorrow.'

Kate raised her eyes to the ceiling and tried not to let her frustration show in her voice. 'Thanks. I'll try her at home. I do have the number.'

'She may not answer. When she has one of her attacks, she usually heavily sedates herself. Er, can I help?'

'No, but thank you. I really do need to speak to her personally.'

'If she calls in, I'll tell her you rang—'

But Kate had ended the call even as she was speaking and was racing back up the stairs to the bedroom. Her pocketbook was on the dresser, and she thumbed through the pages to the notes she had made at the back, before dialling again on the extension phone by the bed. Grey's number rang and rang, but there was no reply.

'Get your skates on, Hayd,' she shouted through the open door, as she stripped off her dressing gown. 'We're gone in five.'

Fifteen minutes later, with Kate driving her new MX5 sports car, they left the house in a flurry of driveway gravel — much to Hayden's horror, forsaking breakfast and even coffee.

'We should get some backup,' he blurted above the roar of the engine, gripping the edges of his seat with both hands as she gunned the powerful little car along the straight out of the village.

'No way,' she replied. 'We have no proof of what we've come up with. It's a theory. We'd be hung out to dry if it transpired that we were barking up the wrong tree.'

He closed his eyes as she pulled out to overtake a farm tractor on the approach to a sharp bend, returning to their correct side of the road with only yards to spare between themselves and an oncoming, horn-blaring lorry.

'So, if it's only a theory, can we slow down a bit?' he asked anxiously.

Her face was set into an expression of grim determination. 'Theory or not, we still need to get there PDQ, in case we happen to be right,' she said. 'Let's pray we're not already too late.'

'Let's just pray we get there,' Hayden retorted.

* * *

Talbot's house was in darkness and it looked completely dead to the world. Kate approached the front door and rapped the wrought-iron knocker several times. 'Miss Talbot, it's Detective Sergeant Kate Lewis,' she shouted and stepped back to look up at the top windows when there was no response.

She felt her heart start to beat a little faster. 'She must be here,' she said. 'Especially if she's as ill as Carla Jameson said.'

'No sign of a car, though, is there? And no garage hiding one,' Hayden added helpfully.

Kate knocked again, harder this time. Still nothing.

Hayden vanished and returned a short time later shaking his head. 'Place is locked up at the back tighter than a duck's you know what,' he said. 'Perhaps the naughty headmistress is playing truant herself?'

Kate's mouth tightened. 'This isn't a joke, Hayd. Something could have happened to her — like the rest of her bloody friends.'

'I can't see Grey picking her off now, so close to his last hit. I mean, he must see how it would look with him as the last man standing.'

'Why? He already knew he'd blown it with Lizzie Johnson's bogus accident well before he murdered Danny Aldridge and Robert Chalmers, yet he still went ahead with their killings. Why would he hold back on wasting Jennifer Talbot now? It seems to me that he's a man in a hurry and he is fully aware of the fact that whatever we might suspect, we have absolutely no proof against him. So why not finish his business and walk away owning the total investment? He's probably already got some bolt-hole lined up in the Caribbean for him to retire to afterwards.'

Hayden ran a hand through his untidy thatch. 'Okay, you have a point, but how do we play it now? Knock on Grey's door and say, "Oh, hello, Mr Grey, can we check your house to see if you have a dead body knocking around anywhere?".'

Kate glared at him. 'Will you pack in the funnies, Hayd?' she snapped. 'I'm not in the mood.' She released her breath in a frustrated hiss and went on in a more conciliatory tone. 'Where the hell is she, Hayd? Not here, or at school. No car in evidence, even though she's supposed to be at home, laid up with a migraine. So where?'

'She could have gone to the chemist for more tablets — even to the doctor's — or maybe she felt better and has gone shopping.'

She snorted. 'You don't believe that any more than I do. We have to find her.'

He made a face. 'Well, I don't know how you propose doing that. As you've already said, we've checked the house and the school and there's nowhere else we know of. I hate to say it, but Julian Grey's *is* the only place left. That's if he's at home and not already out and about.'

Kate jerked her pocketbook from her coat and checked the back pages again. 'Only one way to find out,' she murmured, dialling another number.

She didn't expect an answer at that time in the morning from a commercial company and was surprised when a female voice answered.

'Oh, hello,' Kate said. 'My name is Laura Green. and I would like some advice on setting up a future investment portfolio. A colleague at work recommended that I speak to Mr Julian Grey. I know it's early in the morning, but—'

The woman cut her off at once with a haughty, dismissive response. 'Mr Grey is not expected in today. He is out visiting clients. He does not discuss financial matters over the telephone anyway. You would need to make an appointment to see him.'

'I understand,' Kate replied, quickly ending the call before the woman could ask her for personal details.

'Not expected in today, eh?' Hayden commented as Kate cut off. 'If that's true, and to be fair, you know how secretaries often tell porkies to protect their bosses from irritating timewasters like us, it does indicate a planned absence.'

Kate nodded. 'Which would suggest my suspicions might be justified.'

He sighed resignedly. 'Okay, so it seems it has to be Julian Grey's then. But if he does turn out to be there, aside from my earlier suggestion, which you didn't much like, what reason are you actually going to give for calling on him?'

'We could use Chalmer's death as a pretext. Such as, "thought you ought to know . . . as he was a personal friend of yours" and all that.'

'Cutting-edge stuff yet again from the ace gumshoe,' he said drily.

CHAPTER 24

Julian Grey's house seemed to be as dead as Talbot's and, like her cottage, there was no sign of a car there. Things didn't look very encouraging, and they didn't get any better either. Despite knocking repeatedly on the front door and playing with the bell, not so much as a rudely awakened mouse stirred inside the house.

'Last time I was here with Indi, there was a flashy-looking red Porsche and a green Morgan parked where we are,' Kate commented sourly.

'Maybe they're in a garage round the back,' Hayden suggested, pointing to a wide gap between the side of the house and the boundary hedge.

He was right about the garage. It looked like a new build and was constructed of red brick, with a pitched roof and a white UPVC electronic door, which was closed. It looked big enough to accommodate two and a half cars, but there was no way of checking exactly what, if anything, was parked inside. The only other access was via a small side door, which was secured by a business-like padlock.

'Bugger it!' Kate muttered. 'Now we have no way of telling whether he's out somewhere in his car or skulking around inside the house, refusing to answer the door.'

'We could always return to the nick, have breakfast, then come back,' Hayden suggested hopefully.

Kate threw him a dirty look. 'Sod breakfast, Hayd,' she said. 'This is important. We've got a possible murderer on the loose, plus a potential victim who has disappeared and, if not already dead, may be lying injured somewhere needing urgent medical treatment. So, forget your bloody stomach for once, will you?'

'Okay, okay, keep your hair on,' he replied sullenly. 'It was only a suggestion. But what *do* we do then? Hang around here in the hope that Grey materialises, or until we die of malnutrition?'

'No,' she snapped, '*you* do.'

'I do what?'

'You stay here to see if Grey pokes his nose outside the door or returns home in his car, while I head back to Talbot's to see what the state of the poll is there.'

'I say, that's not on. What am I supposed to do if Grey does reappear? We have nothing on him, as I've said before, and in case you hadn't noticed, we're on private property without a warrant.'

She shook her head irritably. 'You don't *do* anything. You find a place where you can conceal yourself — maybe behind the garage — and observe.' Rattled by his continued obstructive attitude, she resorted to sarcasm. 'You know what that means, don't you, Hayden? You watch and wait and if he appears, you ring me. Remember doing that sort of thing at potential crime scenes when you were a woodentop?'

He snorted. 'Damned stupid, if you ask me.'

'I'm *not* asking you,' she snapped back. Then she abruptly added wearily, 'Humour me, fat man, will you? Two ticks and I'll be back.'

Then she was behind the wheel of her MX5 and driving away.

* * *

There was a silver BMW parked in Talbot's driveway. Kate's heart jumped with a mixture of surprise and relief. Talbot was home. She was alive. The headteacher opened the front door to her even before she got to it.

'Ah, Sergeant Lewis,' she said with a fleeting smile. 'I saw you stopped outside and guessed you were coming to see me. Please come in.'

Kate followed her along the hall into her smart living room, accepting a motioned invitation to drop into the armchair she had occupied on her previous visit with Indrani Purewal.

'So, what can I do for you this time,' Talbot asked. She was smiling again, but there was a barely concealed irritation behind it that Kate immediately picked up on.

'Well, I did call earlier actually, but I could get no reply and when I rang the school, they told me you were off sick with a severe migraine.'

'Oh yes, that's quite right. I suffer a lot from migraine attacks, and I nipped out for some more painkillers from the chemist down the road. Haven't been back long actually.'

Kate made a sympathetic grimace. 'Yes, migraines can be awful. Feeling better now, though?'

'Oh yes, thank you. Probably be back at school tomorrow.'

I bet you will be, Kate mused, remembering Hayden's comment about the headteacher playing hooky. Miss Talbot was obviously up to something. She wondered whether she was seeing someone quietly on the firm's time, or simply needed a break.

'I'm afraid I am the bearer of rather bad news,' Kate went on.

Talbot nodded. 'You mean Danny Aldridge?'

Before Kate could answer, Talbot added, 'I heard it on the radio. When they said the fire was at a well-known estate agent's house near Glastonbury, I checked up and was told the dead man was believed to be Danny . . . Terrible.'

Kate shook her head. 'Well, actually I didn't come here to tell you about Danny,' she said. 'You see, there's been a further death. Your friend, Robert Chalmers died yesterday, allegedly as a result of an accident.'

Talbot's hand flew to her mouth and her eyes widened. 'Good grief, poor Bob. You're sure?'

'Positive, I'm afraid.'

'Excuse me.'

She jumped to her feet and, crossing the room to an old-fashioned sideboard, she selected one of three bottles from the top, unscrewed it, and poured herself a stiff measure of what looked like brandy before returning to her seat.

'Oh, I'm sorry,' she said, raising her glass towards Kate, 'how rude of me. Would you like—?'

Kate dismissed the offer with a quick wave of her hand. 'Thanks, no,' she said, giving a short laugh. 'Not on duty.'

'Oh, of course, I should have known. I don't usually drink during the day, but after this terrible news . . .' Then abruptly her jaw dropped as the realisation hit her. 'But hold on a minute, if Bob is dead, that means—'

'Yes,' Kate confirmed, reading her mind, 'three of your former group have all died within the space of a few days. Furthermore, we believe that *all three* were murdered. Only you and Julian Grey are still alive, which is why I am here.'

She leaned forward. 'You think we are in danger?'

'It's very possible. Have you any idea who might have had a grudge against you and your friends — something you did at some time in the past, for instance, that might have made them want to hurt you because of it?'

Talbot hesitated, but then shook her head. Plainly, she was not going to admit to knowing anything about the fatal car accident in which Annie Evans had been killed all those years ago. 'Nothing that I can think of, no.'

Kate accepted her answer with a couple of satisfied nods. She was not about to bring up the subject of Annie Evans herself. In the light of her current suspicions as to the more plausible motive for the killings, it had no bearing on the murders themselves and would only have confused things at a time when clarity was vital. Questions about the Pagan's Clump incident could be asked later.

Instead, she said, 'I understand that you and your four friends took out a financial investment together around thirty years ago, something called a tontine?'

There was a perceptible change in Talbot's manner and her eyes seemed to sharpen. 'That's true. But why are you asking about that?'

'We think it could have a bearing on the murders we are investigating.'

'Oh, er, right. Well, at the time, Jules — Julian — was in the process of starting up his financial adviser business, and he had come across this scheme through a contact. He thought it was a sound long-term investment opportunity for us all to sign up to. We had each received a large sum of money from our parents after graduating from uni, so we decided to go for it. He arranged everything through his firm's solicitor with a well-known international bank, and—' she shrugged —'that was it. Over the years we have all received regular — I suppose you would call them dividends, a bit like a group annuity — and it's been a nice source of income which seems to have kept on growing—'

'For as long as you live, that is,' Kate cut in. 'Some would actually call it a mortality lottery — a sort of financial gamble on living a long life.'

'What's wrong with that? You don't need it when you're dead, do you? The benefit is no good to you then.'

'No, but it *is* to whoever survives, because, as I understand it, the remaining investment transfers to the other members of the group in equal shares, and they get increased payouts as a result. The thing is, that where there are only two survivors left in such a scheme, that puts one of them in a vulnerable position, and you have to ask yourself how you feel about that.'

Talbot's eyes narrowed behind the blue-tinted spectacles. 'What are you suggesting? That Julian has been killing all of us to get hold of our shares of the money?'

Kate didn't answer. She simply stared at her and waited for the penny to drop.

It didn't take long. 'Is that really why you're here?' Talbot gasped. 'Because you think he's planning to kill me? The very idea is preposterous.'

'Have you seen him lately?' Kate asked quietly, without confirming or denying the assertion. 'I've just come from his place, and there doesn't appear to be anyone there.'

'He's probably in his office at work. He does have a business to run, you know.'

'He wasn't there when I rang. According to his secretary, he's out visiting clients.'

'There you are then.'

'If that really *is* what he is doing. In fact, he could be on his way here at this very moment . . .'

Talbot shook her head definitely several times. 'If he is, it wouldn't be to kill me, I assure you. He's far too gentle a man to be a cold-blooded killer. He doesn't have it in him — I should know. We've been friends for over thirty years.'

'People can change. Especially if money is involved.'

'Maybe they can, but I can't see Jules callously burning someone to death in their own home or tossing them off a high-rise balcony.'

Kate froze. 'How did you know Robert Chalmers fell from a high-rise balcony?' she said.

For the first time, Talbot seemed to falter. 'Well, you– you told me that's how he died.'

Kate shook her head. 'No, I didn't. I said he'd had an accident. I never said how it had happened?'

'Then I must have read it in the newspapers or heard it on the radio.'

'I wouldn't have thought so. As far as I know, the story hasn't broken publicly yet.'

The eyes behind the blue-tinted spectacles met Kate's gaze in a shocked, fixed stare and then the next instant, Jennifer Talbot's mouth suddenly twisted into an unpleasant, humourless grin. 'Sod it!' was all she said.

* * *

Hayden was bored. Standing about in what had developed into a very cold winter's afternoon was not his idea of enjoyment, coupled with which, he was so hungry that, as the phrase went, he could have eaten a scabby horse.

Finally, fed up with counting bricks in the garage wall, he left his hiding place to check out the back garden, which was accessed via a wrought-iron gate between the end of the garage and the wall of the house. It turned out to comprise around a quarter of an acre of neatly manicured lawn, sloping away from a walled patio between beds packed with evergreen shrubs to a line of trees marking the furthest boundary of the property. There was a cedar-wood shed in the left-hand corner and a very large pond in the right. All nicely balanced, but to Hayden's mind, a bit too formal.

For something to do, he followed a paved path which cut across the lawn through a series of rose arches to the pond, wondering if Grey's extravagant tastes stretched to heated water and exotic fish. As it transpired, Hayden never got the chance to find out. He had something a bit more serious to think about.

The man was lying face down and partially submerged in the middle of the pond, jammed between two big terracotta pots, with the patterned dressing gown he was wearing spread out around him like a deflated parachute. It was obvious he was dead even before Hayden managed to haul him to the side and manhandle him out on to the paved area at the rear of the gazebo, and it wasn't difficult to identify him. The name *Julian* was embroidered in fancy, gold-coloured lettering on the breast pocket of his dressing gown!

* * *

The tense silence which had settled on the room was broken only by the buzzing of Kate's mobile she had earlier set on "silent". It was now vibrating frantically against her thigh. But she made no attempt to answer it, and was relieved that, buried as it was in her trouser pocket under her thick coat, the sound was muted enough to escape Talbot's attention and risk spooking her. There was a very good reason for not wanting to spook her too. The tiny pistol she was now holding in one hand was pointing directly at Kate's chest.

How she had managed to get hold of it, then produce it seemingly from thin air had at first seemed like some miraculous sleight of hand, but in fact, it must have been tucked away in a drawer in the sideboard and, after making her excuse about needing a drink, perhaps sensing a possible impending problem, she had surreptitiously slipped it into the pocket of the short coat she was wearing. *A clever, dangerous cookie, this one*, Kate mused, *who was prepared for every eventuality and should not be underestimated.*

'Pretty little thing, isn't it?' Talbot said suddenly, picking up on Kate's stunned reaction to the production of the pistol. 'My late father got it for me on a business trip to the States when I was fifteen. He was worried about the rise in violent crime in the UK at the time and he wanted me to have some form of protection when I was out partying late at night. It's a Beretta Bobcat, what they call a pocket pistol, and it fits so nicely into one's evening bag. How he managed to smuggle it into the country, I have no idea, but though he did teach me how to shoot, I have never had much use for it — until now, that is. Ironic, isn't it? He got it so I could protect myself against nasty criminals and here I am using it as one of them. Poor Daddy would turn in his grave.'

'I should think *Daddy* would be more likely to turn in his grave over the fact that his daughter has become a sadistic killer,' Kate grated. 'Didn't it bother you, brutally murdering all those so-called friends of yours the way you did?'

Talbot pursed her lips, then frowned. 'Well, I didn't enjoy it, if that's what you mean. But, as a "mere teacher", I'd always been the odd one out in the group, with the others lording it over me because of their inflated egos and even bigger bank balances. So, at the same time I suppose I did nurse a sneaking sense of satisfaction that they were getting their comeuppances.'

She gave an exaggerated sigh. 'Principally, though, it was a case of needs must. You see, I had made a decision to retire from the purgatory of having to teach all those horrid little brats I had given half my life to, and I had put a down payment on a nice bungalow in the Seychelles. But just when I thought my future retirement in the sun was assured, the vendors upped the price and I was forced to pay another large sum to secure the property, which took nearly all of my remaining savings. A head's pension is not too bad, but I knew it would not be enough on its own to enable me to live comfortably into old age. As the sole survivor of Jules's tontine scheme, however, I realised that the substantial regular income I'd receive from the investment would give my finances the extra boost needed. So, it was a no-brainer really. Them or me.'

She sighed. 'Killing Lizzie was the worst one, I suppose, because she was my first, and it all went a bit pear-shaped too. Mind you, the plan was good enough. I telephoned her to suggest I popped round for a drink and a chat, like in the old days, and she jumped at the idea. I knew she was on diazepam for her nerves and was a whisky drinker, so I took a bottle of scotch round with me, plus a bottle of brandy for myself. I doctored the scotch with a massive dose of diazepam from the prescription box I found in her kitchen and when I thought she was on the way out, I put her to bed and got stuck into setting up the suicide scene.'

She grimaced. 'But Sod's Law being what it was, she came round as I was artistically arranging the diazepam blister packs on the bed, and she tried to get up. So, I had no choice but to finish her off, using the plastic bag I had brought the bottles in.' She screwed up her face in disgust. 'Unfortunately, she was a lot stronger than I thought possible and it all ended rather messily. Not only that, but it evidently put paid to my original plan to rig the whole thing up as a suicide.'

'So, why carry on with the killing once you realised your plan had backfired?'

Talbot shrugged. 'I had to if I was to achieve what I had set out to do, though I have to say the three boys were a lot easier to dispose of than poor Lizzie. Take Danny, for instance. He was always pissed and when I rang his office ostensibly to speak to him and found he hadn't been in for two days, I guessed he had to be on a bender, which suited me perfectly. I knew he was having major work carried out on his house, as he'd complained a while ago about the smell from all the paint tins, solvents and other inflammables the builders had stored in one of the rooms. So, I moseyed along there armed with a can of petrol and a lighter and broke in through an insecure window. Within minutes half the house was lit up like the fourth of July. A case of job well done.'

'You call deliberately burning someone to death a job well done?'

'It's all about perspectives, isn't it, Sergeant? From my perspective, it was a successful result, never mind the physical nature of things. For Danny, doubtless not so.'

Kate couldn't repress a shudder as she remembered Danny Aldridge's contorted blackened corpse. 'I saw Danny's remains,' she told her. 'It was a horrific sight I'll never forget. He must have died in agony.'

'Fortunately, I didn't see them, as I'm a bit squeamish about that sort of thing,' Talbot replied. 'In fact, I didn't even see him before the fire either. I knew he was still in the house because his Merc was parked out front, and that was enough as far as I was concerned, but the fire took hold so quickly, it practically singed my eyebrows, and I couldn't get out the way I'd got in—'

'No, you left via the kitchen at the other end of the building,' Kate finished for her, 'where you attacked one of my officers who confronted you.'

Talbot raised an eyebrow. 'What was I supposed to do? Hold out both wrists and say, "It's a fair cop," or stay there and burn to a cinder like Danny? I only gave that little lady cop a tap on the head with a torch I was carrying anyway—'

'A tap on the head that killed her!'

'What?' Talbot seemed ruffled for a moment, but quickly recovered and shook her head. 'Oh dear, that's unfortunate. It was, as I've said, nothing more than a tap.'

Kate nodded grimly. 'The same sort of tap that sent Robert Chalmers pitching over the wall of his balcony?'

'Actually, I didn't hit Bob with anything at all. I didn't have to. You see, I had arranged to meet him at his flat in Bristol on the pretext of seeking his advice on a bogus IT programme I said my school were thinking of setting up. Obviously already counting the brownie points he could earn with his bosses if he could secure a deal off the back of that on behalf of his company, he took an afternoon off to see me. Then shortly after I had arrived and we were having a quiet drink together, you forced my hand by turning up at the front door. As soon as I heard your voice on the intercom, I knew I had to act quickly. So, on your way up, I invited Bob to look at something down in the street. It was then simply a case of upending him when he was bending over the wall. No tap on the head there, you see, but a bit of a fatal free fall.'

'I did hear you running off down the stairs,' Kate admitted, 'but I lost you in the basement car park. I should have tumbled to the fact that those quick, light steps were obviously made by a woman in heels, but sadly, it didn't occur to me at the time.'

'Sod's Law I think that's called,' Talbot patronised. Then goaded, 'Even happens to really good detectives too, I would imagine.'

Kate didn't rise to the bait. 'And by now, I suppose, you've already wasted Julian?' she said grimly, thinking of the unanswered call on her mobile, which she guessed had been Hayden desperately trying to contact her.

''Fraid so.' Talbot flicked her wrist to consult her watch, but her pistol remained firmly trained on Kate in her other hand. 'Not long ago either. Got back from his place a few minutes before you arrived here.'

'So, no trip to the chemist then?' Kate said sarcastically.

'Not much point really, when I hadn't even the touch of a headache and I had already arranged to meet up with Jules for coffee anyway.'

'And what reason did you give *him* for suggesting that cosy, little tête-à-tête? To discuss his funeral and whether he would prefer burial or cremation?'

Talbot chuckled and waggled a finger at her in mock admonishment. 'Now, now, that's not nice, Sergeant. You should show more respect for the dead. But no, I simply appealed to his greed in the same way as I had done with Bob. I said I was thinking of taking out another major investment and needed his financial advice. Then, after the meaningless chit-chat, I asked if I could see the new pond, which I knew he had recently installed in his back garden.

'He was only too pleased to oblige and to show off his expensive golden carp. When I asked him why one of the stupid fish was floating on its side, he foolishly bent down to take a look. I had a rock from the side of the pond in my hand and I will admit that I did use more than a little tap in his case. Then I dumped him in his beloved pond with all the other pond life and held him down until he couldn't take in any more water. Your colleagues will probably see quite a nasty injury to the side of his head, when they eventually find him, but hopefully they will conclude he tripped and fell, hitting his head on the very rock I had carefully put back in place . . . Anything else you'd like to know, Sergeant?'

Talbot's face now wore a self-satisfied smirk and the eyes behind the blue-tinted lenses of her spectacles seemed to carry a glint of triumph. She was plainly on a high. Confident that, as Grey's body had not yet been discovered and Kate's visit had been prompted by nothing more than a genuine concern for her safety, none of the detective's colleagues were likely to be steaming in any time soon to rescue her and feel the collar of the real killer. Without a doubt, the police had been outwitted at every turn by an adversary a lot cleverer than them. No one, outside the four walls of her cottage knew, or would ever know, what she had done, so she could afford to indulge her vanity and spend a few moments gloating over her success; enjoying the fifteen minutes of fame — or in her case, infamy — Andy Warhol had claimed everyone would experience once in their lifetime.

But it was what was going to happen after that which bothered Kate, and she felt her stomach muscles tense and a trickle of perspiration glide down her backbone as she contemplated the little pistol in Talbot's hand, which seemed to have developed a mesmeric quality all of its own, as she stared into that wicked black muzzle.

As an experienced police officer who had spent most of her police service at the coalface, this was not the first time she had been in perilous situations like this. In fact, looking back, she seemed to have made a habit of it. But there had always been an opportunity to turn the tables on her adversary, or to effect an escape. In this case, she couldn't for the life of her — and she thought that literally — see a way out of her predicament. She considered a sudden lunge across the room to wrest the gun from Talbot's hand and overpower her but dismissed the idea as wishful thinking. In a good detective film, the heroine would have been an exponent of the martial arts, or at the very least a muscle-bound toughie who knew all the right moves, but she was neither and this wasn't a scene from a film: this was reality and from her perspective the odds on survival would have been a bookie's nightmare.

Her eyes flicked quickly around the room, trying to avoid any give-away head movement, and her heart jumped. One of the patio doors was a quarter open. She could see that yet another winter mist was beginning to drift in off the marshes, its telltale whiteish spirals floating across the garden like an army of ghosts. She could even smell its dank, earthy presence from inside the room. It was reminiscent of a newly dug grave, which, in a morbid sense, seemed horribly appropriate under the circumstances. Soon it would be difficult to even see the trees and shrubberies. If only she could somehow distract Talbot and get through that door . . .

'You would never make it,' Talbot said, easily reading her body language. 'There's something you should know before you try anything stupid. I have grown up with firearms. My dad was an ex-soldier and ran a local firearms club. He taught me well and, though I haven't fired a gun in years, I haven't forgotten what I learned.'

'So, are you going to shoot me in here?' Kate asked, partially losing her voice halfway through the question. 'It would leave a nice telltale hole in the chairback if it went straight through and a distinctive change of colour to the cushions.'

But Talbot never answered. The distraction Kate had been looking for came from the most unexpected source. The marked police car had arrived on a "silent approach" tactic and the next instant its powerful strobe was blazing in the window and sending a pulsing blue and red wash across the ceiling.

As doors slammed and heavy feet pounded the driveway, Talbot leaped to her feet in a panic. Then, waving the pistol towards the patio doors, she literally snarled at Kate. 'Out! *Now!*'

In her super agitated state, refusal would have been fatal and, as fists pounded the front door, and a deep voice shouted unnecessarily, 'Police. Open up!' Kate allowed herself to be forced ahead of her captor through the doors into the garden.

The mist had thickened appreciably in the last few minutes, and it couldn't have come at a more opportune moment for Talbot. Even so, she only just managed to get clear, jerking off a warning shot in the direction of a heavy-set uniformed figure that suddenly appeared round the side of the house, as she pushed Kate ahead of her into the deepening gloom. Then they were stumbling along a gravel path between tall shrubs towards the end of the garden.

'That was stupid,' Kate panted as Talbot forced her through an open gateway into a field. 'The call will now go out that you're armed.'

'Good,' Talbot grated close to her ear. 'Then they'll keep their distance, won't they?'

Kate stopped, turning slightly. 'They'll deploy an ARV — an armed response vehicle — which means you'll be a target.'

Talbot dug the pistol into her back. 'Keep moving,' she rapped. 'And remember, if I become a target, so will you.'

* * *

Kate's feet were soaked from the squelchy, waterlogged grass, and she was bitterly cold. The mist seemed to have closed in on them like a shroud and a fine drizzle was now falling through it.

'Do you know where you're going?' she threw back over her shoulder. 'We're on a marsh. There could be bogs everywhere.'

'Keep going,' Talbot replied. 'There's a rhyne to your right. All we have to do is to keep it and the willows bordering it in view and follow it along.'

For the first time, Kate noticed the greyish shapes, like ghostly sentinels, some twenty feet away, forming a ragged irregular line.

'I know this countryside like the back of my hand,' Talbot went on, breathlessly. 'I walk it regularly.'

As she spoke, another grey shape appeared directly in front of them, this time not a willow tree but what looked like some kind of large barn.

'In there,' Talbot wheezed, 'and no nonsense.'

The barn was old and badly holed, with a flat roof and a pair of double doors on one side that seemed to be hanging on to their hinges in desperation. Inside, the floor was covered in an evil-smelling sludge that had probably been hay when the English Civil War was at its height, Kate thought cynically, as she sank into it above her ankles. There was a high window at the far end of the building which admitted some light, but overall, the place was almost as gloomy as the world outside.

'So where to now?' Kate panted, turning to stare at Talbot. 'You reckon my colleagues won't find you in here? It's the first place they'll look.'

'Shut it!' Talbot retorted. 'Let me think.'

She was clearly in a panic and the pistol in her hand was erratically wandering from side to side. Kate thought about trying to take it off her, but then ditched the idea as too risky, praying instead that, if the weapon had a safety catch, it was on! But she had no intention of trying to find out.

'We're safe for the moment,' Talbot said suddenly, breathing more evenly. She was obviously trying to convince herself, but Kate didn't share her analysis of the situation with the use of the word "we". She had never felt so unsafe for a long time.

Risking winding her up still further, Kate said, 'Once this mist clears, they'll put a chopper up, you know that, don't you? And they'll almost certainly have already called for dogs. You don't stand a chance. For heaven's sake give it up.'

The little pistol tasted of cold metal as it rammed into Kate's mouth, drawing blood from her split lip and rattling against her teeth. 'I said, shut it!' Talbot snarled, no longer the cool, phlegmatic head teacher, who took everything in her stride. 'Another word, and I swear, I'll blow your head off!'

Kate froze and stayed frozen for a few seconds after the gun was withdrawn. Talbot was very close to losing it altogether and the old maxim of discretion being the better part of valour seemed particularly appropriate under the present circumstances.

'Right, we're leaving,' Talbot said again, waving her pistol in Kate's face and signalling towards the double doors. 'We have to get to the road on the other side of these fields.'

The going got a lot harder and wetter after that. Stumbling almost blindly through the dense swirling blanket that enveloped them, they found themselves having to negotiate large tufts of grass that had forced their way up out of the saturated ground, acting like a sponge and partially submerging their feet in icy water at every other step. Kate was already exhausted, but Talbot had no intention of giving up and pushed her on none too gently with her pistol. 'The road can't be far now,' she said, but then called Kate to a halt. 'Where's the rhyne we were following?' she demanded, panic even more pronounced in her voice. Kate turned to see her frantically peering about her in the mist. 'We must have moved away from it . . . Quick, back. This way, I think.'

But it wasn't. After a short distance, she ordered Kate in another direction. Again, there was no sign of the willows marking the edge of the rhyne. But they had blundered into an even more soggy area, where the tufted grass had given way to what Kate could see were patches of thick, bouncy vegetation, interspersed with pools of dark water, and what ground there was beneath their feet felt as if it were moving. They had wandered into a quaking bog.

She came to an abrupt stop. 'We're in a bog,' she warned, turning to face her captor. 'We have to go back.'

But Talbot was not listening. Instead, she had whirled round and was staring hard into the mist, even though she couldn't see anything beyond a couple of yards. The excited barking of dogs had erupted from somewhere behind them and it had plainly unnerved her. Kate didn't give her time to recover either. Regardless of the boggy hazard she had pointed out, she made the most of the distraction and promptly melted into the chilling gloom.

The first shot went wide, and the second. Fortunately, there was no third, but Kate's luck didn't hold. Moments later, she failed to spot a water-filled hollow in front of her and put her foot in it. At once, she felt the sinews in her ankle tear as she twisted it and tumbled to the ground with a sharp cry of pain. Unable to stand on her leg, or even try to crawl anywhere, her escape bid was totally compromised, and she had to face the fact that she was now helpless, her only protection being her dubious invisibility in the mist.

As she thought about that, she heard the telltale splashing and squelching sounds of Talbot searching for her close by, and she forced herself up into a sitting position, rocking herself backwards and forwards on her haunches with gritted teeth to stop herself making a noise, while she gripped her lower leg with both hands in a futile effort to shut off the vicious needle-like spasms ripping through the muscles. Her one hope was that Talbot would not be able to find her and, under the pressure of imminent capture by the police search party scouring the fields with their dogs, she would finally give up and flee. But venom is a compulsive driver and Kate guessed that by now Talbot would be full of it. Perhaps realising it was all over for her, she would be determined to destroy the one person she blamed for her present predicament before her perverted dreams ended in a police cell, and that was not the most reassuring thought Kate needed. As it turned out, fickle Fate seemed only too pleased to help the sadistic killer get what she wanted too.

Kate saw Talbot emerge from the mist suddenly, a hazy shadow that gained substance almost immediately, forming up on the far side of a patch of thick, green-brown vegetation, with the hand clutching the pistol outstretched towards her. With nowhere to run to and no ability to do so anyway in her present condition, she watched as the woman advanced slowly towards her, obviously enjoying every moment of her revenge and keen to put a bullet in her target's head at point-blank range.

Strangely enough, Kate didn't really care anymore. Cold, soaked to the skin and in so much pain, she felt only that she wanted it all to stop. For the shutters to come down, so she could drift off into peaceful oblivion. There was no fight in her anymore. She was done. She only hoped Hayden would find it in him to understand. But then, the old fire in her belly was suddenly rekindled with what Talbot had meant to be her parting taunt.

'Time to join your stupid colleague,' she sneered. 'Maybe they'll do you a joint funeral.'

At once Kate thought of Indrani Purewal, her dear friend and colleague, brutally and senselessly wasted to enable a callous, arrogant killer to achieve her vile ambitions, and she was almost overcome by a hatred she had never thought was in her; a hatred that she now knew would never be satisfied.

So, Talbot would lose everything when she was put before the court: her liberty, her respect, her ill-gotten gains, but she would still be alive, with the possibility of earning parole from some naive review board on humanitarian grounds after ten to fifteen years tucked away in a nice comfortable cell. Maybe she would even write a book based on her life story and maybe it would be made into a film. She would be old by then, of course, but she would still be alive!

The police dogs were closer now. Kate could even hear the jangle of their harnesses. But they would be too late. The scent they had been following would simply produce her own corpse with half its head missing!

But Kate was wrong. There would be no corpse with half her head missing, no nice comfortable cell for Talbot, no book or film of her despicable crimes. At the last hurdle, Fate had suddenly changed his mind.

Talbot never got to within a yard of her before it happened and then, as Kate watched, the grim finale was played out right in front of her. How she herself had missed the bog she would never know, but Talbot didn't. She stepped straight into it. She must have wondered what was happening, as her feet sank into the soft, wet peat lurking beneath the carpet of floating vegetation. She tried to pull herself out, grabbing handfuls of grass and sphagnum moss from the edge, but it all came out of the ground and there was nothing else for her to hold on to. She cried out to Kate when the level of mud and slime reached her chest, but the woman sitting gripping her ankle in pain on the one piece of firm ground in front of her was in no position to help anyone and she stared at her with a cold, hard gaze that held not the slightest trace of humanity and might have been carved from stone.

The dogs were practically on top of them, and Kate heard the rough male voice shout a warning, 'Steady. We're on the edge of a bloody bog.' She could have called out to attract their attention immediately and they might even have managed to pull Talbot free in time. But she didn't, and when the dogs found her moments before Hayden burst in on the scene like a runaway express train, she was still sitting there, massaging her ankle and staring blankly at the spot where Talbot had disappeared, with a last obscene gurgle from the peat bed that had claimed her . . .

AFTER THE FACT

Kate had only been to police headquarters once in her career — excepting her extended interview for the job of a police officer in the first place — and that had been for promotion to the rank of sergeant quite a few years ago. All her other sideways moves had been made at local level. Now sitting on the uncomfortable straight-backed chair in the office of the secretary to the Assistant Chief Constable, Personnel, Kate glanced at her watch and frowned. Why she was here, she hadn't the slightest idea. The imperious summons had arrived in an email to her superintendent, George "Birdie" Rutherford, the day before and he had remained totally impassive when he'd passed it on, giving nothing away.

The little worms of anxiety that had started crawling around her insides as soon as she'd heard must have tripled in size by now. ACC (P), as he was officially referred to, dealt with all kinds of personnel matters, which included postings, transfers, sickness and discipline issues. It was only in the last couple of weeks that she had returned to full operational duty after recovery from the ankle injuries she had sustained in the Talbot case. Could this be anything to do with that, she wondered? Did the powers-that-be think she was not fit enough to remain in the force? Then there was the DCI at Bridgwater. He had always hated her, had tried to get her disciplined and thrown out at every opportunity. Could this interview be anything to do with him? Was she being taken off CID perhaps or moved to another station? All these thoughts crowded her mind as she sat there twisting her fingers together in her lap, while the buxom, middle-aged secretary carried on using the keyboard of her computer without so much as an attempt at polite conversation.

It was now six months since the conclusion of the Talbot case and Kate had recovered well from the torn ligaments in her ankle, though she still had to wear a tight crepe bandage for support. The world itself had moved on a league in those six months and for most people the case was past history, but for Kate the whole thing would be forever indelibly etched on her memory.

Flowers were what she knew she would always remember most; masses and masses of beautiful flowers, releasing their overpowering perfume into the small, packed building. Indrani Purewal's send-off had been a big event, with relatives and friends in their traditional saris mixing with the late detective's former police colleagues, including the chief constable and other senior officers from headquarters who had put in an appearance to pay their respects. Her elderly parents were not wealthy people, but the force had paid for their return flight from the Punjab in India and their accommodation at a smart hotel a few miles from Highbridge, which Kate thought was a nice touch. Nevertheless, she had really felt for them, admiring the way these dignified, elderly people had handled their terrible loss. Finally flying back to India to spread their beloved daughter's ashes over the waters of their sacred Ganges River, they had been left with nothing more than memories of a brave daughter who had come to Britain to fulfil a childhood dream of becoming a police detective and had been cruelly cut down little more than a year after being appointed. What was it the old sweats in the force often said? "Life's a bitch and then you die".

The funeral had marked the final chapter in a horrific, complicated case, which Kate knew would haunt her for the rest of her days. Once again, she had escaped death by the narrowest of margins — something that had become rather a habit for her in her police career over the years. But even now, she still couldn't remember much about those final moments crouched on the edge of that quaking bog. She had no recollection of Talbot's cries for help as she had watched with an unashamed sense of satisfaction the killer of her friend and colleague slowly disappear into the choking mud. All she could recall was being swept up in Hayden's arms after he had suddenly burst recklessly out of the mist to carry her to safety. It was as if her mind had buried the memory in her subconscious and locked the door against retrieval.

Talbot's body had eventually been recovered after a major search operation by an expert team and, following the necessary legal formalities, permission had been given by the local authority for her cremated remains to be interred in the graveyard at the crematorium with nothing more than a simple plaque to mark the spot — or was it more like a stain?

As for the case itself, that had been filed in the police archives as a *Detected — No Proceedings,* and the Reverend Arthur Taylor had been released from custody without charge, after the CPS had decided that a prosecution for wasting police time was "not in the public interest".

True to form, once the drama attached to the case was over, it hadn't taken long for the press feeding frenzy to fizzle out completely, and there had been little interest in the inquests into the deaths of the five friends whose callous behaviour thirty years before had started it all. Even Debbie Moreton had been unable to keep things going — and finally given up trying to make political capital out of the way the police had handled the investigation, latching on to other, more sensational stories instead.

The brutal murder of the young police detective herself, which at the time had made headlines in the national newspapers, featured as the number one story on all the main television channels and had also got a mention in Parliament's hallowed House of Commons chamber, was no longer a public interest story but had been relegated to the status of just another tragic episode in UK crime history. As memories dulled, and the world returned to business as usual, the sacrifice of the brave young woman who had died trying to rescue someone from a burning house had become nothing more than an anonymous crime statistic! Such was life — and

death . . .

'I *said* the Assistant Chief Constable will see you now, Sergeant,' the slightly irritated voice broke in on Kate's recollections. 'Please go *in*.'

Kate jumped. She had been so lost in her reverie that she hadn't heard the secretary's voice.

Swallowing hard, she got up, giving her an apologetic smile. Then smoothing down her skirt, she knocked on the walnut-panelled door and went straight in.

* * *

Hayden was waiting in the headquarters car park when Kate came out again, his brows knitted together in an anxious frown, as he studied her white face.

'What is it?' he asked, the concern evident in his tone. 'What did the old man want to see you about?'

Kate climbed into the front passenger seat of his smart Mk II Jaguar and promptly burst into tears.

'Gordon Bennett!' he exclaimed. 'Don't tell me you got the push?'

She turned her face, streaming with tears, towards her. 'No, Hayden,' she said, 'it's far worse than that.'

'Worse? What–what do you mean? What could be worse?'

Suddenly the smile broke through the tears, and he read the devilment in her eyes.

'At last,' she exclaimed, throwing her arms around his neck, 'after all these years of rejection, I've got it! Can you believe it? "Go It Alone Kate" is being promoted to DI at Bristol.'

He tore himself free, looking staggered. 'DI?' he exclaimed. 'Good Lord! Well, flipping heck, congratulations! But–but I don't understand. Why is that worse?'

'Because, my sweet, darling,' she said, squeezing him tight, 'from now on, you will have to call me Ma'am!'

THE END

THE JOFFE BOOKS STORY

We began in 2014 when Jasper agreed to publish his mum's much-rejected romance novel and it became a bestseller.

Since then we've grown into the largest independent publisher in the UK. We're extremely proud to publish some of the very best writers in the world, including Joy Ellis, Faith Martin, Caro Ramsay, Helen Forrester, Simon Brett and Robert Goddard. Everyone at Joffe Books loves reading and we never forget that it all begins with the magic of an author telling a story.

We are proud to publish talented first-time authors, as well as established writers whose books we love introducing to a new generation of readers.

We won Trade Publisher of the Year at the Independent Publishing Awards in 2023 and Best Publisher Award in 2024 at the People's Book Prize. We have been shortlisted for Independent Publisher of the Year at the British Book Awards for the last five years, and were shortlisted for the Diversity and Inclusivity Award at the 2022 Independent Publishing Awards. In 2023 we were shortlisted for Publisher of the Year at the RNA Industry Awards, and in 2024 we were shortlisted at the CWA Daggers for the Best Crime and Mystery Publisher.

We built this company with your help, and we love to hear from you, so please email us about absolutely anything bookish at feedback@joffebooks.com.

If you want to receive free books every Friday and hear about all our new releases, join our mailing list here: www.joffebooks.com/freebooks.

And when you tell your friends about us, just remember: it's pronounced Joffe as in coffee or toffee!

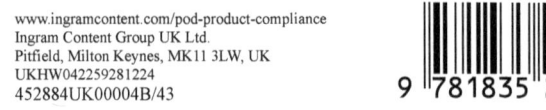